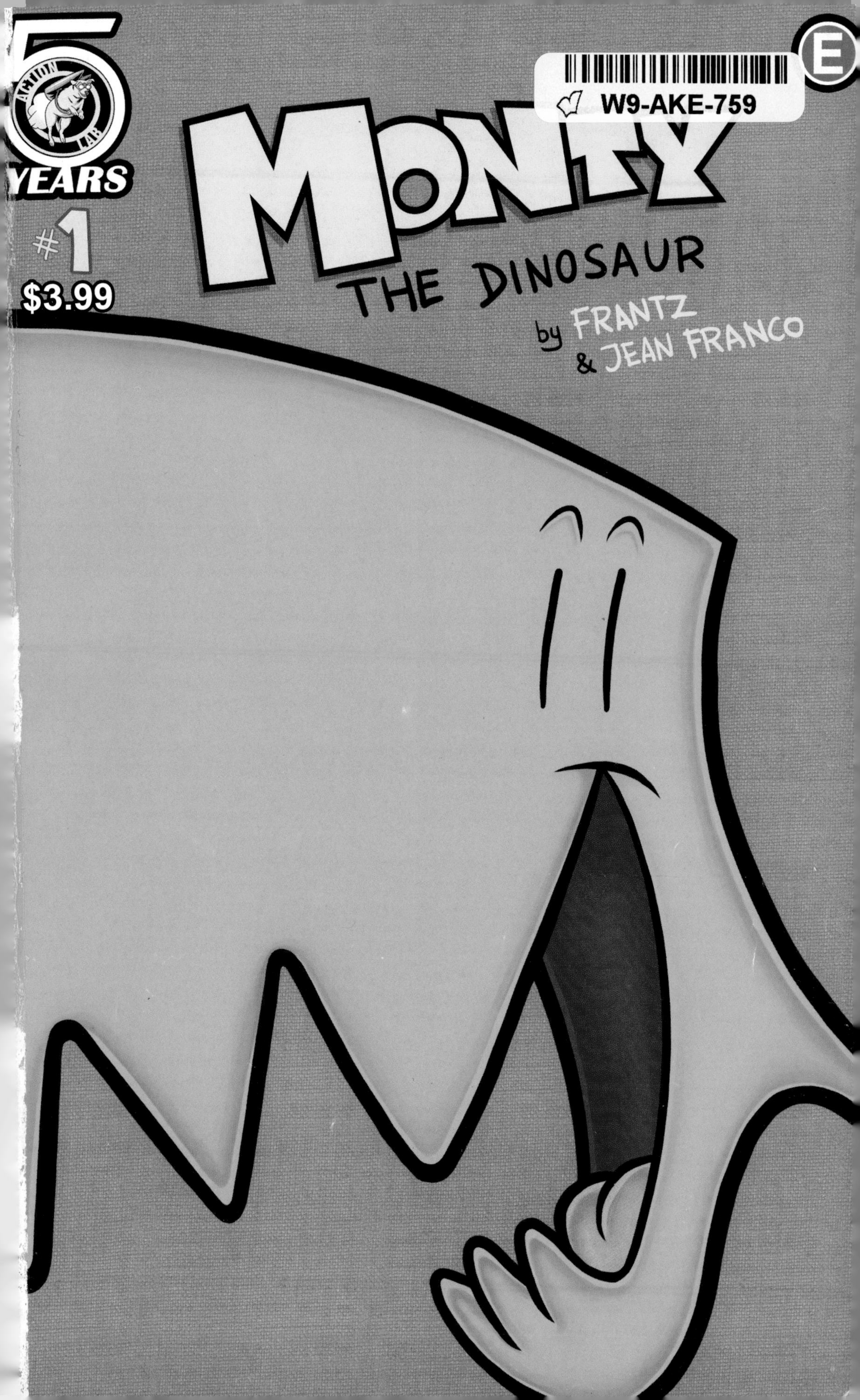
5 YEARS
ACTION LAB
#1
$3.99
E
MONTY
THE DINOSAUR
by FRANTZ
& JEAN FRANCO

# MONTY
## THE DINOSAUR
-ISSUE ONE-

Written by:
**Bob Frantz**
@bfrantz19

Art by:
**Jean Franco**
facebook.com/jeanfrancodg

Variant cover by:
**Eryk Donovan**

Edited By:
**Mike Exner III**
@mikeexnerIII

Inspiration:
**Sophie and Bobby Frantz**

Special thanks to:

Stephanie Frantz, without your love none of this would be possible.
Mom and Roger, Dad, Erin, Drew Moss, Anton Kromoff, Kevin Cuffe,
Hoyt Silva, Mike Federali, Shane Berryhill, Eryk Donovan, Brad Iten,
The Bass Family (best in-laws ever),The Deans Family, The Cosely Family.

Bryan Seaton: Publisher • Dave Dwonch: President • Shawn Gabborin: Editor In Chief
Jason Martin: Publisher-Danger Zone • Jamal Igle: Vice-President of Marketing
Jim Dietz: Social Media Director • Nicole DAndria: Editor • Chad Cicconi: Lord of the Flies
Colleen Boyd: Submissions Editor.

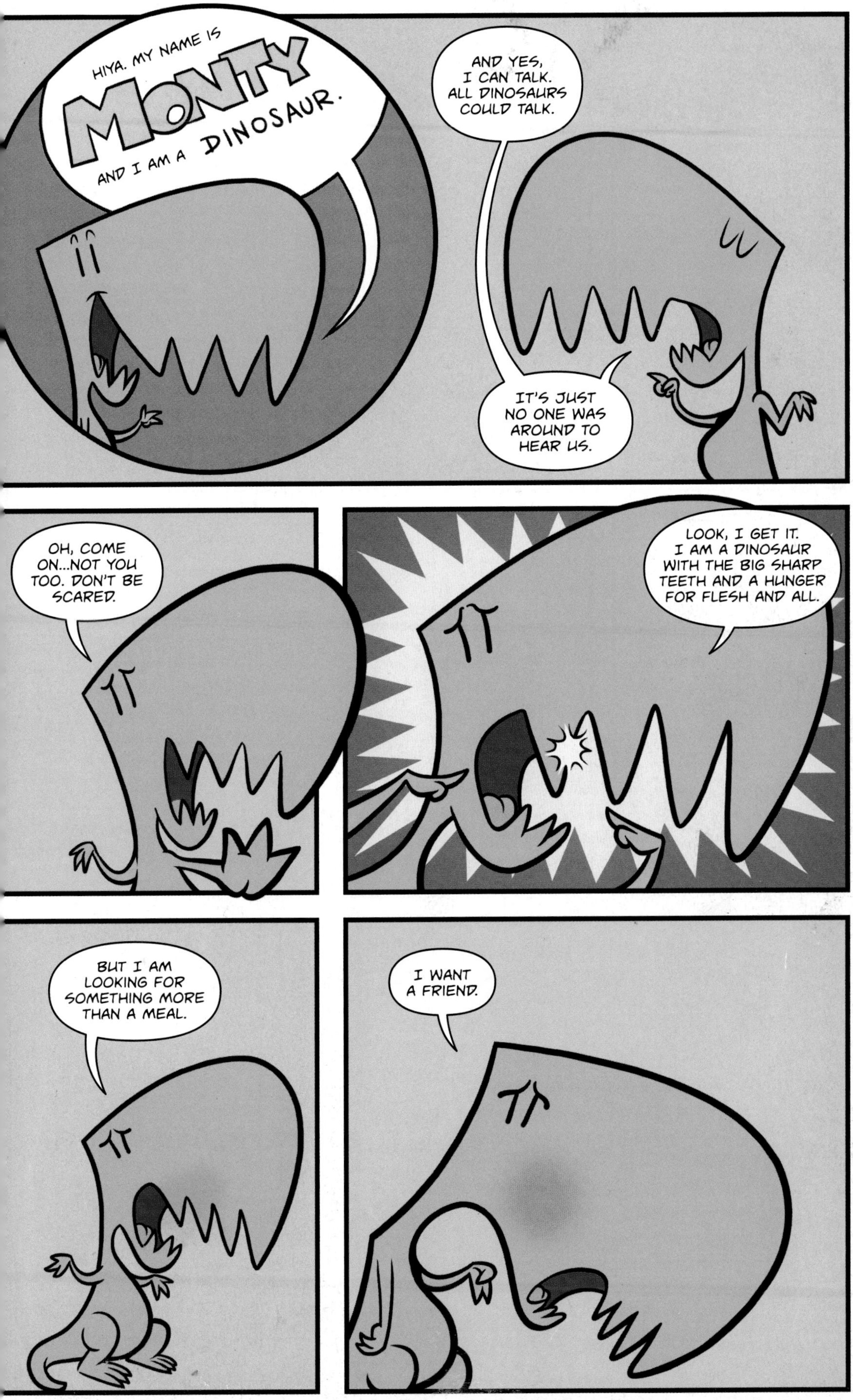

HIYA. MY NAME IS MONTY AND I AM A DINOSAUR.
AND YES, I CAN TALK. ALL DINOSAURS COULD TALK.
IT'S JUST NO ONE WAS AROUND TO HEAR US.
OH, COME ON...NOT YOU TOO. DON'T BE SCARED.
LOOK, I GET IT. I AM A DINOSAUR WITH THE BIG SHARP TEETH AND A HUNGER FOR FLESH AND ALL.
BUT I AM LOOKING FOR SOMETHING MORE THAN A MEAL.
I WANT A FRIEND.

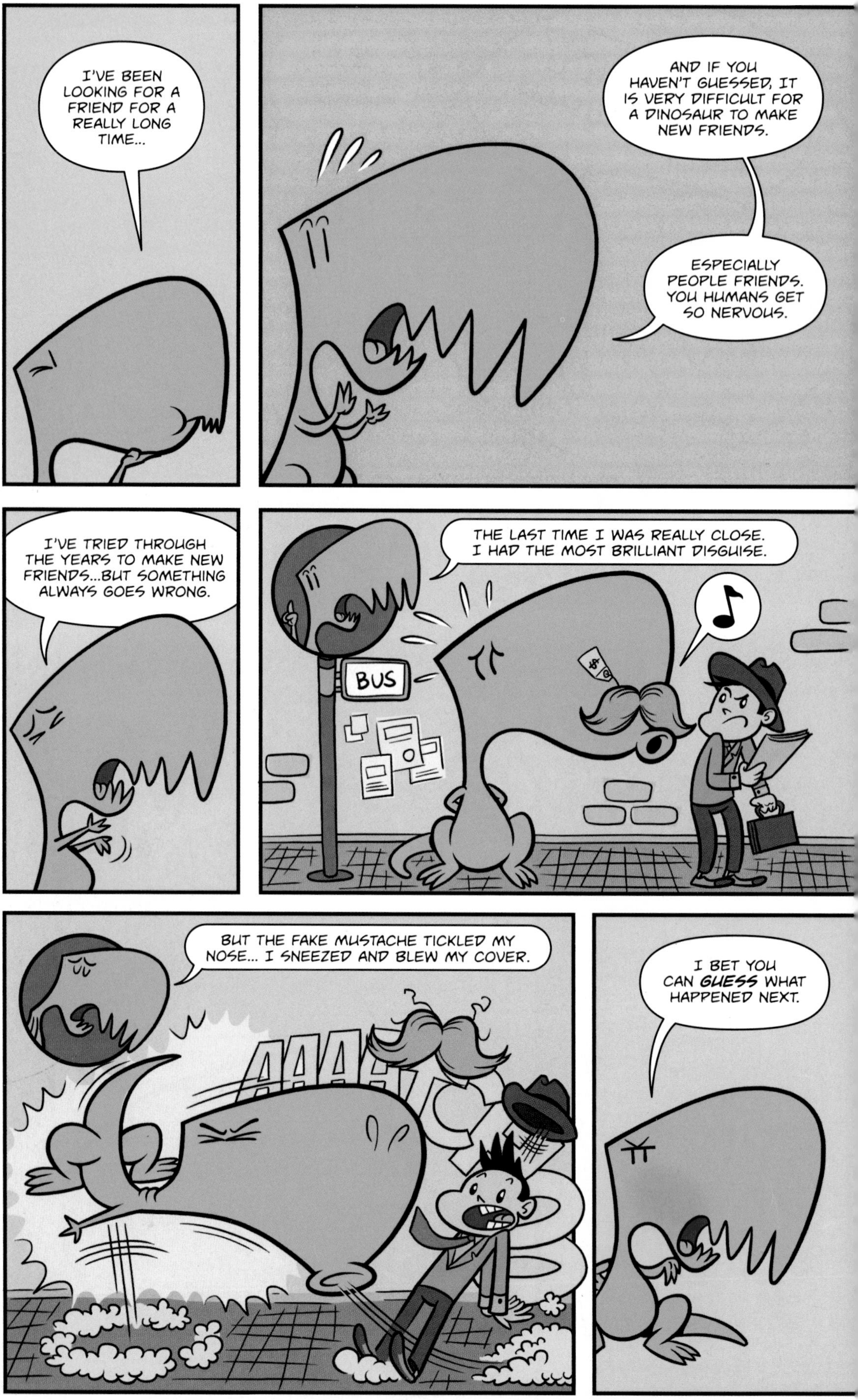

I'VE BEEN LOOKING FOR A FRIEND FOR A REALLY LONG TIME...
AND IF YOU HAVEN'T GUESSED, IT IS VERY DIFFICULT FOR A DINOSAUR TO MAKE NEW FRIENDS.
ESPECIALLY PEOPLE FRIENDS. YOU HUMANS GET SO NERVOUS.
I'VE TRIED THROUGH THE YEARS TO MAKE NEW FRIENDS...BUT SOMETHING ALWAYS GOES WRONG.
THE LAST TIME I WAS REALLY CLOSE. I HAD THE MOST BRILLIANT DISGUISE.
BUS
BUT THE FAKE MUSTACHE TICKLED MY NOSE... I SNEEZED AND BLEW MY COVER.
I BET YOU CAN GUESS WHAT HAPPENED NEXT.

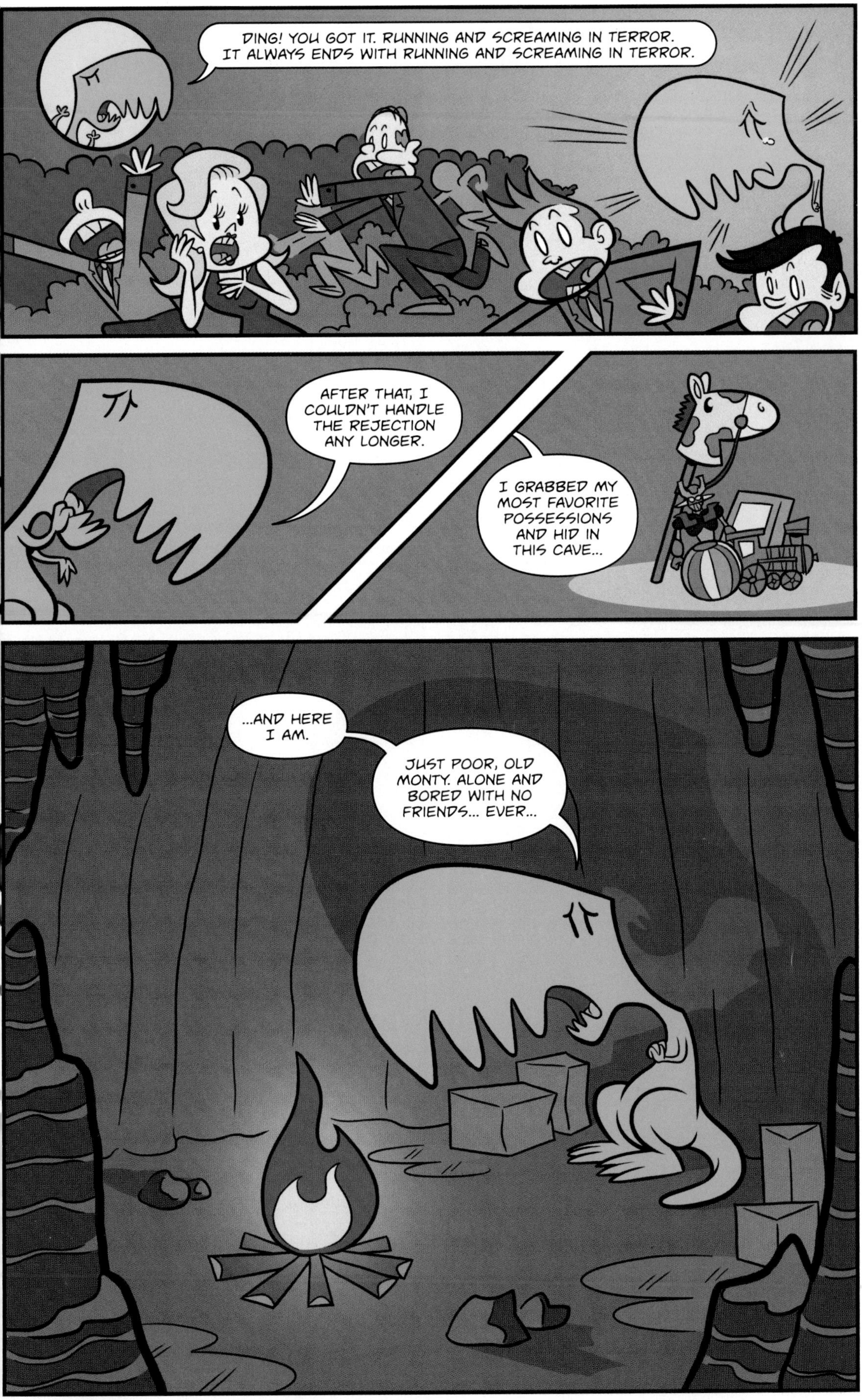
DING! YOU GOT IT. RUNNING AND SCREAMING IN TERROR. IT ALWAYS ENDS WITH RUNNING AND SCREAMING IN TERROR.
AFTER THAT, I COULDN'T HANDLE THE REJECTION ANY LONGER.
I GRABBED MY MOST FAVORITE POSSESSIONS AND HID IN THIS CAVE...
...AND HERE I AM.
JUST POOR, OLD MONTY. ALONE AND BORED WITH NO FRIENDS... EVER...

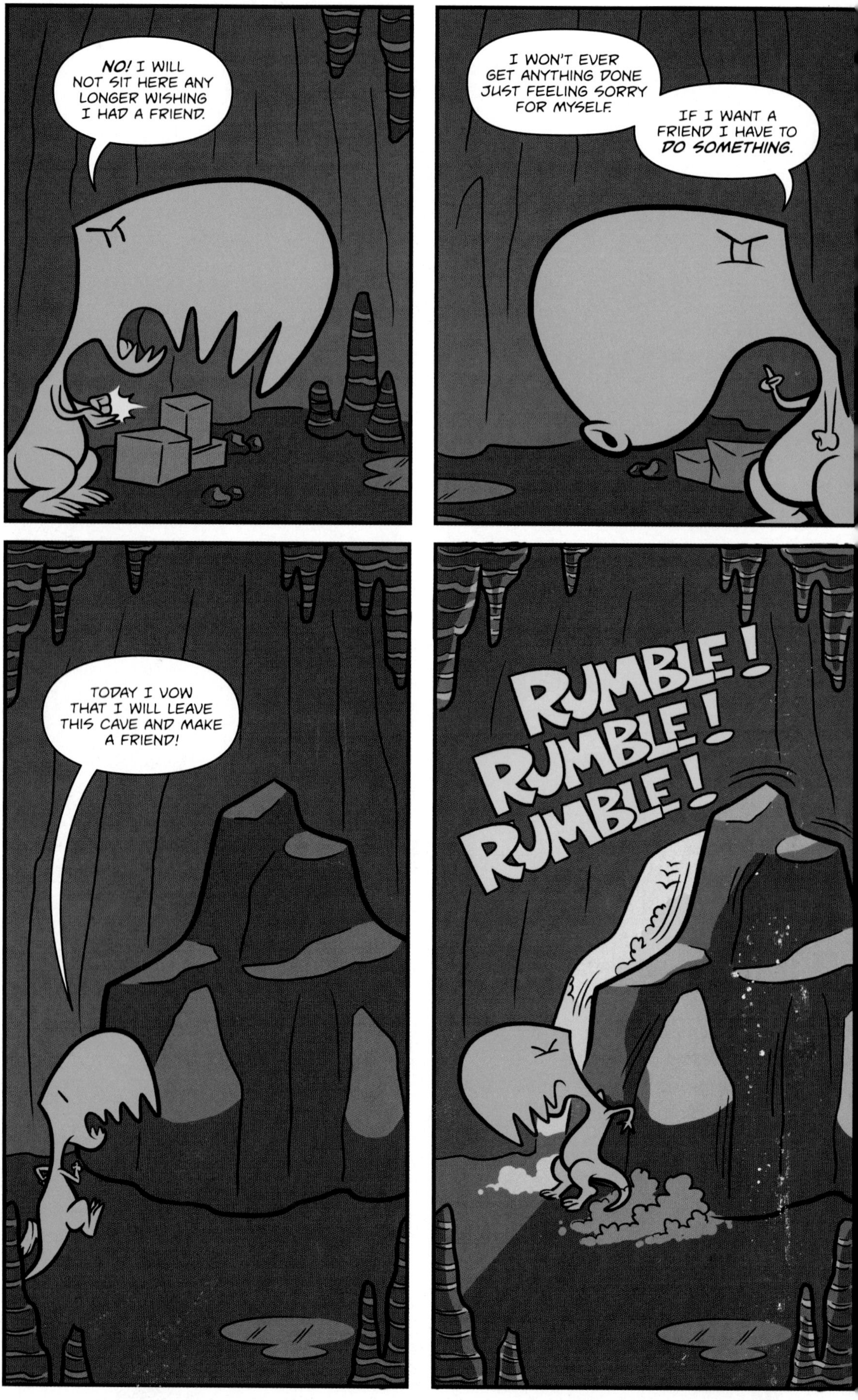
NO! I WILL NOT SIT HERE ANY LONGER WISHING I HAD A FRIEND.
I WON'T EVER GET ANYTHING DONE JUST FEELING SORRY FOR MYSELF.
IF I WANT A FRIEND I HAVE TO DO SOMETHING.
TODAY I VOW THAT I WILL LEAVE THIS CAVE AND MAKE A FRIEND!
RUMBLE! RUMBLE! RUMBLE!

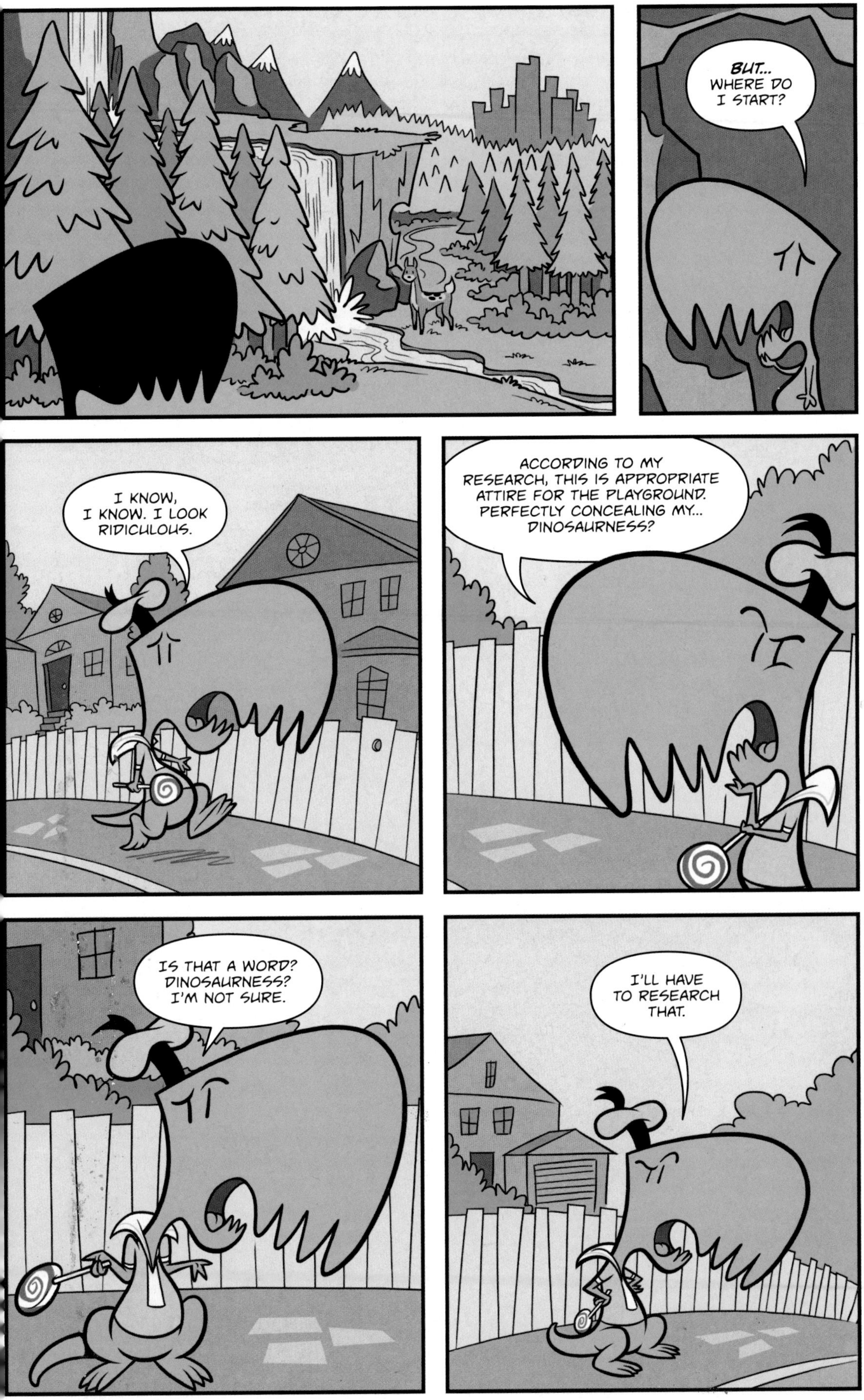
BUT... WHERE DO I START?
I KNOW, I KNOW. I LOOK RIDICULOUS.
ACCORDING TO MY RESEARCH, THIS IS APPROPRIATE ATTIRE FOR THE PLAYGROUND. PERFECTLY CONCEALING MY... DINOSAURNESS?
IS THAT A WORD? DINOSAURNESS? I'M NOT SURE.
I'LL HAVE TO RESEARCH THAT.

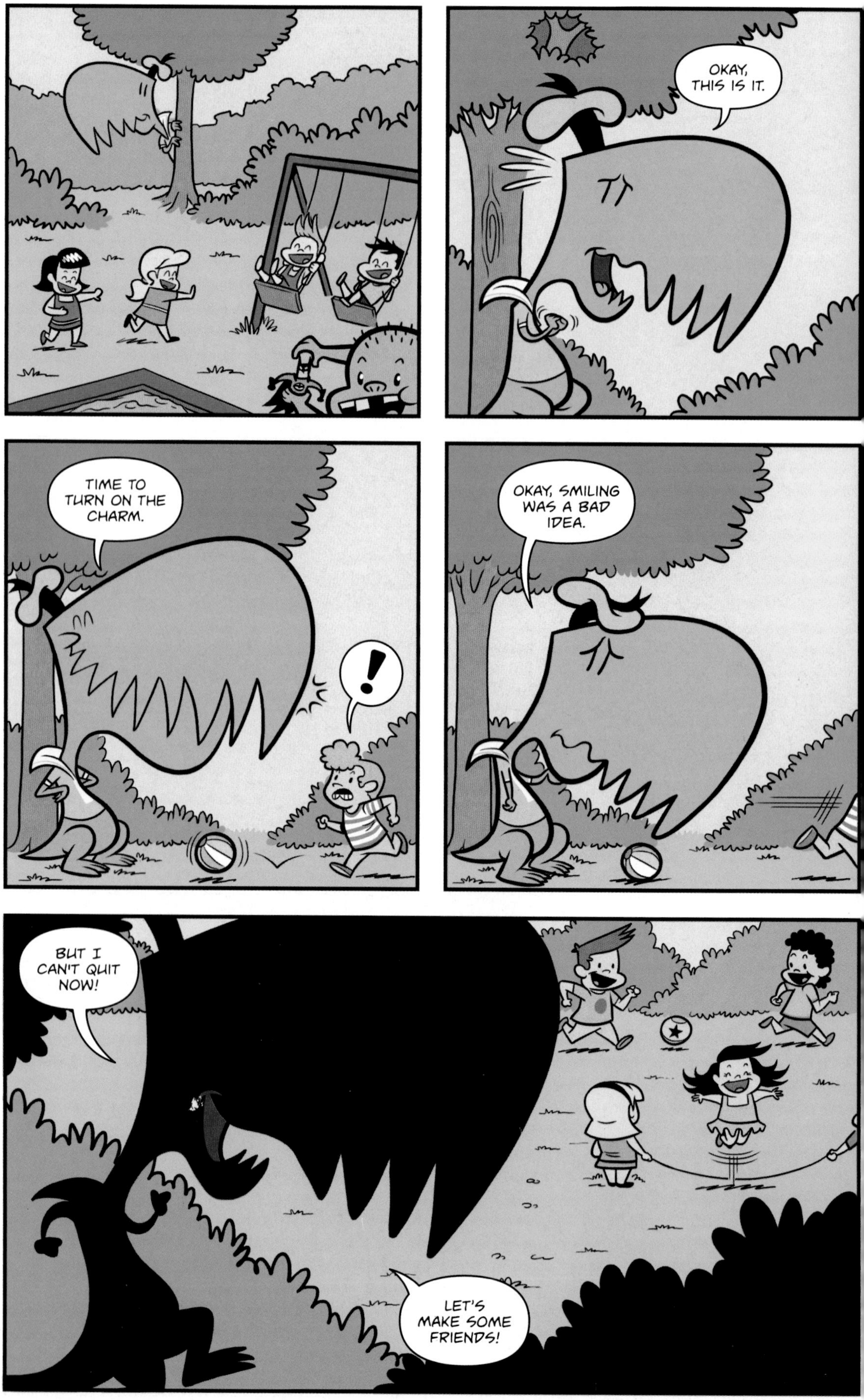
OKAY, THIS IS IT.
TIME TO TURN ON THE CHARM.
!
OKAY, SMILING WAS A BAD IDEA.
BUT I CAN'T QUIT NOW!
LET'S MAKE SOME FRIENDS!

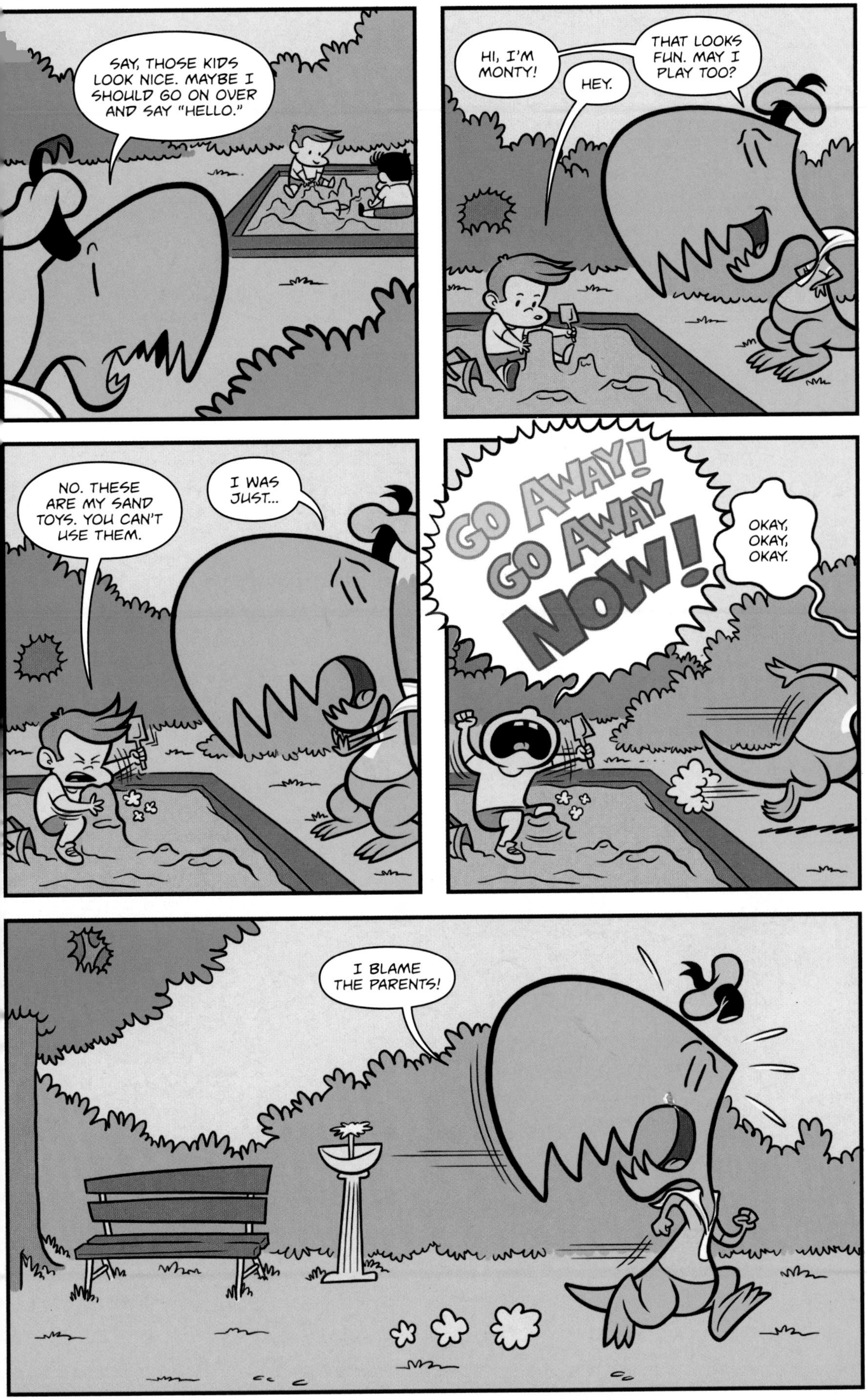
SAY, THOSE KIDS LOOK NICE. MAYBE I SHOULD GO ON OVER AND SAY "HELLO."
HI, I'M MONTY!
HEY.
THAT LOOKS FUN. MAY I PLAY TOO?
NO. THESE ARE MY SAND TOYS. YOU CAN'T USE THEM.
I WAS JUST...
GO AWAY! GO AWAY GO AWAY NOW!
OKAY, OKAY, OKAY.
I BLAME THE PARENTS!

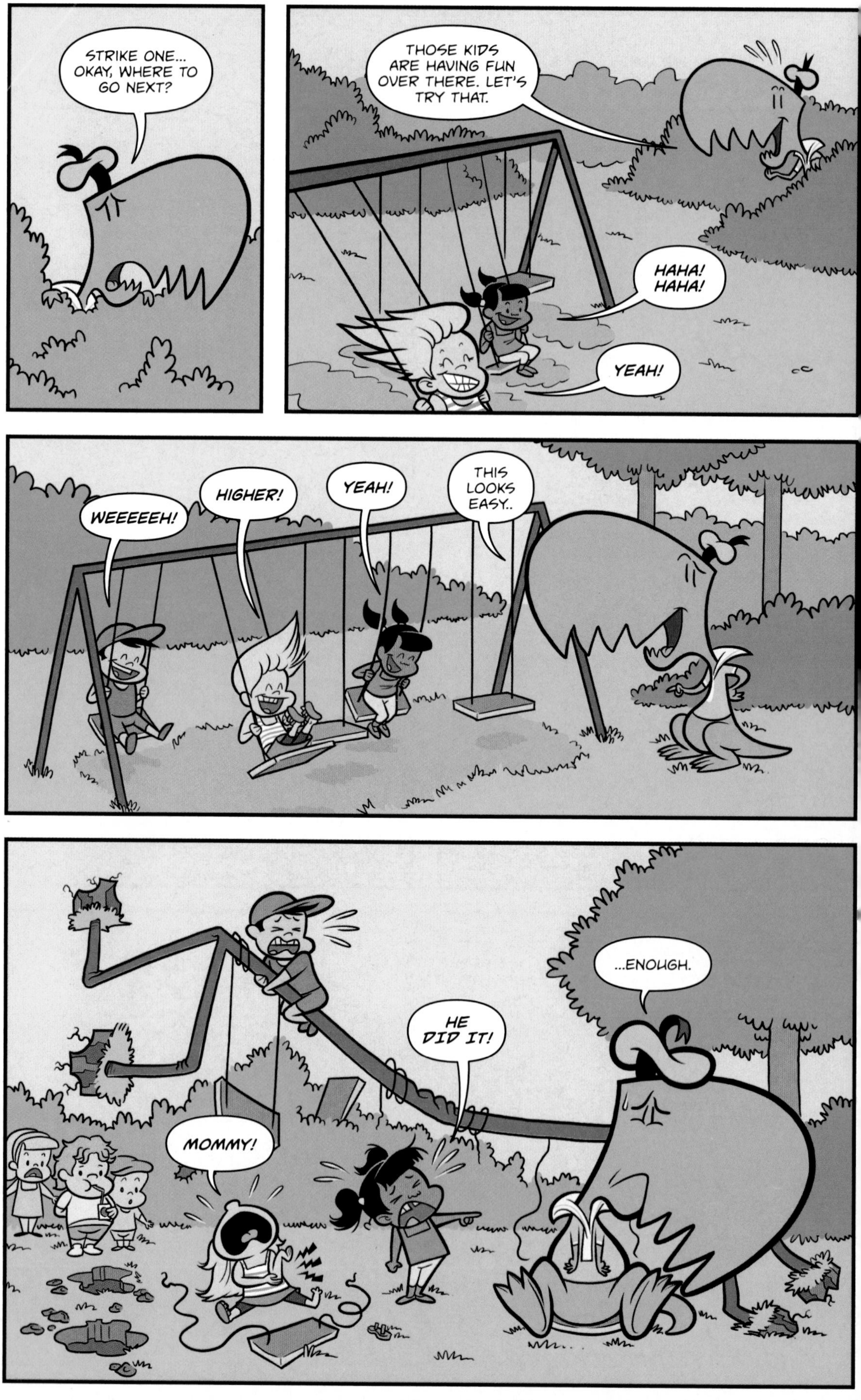
STRIKE ONE... OKAY, WHERE TO GO NEXT?
THOSE KIDS ARE HAVING FUN OVER THERE. LET'S TRY THAT.
HAHA! HAHA!
YEAH!
WEEEEEH!
HIGHER!
YEAH!
THIS LOOKS EASY..
...ENOUGH.
HE DID IT!
MOMMY!

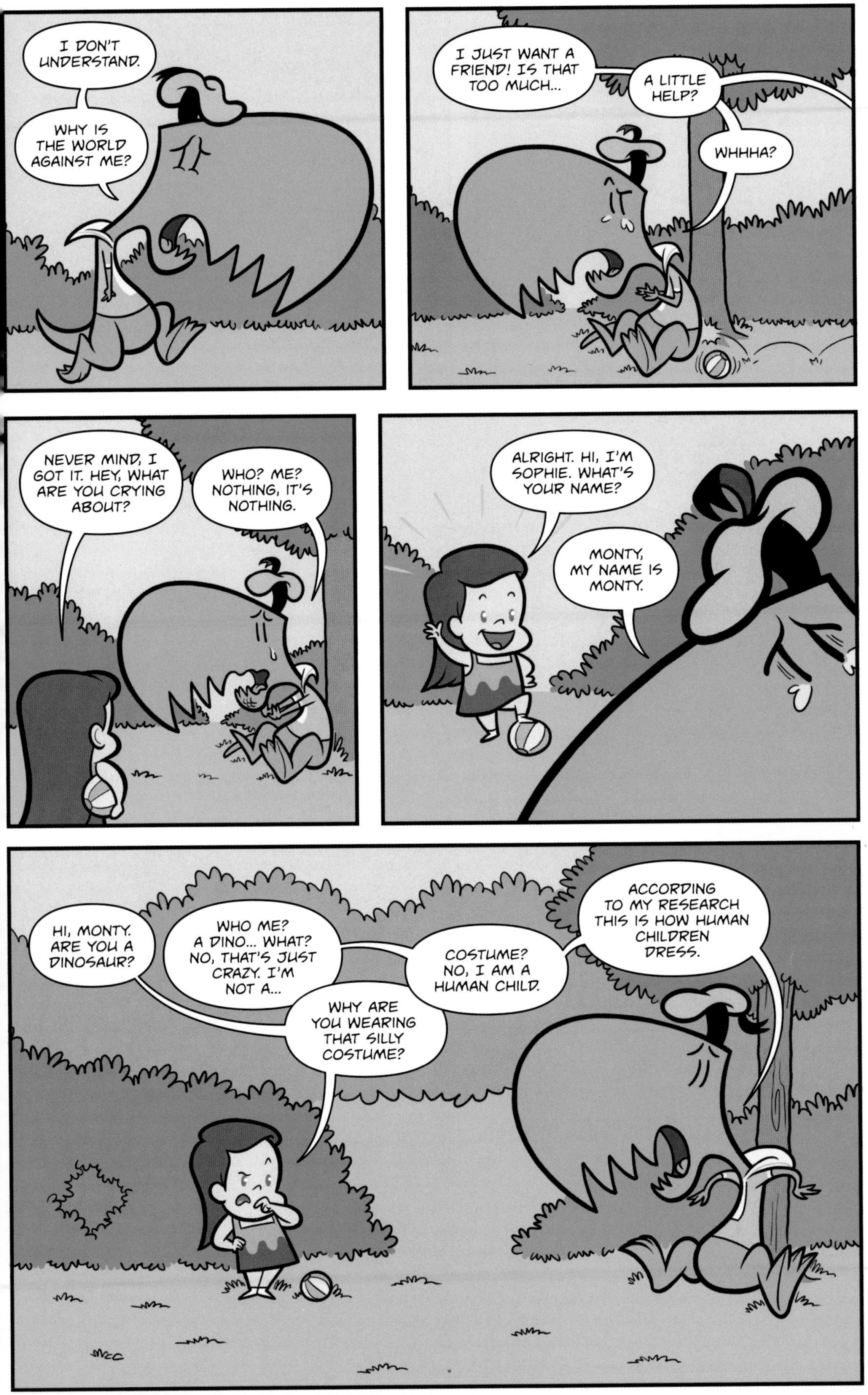

I DON'T UNDERSTAND.
WHY IS THE WORLD AGAINST ME?
I JUST WANT A FRIEND! IS THAT TOO MUCH...
A LITTLE HELP?
WHHHA?
NEVER MIND, I GOT IT. HEY, WHAT ARE YOU CRYING ABOUT?
WHO? ME? NOTHING, IT'S NOTHING.
ALRIGHT. HI, I'M SOPHIE. WHAT'S YOUR NAME?
MONTY, MY NAME IS MONTY.
HI, MONTY. ARE YOU A DINOSAUR?
WHO ME? A DINO... WHAT? NO, THAT'S JUST CRAZY. I'M NOT A...
WHY ARE YOU WEARING THAT SILLY COSTUME?
COSTUME? NO, I AM A HUMAN CHILD.
ACCORDING TO MY RESEARCH THIS IS HOW HUMAN CHILDREN DRESS.

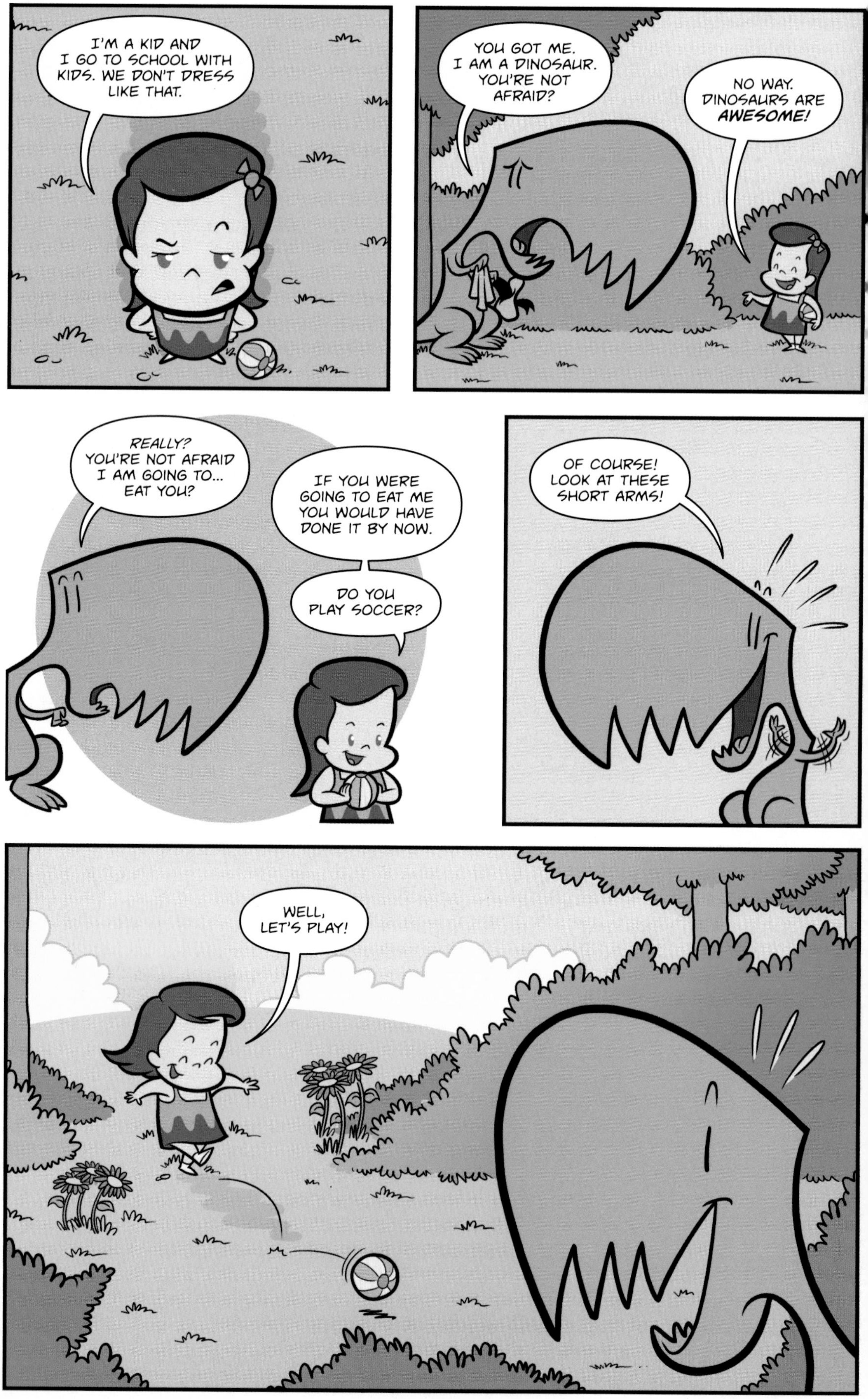
I'M A KID AND I GO TO SCHOOL WITH KIDS. WE DON'T DRESS LIKE THAT.
YOU GOT ME. I AM A DINOSAUR. YOU'RE NOT AFRAID?
NO WAY. DINOSAURS ARE AWESOME!
REALLY? YOU'RE NOT AFRAID I AM GOING TO... EAT YOU?
IF YOU WERE GOING TO EAT ME YOU WOULD HAVE DONE IT BY NOW.
DO YOU PLAY SOCCER?
OF COURSE! LOOK AT THESE SHORT ARMS!
WELL, LET'S PLAY!

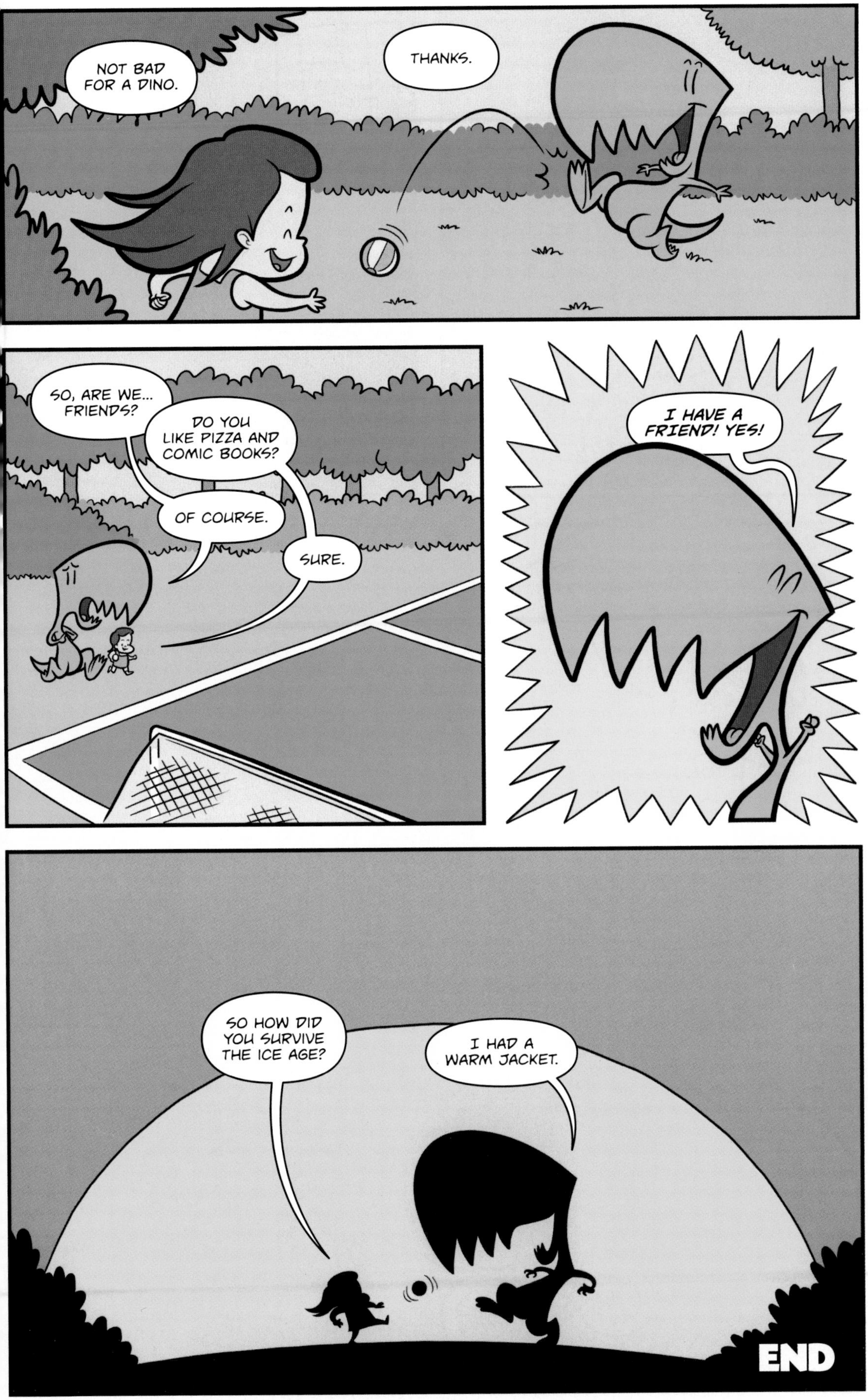
NOT BAD FOR A DINO.
THANKS.
SO, ARE WE... FRIENDS?
DO YOU LIKE PIZZA AND COMIC BOOKS?
OF COURSE.
SURE.
I HAVE A FRIEND! YES!
SO HOW DID YOU SURVIVE THE ICE AGE?
I HAD A WARM JACKET.
END

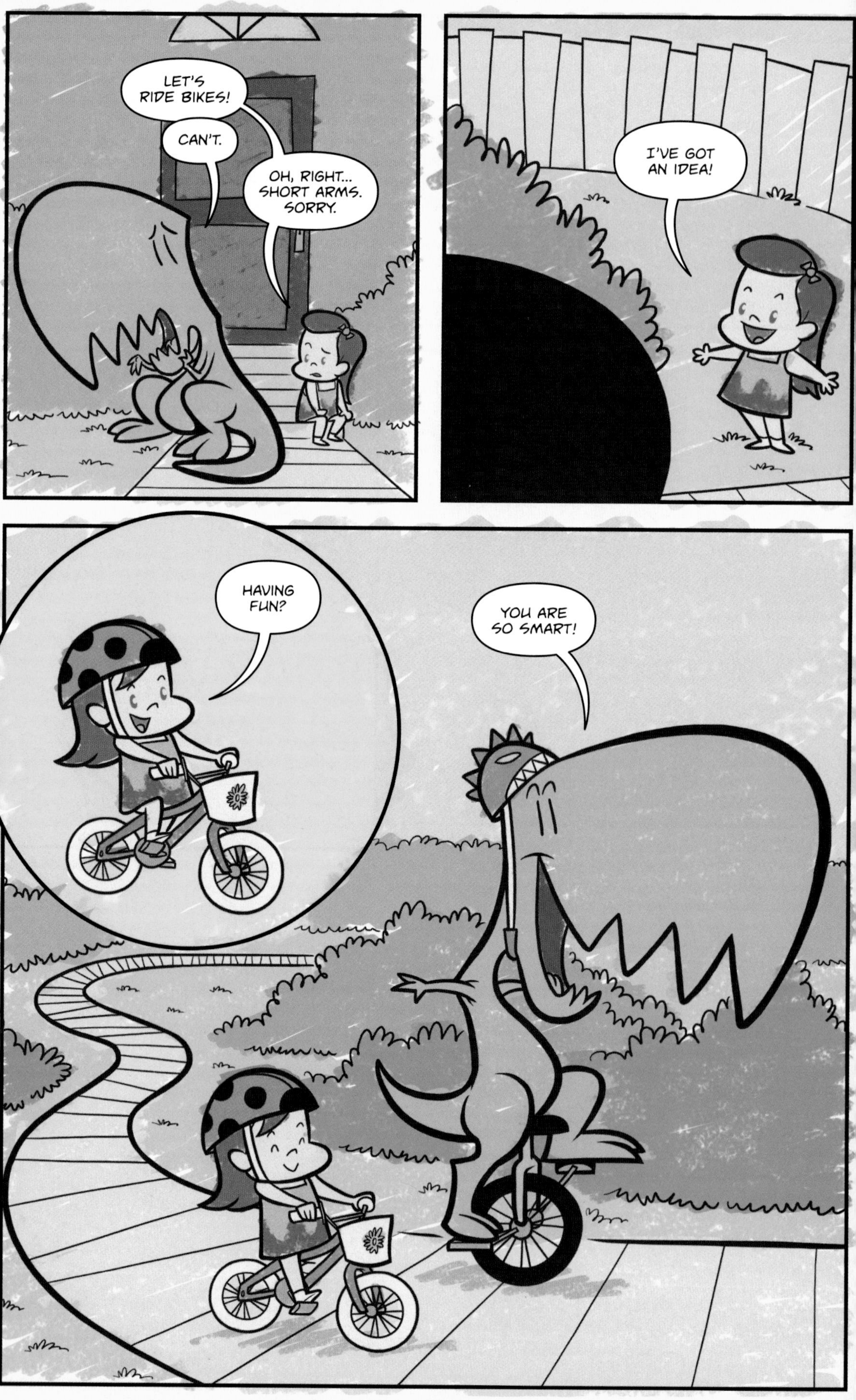
LET'S RIDE BIKES!
CAN'T.
OH, RIGHT... SHORT ARMS. SORRY.
I'VE GOT AN IDEA!
HAVING FUN?
YOU ARE SO SMART!

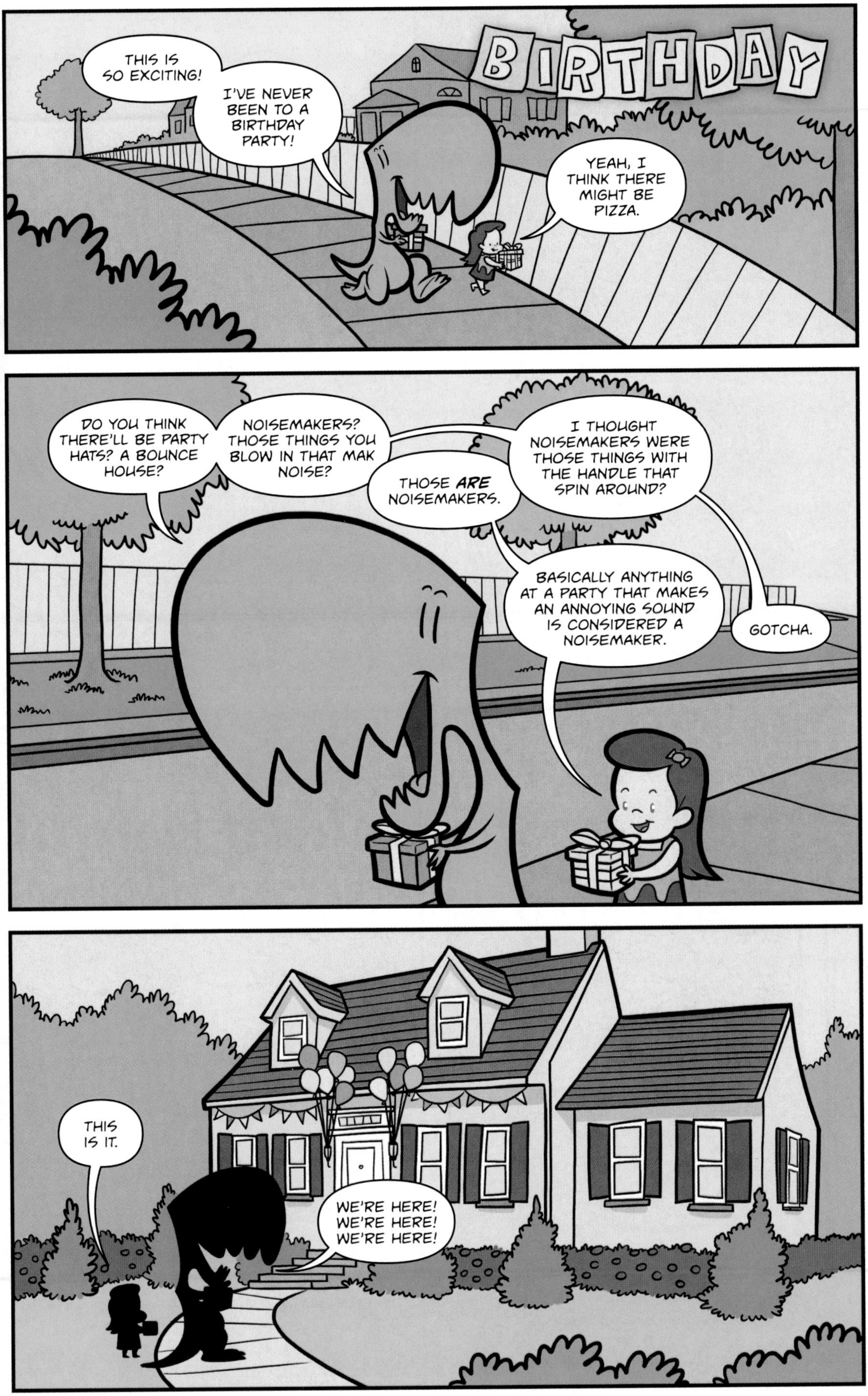
BIRTHDAY
THIS IS SO EXCITING!
I'VE NEVER BEEN TO A BIRTHDAY PARTY!
YEAH, I THINK THERE MIGHT BE PIZZA.
DO YOU THINK THERE'LL BE PARTY HATS? A BOUNCE HOUSE?
NOISEMAKERS? THOSE THINGS YOU BLOW IN THAT MAK NOISE?
I THOUGHT NOISEMAKERS WERE THOSE THINGS WITH THE HANDLE THAT SPIN AROUND?
THOSE **ARE** NOISEMAKERS.
BASICALLY ANYTHING AT A PARTY THAT MAKES AN ANNOYING SOUND IS CONSIDERED A NOISEMAKER.
GOTCHA.
THIS IS IT.
WE'RE HERE! WE'RE HERE! WE'RE HERE!

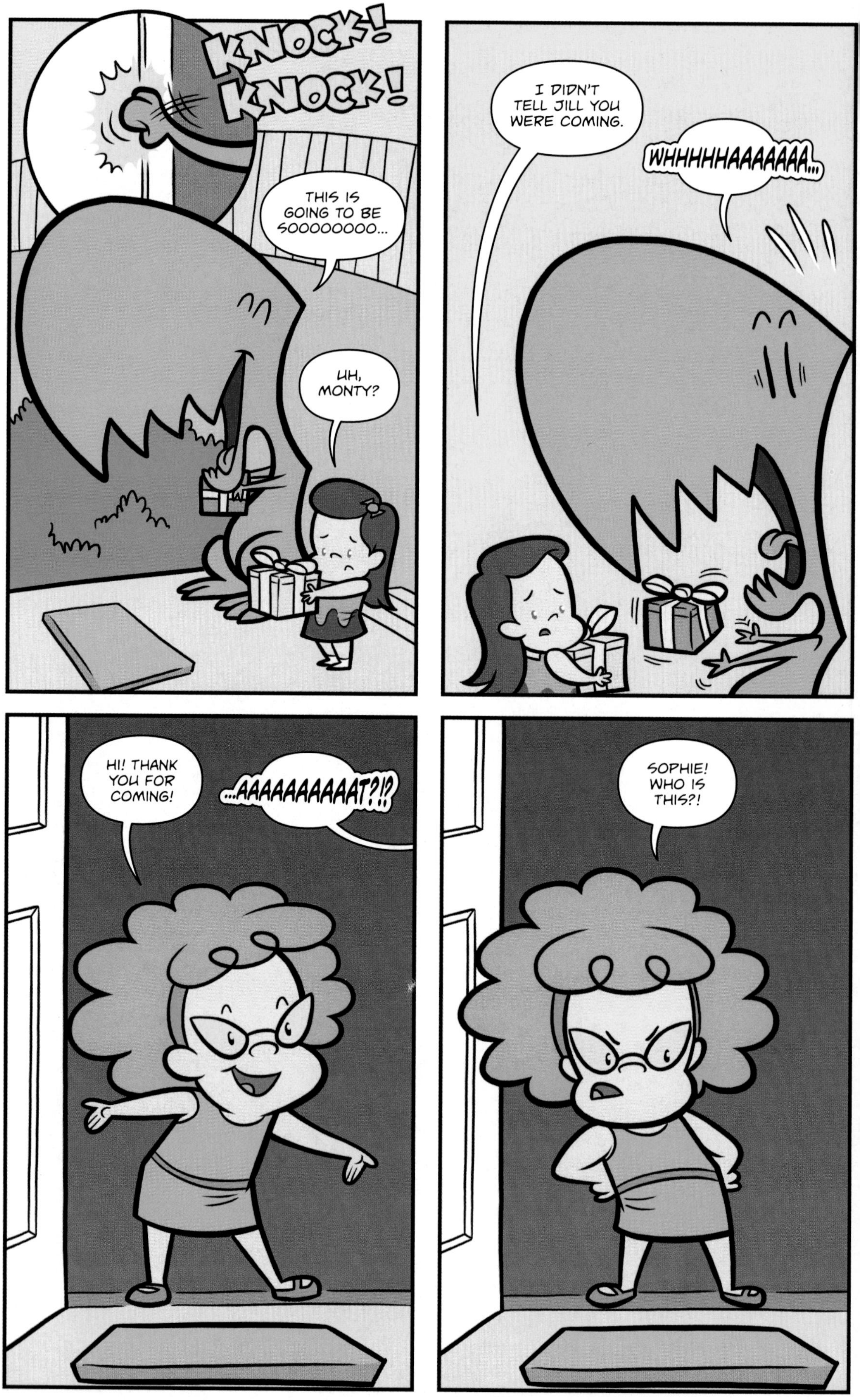
KNOCK! KNOCK!
THIS IS GOING TO BE SOOOOOOOO...
UH, MONTY?
I DIDN'T TELL JILL YOU WERE COMING.
WHHHHHAAAAAAA...
HI! THANK YOU FOR COMING!
...AAAAAAAAAAT?!?
SOPHIE! WHO IS THIS?!

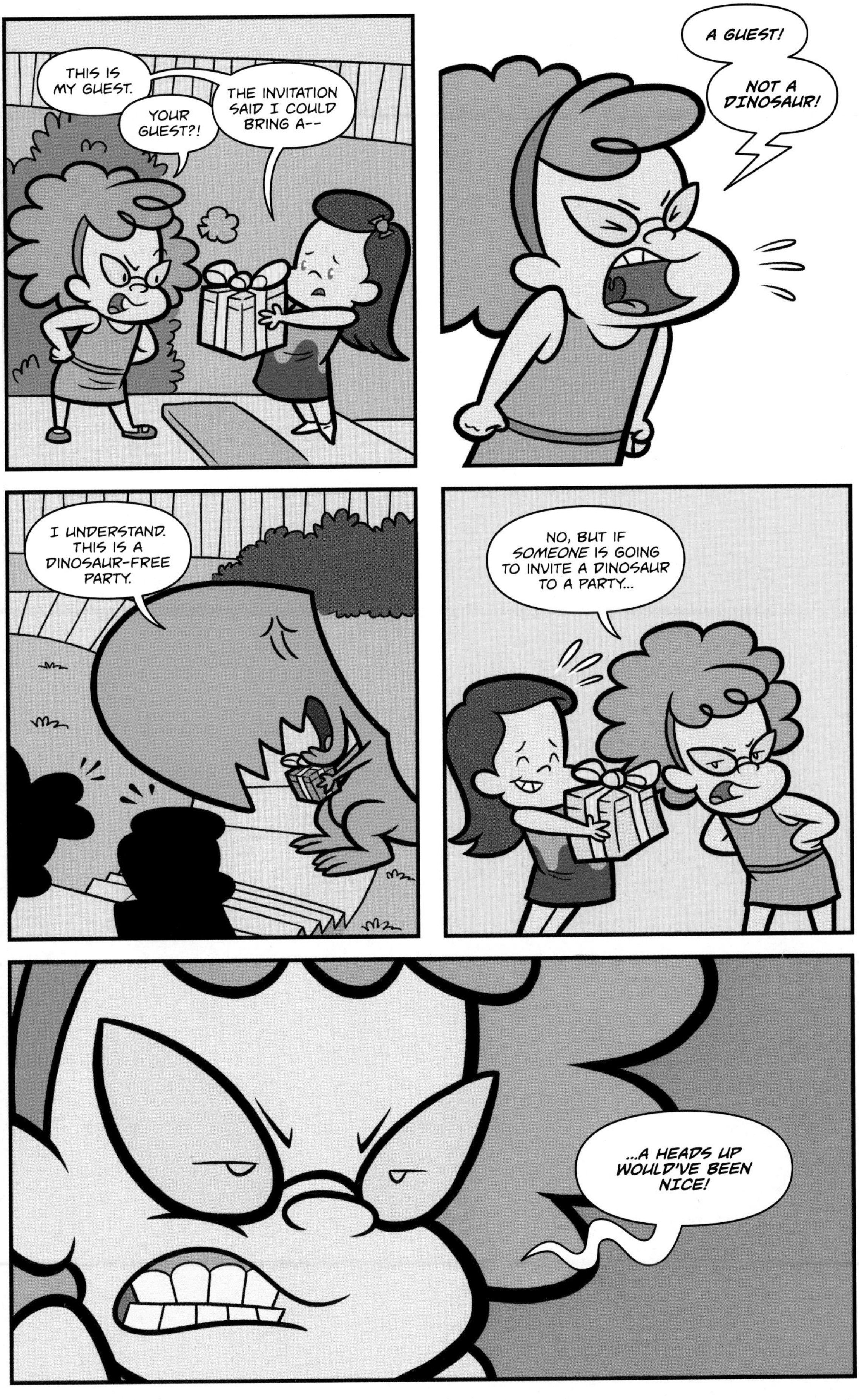
THIS IS MY GUEST.
YOUR GUEST?!
THE INVITATION SAID I COULD BRING A--
A GUEST!
NOT A DINOSAUR!
I UNDERSTAND. THIS IS A DINOSAUR-FREE PARTY.
NO, BUT IF SOMEONE IS GOING TO INVITE A DINOSAUR TO A PARTY...
...A HEADS UP WOULD'VE BEEN NICE!

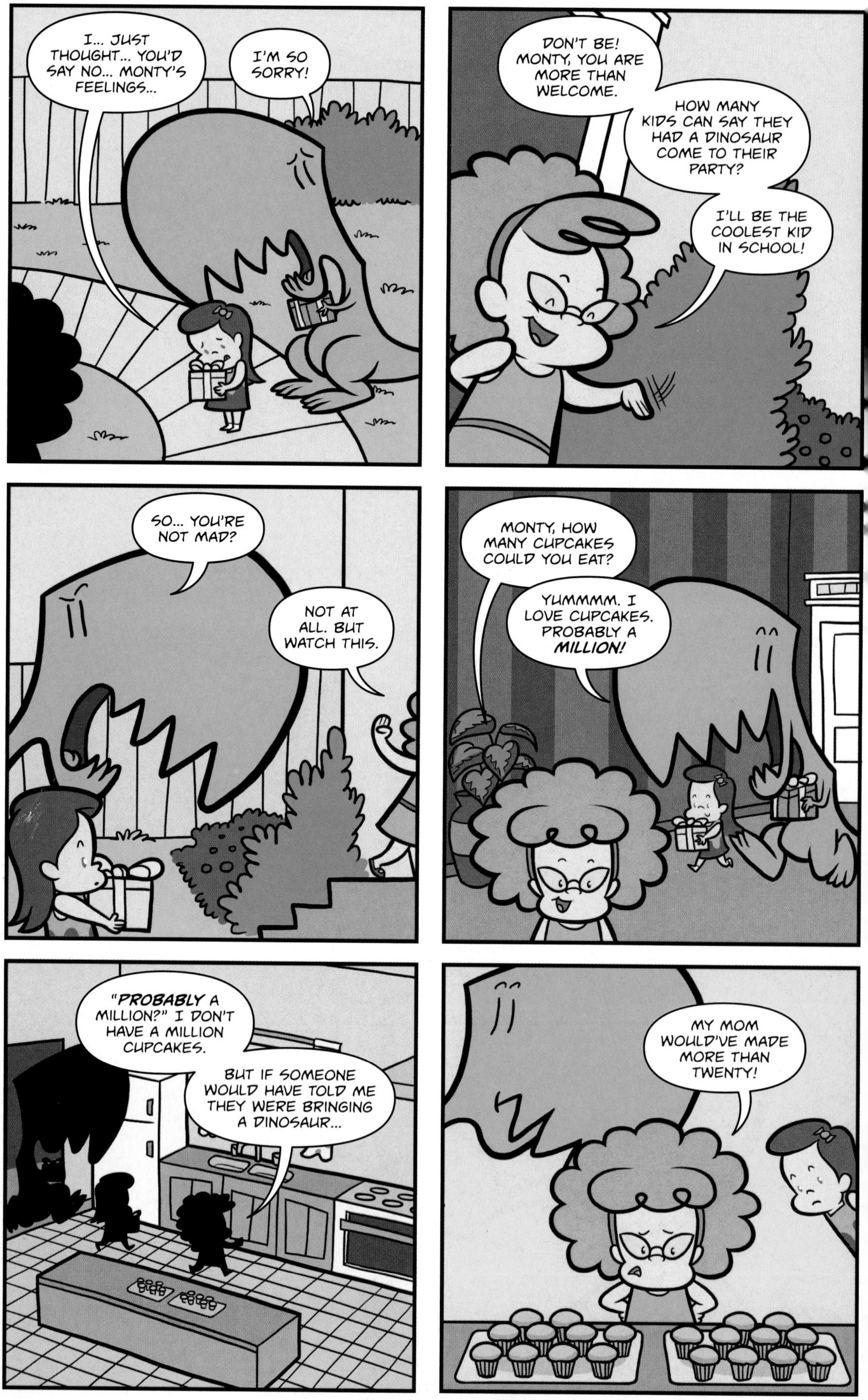
I... JUST THOUGHT... YOU'D SAY NO... MONTY'S FEELINGS...
I'M SO SORRY!
DON'T BE! MONTY, YOU ARE MORE THAN WELCOME.
HOW MANY KIDS CAN SAY THEY HAD A DINOSAUR COME TO THEIR PARTY?
I'LL BE THE COOLEST KID IN SCHOOL!
SO... YOU'RE NOT MAD?
NOT AT ALL. BUT WATCH THIS.
MONTY, HOW MANY CUPCAKES COULD YOU EAT?
YUMMMM. I LOVE CUPCAKES. PROBABLY A *MILLION!*
"*PROBABLY* A MILLION?" I DON'T HAVE A MILLION CUPCAKES.
BUT IF SOMEONE WOULD HAVE TOLD ME THEY WERE BRINGING A DINOSAUR...
MY MOM WOULD'VE MADE MORE THAN TWENTY!

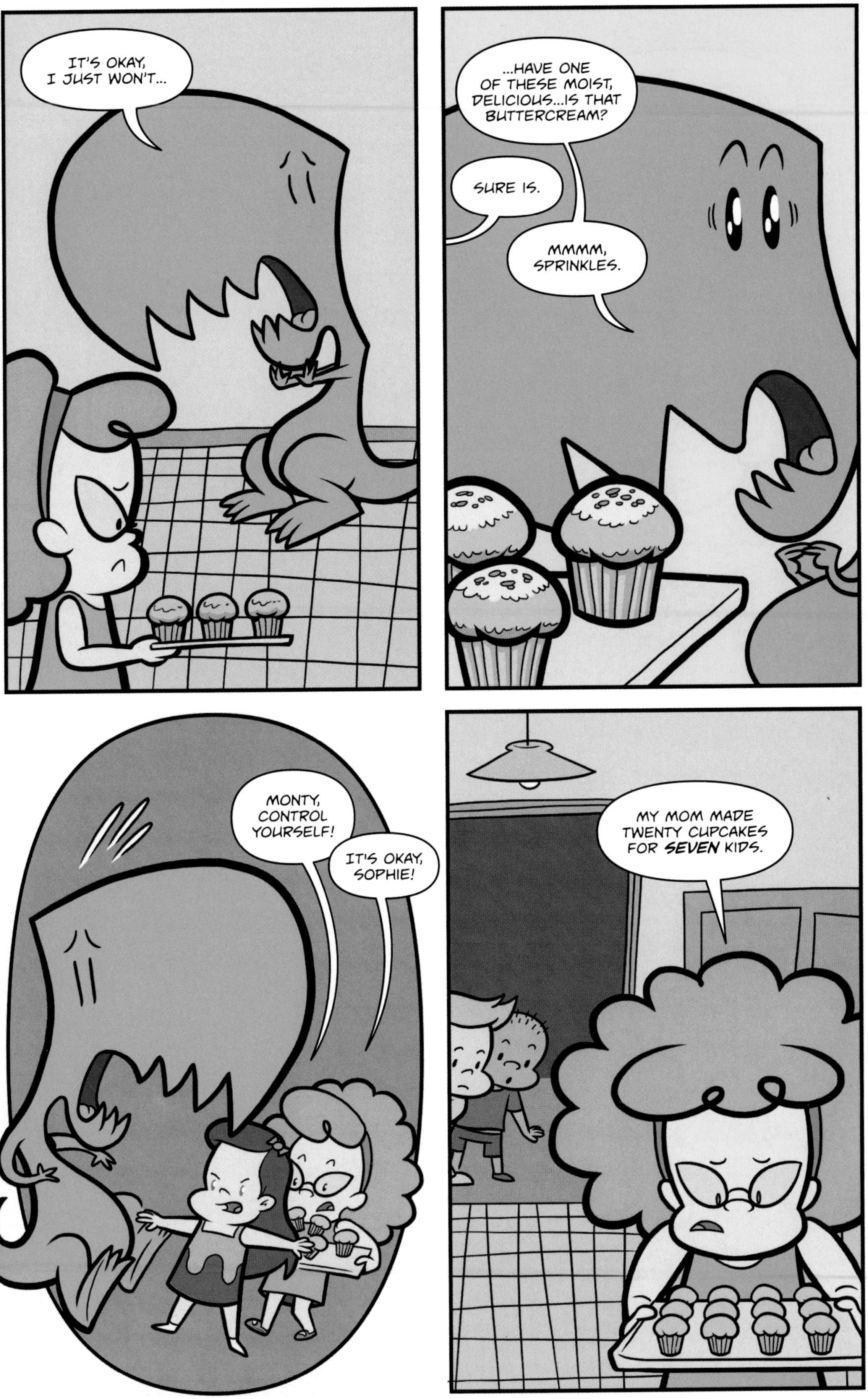
IT'S OKAY, I JUST WON'T...
...HAVE ONE OF THESE MOIST, DELICIOUS...IS THAT BUTTERCREAM?
SURE IS.
MMMM, SPRINKLES.
MONTY, CONTROL YOURSELF!
IT'S OKAY, SOPHIE!
MY MOM MADE TWENTY CUPCAKES FOR **SEVEN** KIDS.

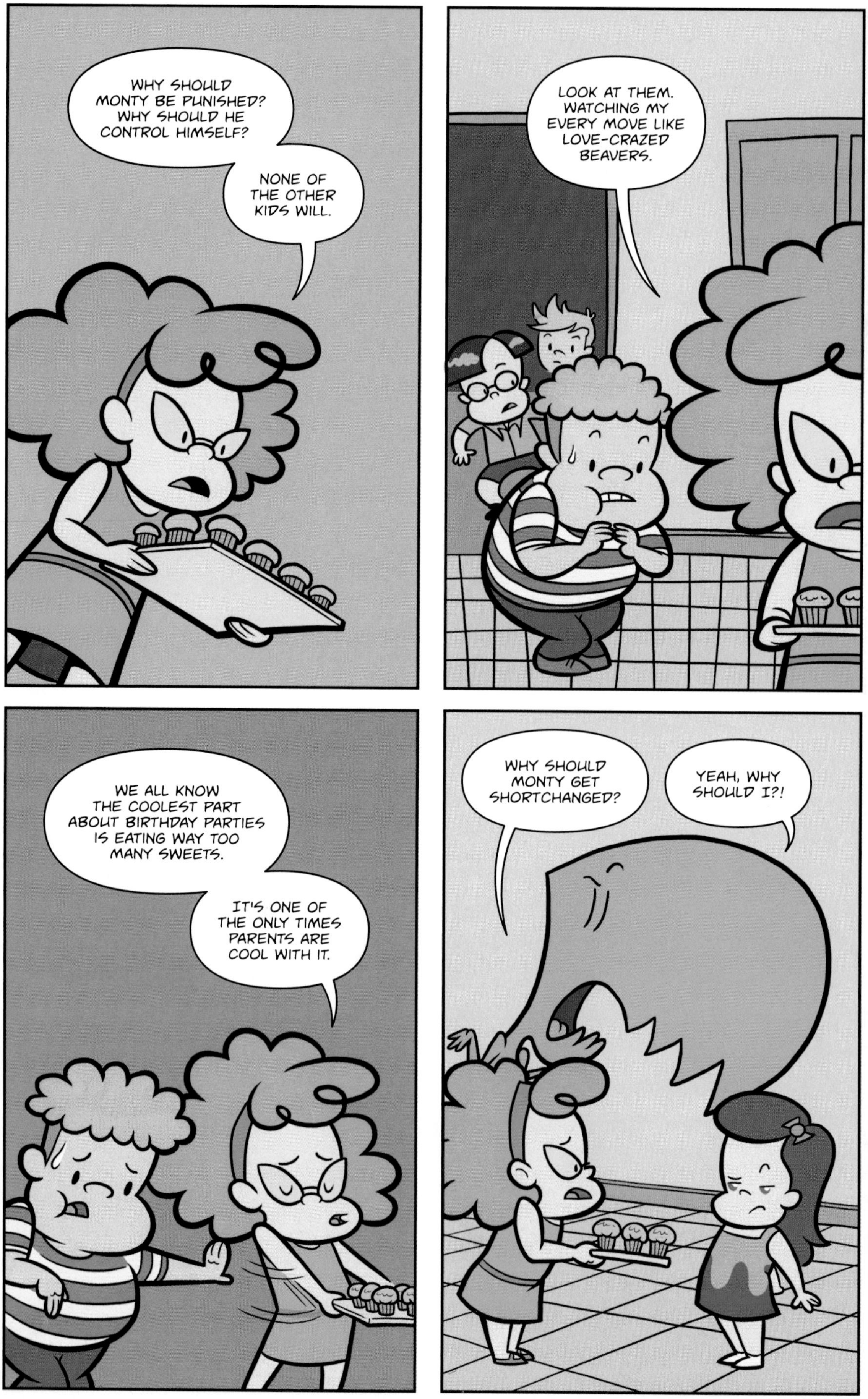
WHY SHOULD MONTY BE PUNISHED? WHY SHOULD HE CONTROL HIMSELF?
NONE OF THE OTHER KIDS WILL.
LOOK AT THEM. WATCHING MY EVERY MOVE LIKE LOVE-CRAZED BEAVERS.
WE ALL KNOW THE COOLEST PART ABOUT BIRTHDAY PARTIES IS EATING WAY TOO MANY SWEETS.
IT'S ONE OF THE ONLY TIMES PARENTS ARE COOL WITH IT.
WHY SHOULD MONTY GET SHORTCHANGED?
YEAH, WHY SHOULD I?!

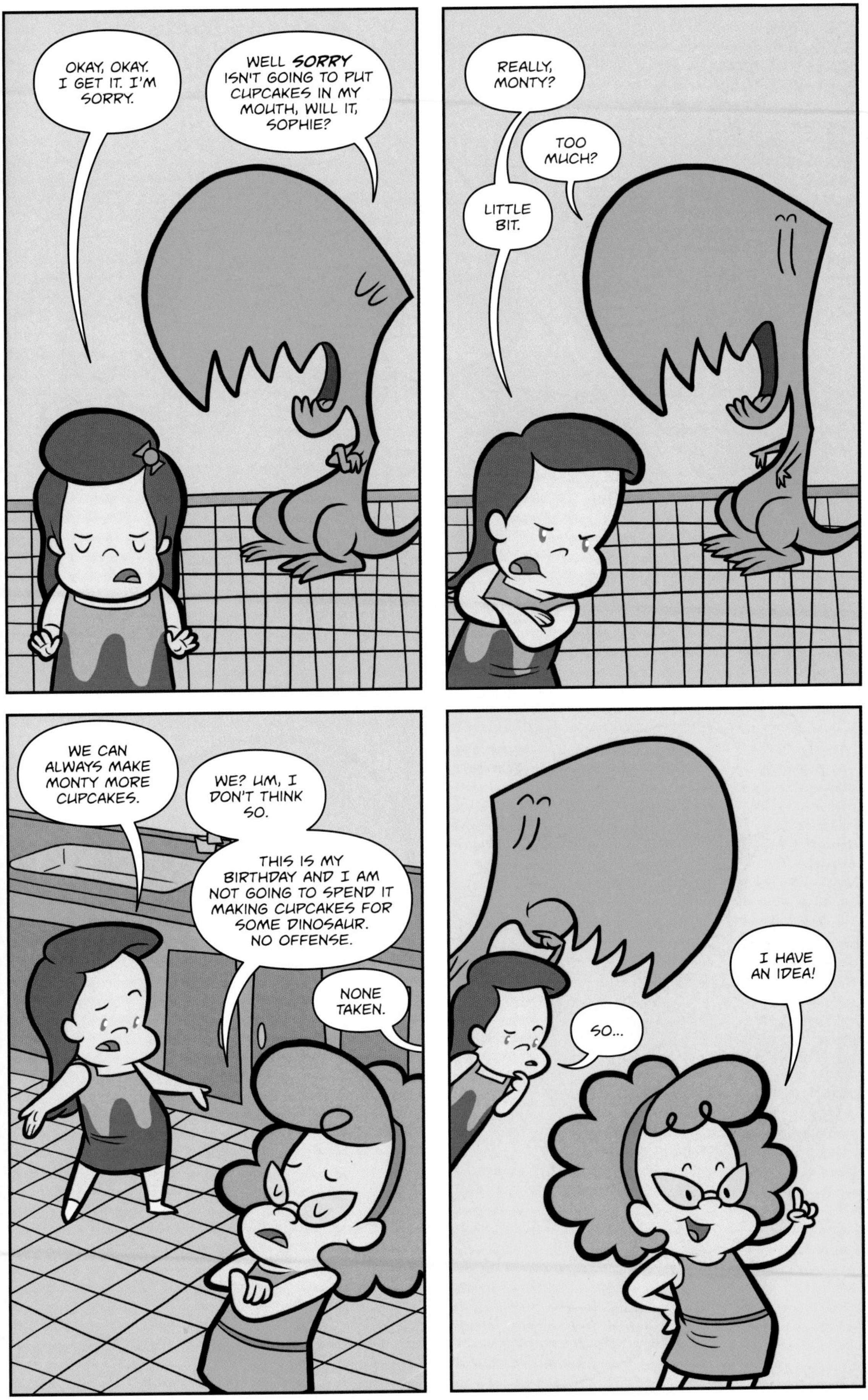
OKAY, OKAY. I GET IT. I'M SORRY.
WELL SORRY ISN'T GOING TO PUT CUPCAKES IN MY MOUTH, WILL IT, SOPHIE?
REALLY, MONTY?
TOO MUCH?
LITTLE BIT.
WE CAN ALWAYS MAKE MONTY MORE CUPCAKES.
WE? UM, I DON'T THINK SO.
THIS IS MY BIRTHDAY AND I AM NOT GOING TO SPEND IT MAKING CUPCAKES FOR SOME DINOSAUR. NO OFFENSE.
NONE TAKEN.
SO...
I HAVE AN IDEA!

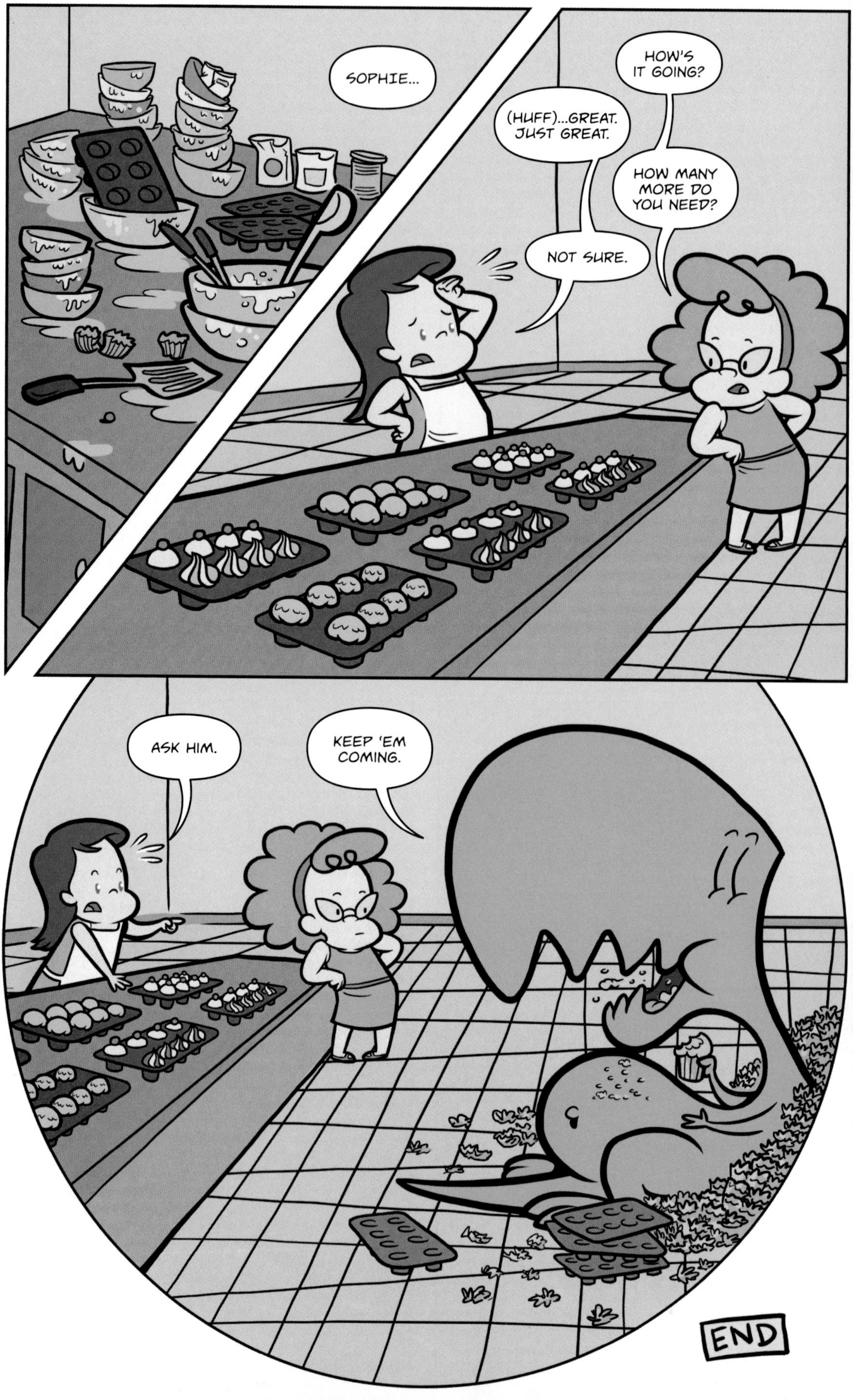
SOPHIE...
HOW'S IT GOING?
(HUFF)...GREAT. JUST GREAT.
HOW MANY MORE DO YOU NEED?
NOT SURE.
ASK HIM.
KEEP 'EM COMING.
END

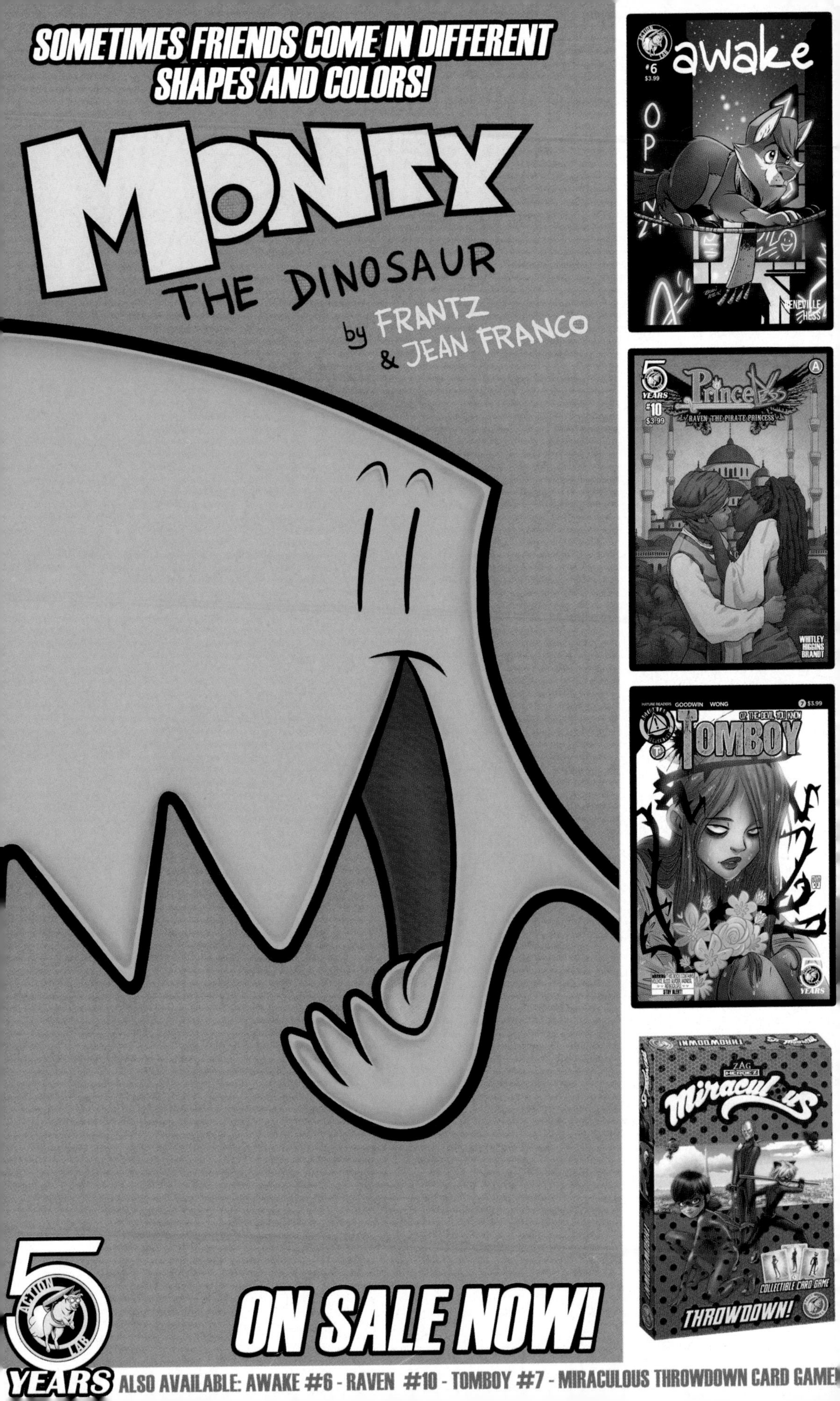
SOMETIMES FRIENDS COME IN DIFFERENT SHAPES AND COLORS!
MONTY THE DINOSAUR
by FRANTZ & JEAN FRANCO
awake
#6 $3.99
BENEVILLE HESS
Princeless
#10 $3.99
RAVEN THE PIRATE PRINCESS
WHITLEY HIGGINS BRANDT
GOODWIN WONG
7 $3.99
OZ: THE DEVIL YOU KNOW
TOMBOY
miraculous
THROWDOWN!
COLLECTIBLE CARD GAME
5 YEARS
ON SALE NOW!
ALSO AVAILABLE: AWAKE #6 - RAVEN #10 - TOMBOY #7 - MIRACULOUS THROWDOWN CARD GAME!

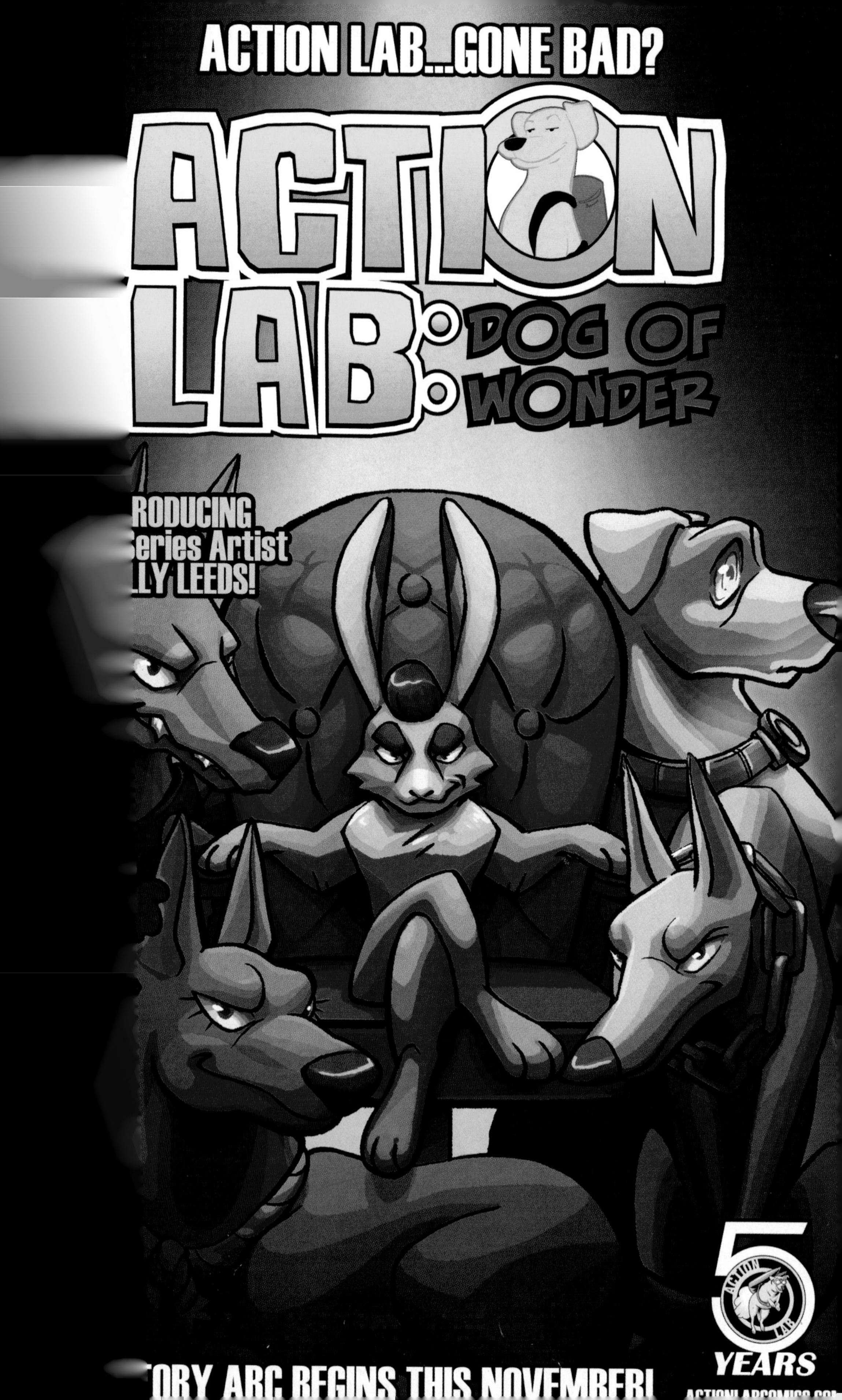

ACTION LAB...GONE BAD?
ACTION LAB: DOG OF WONDER
RODUCING
eries Artist
LLY LEEDS!
5
ACTION LAB
YEARS
TORY ARC BEGINS THIS NOVEMBER!

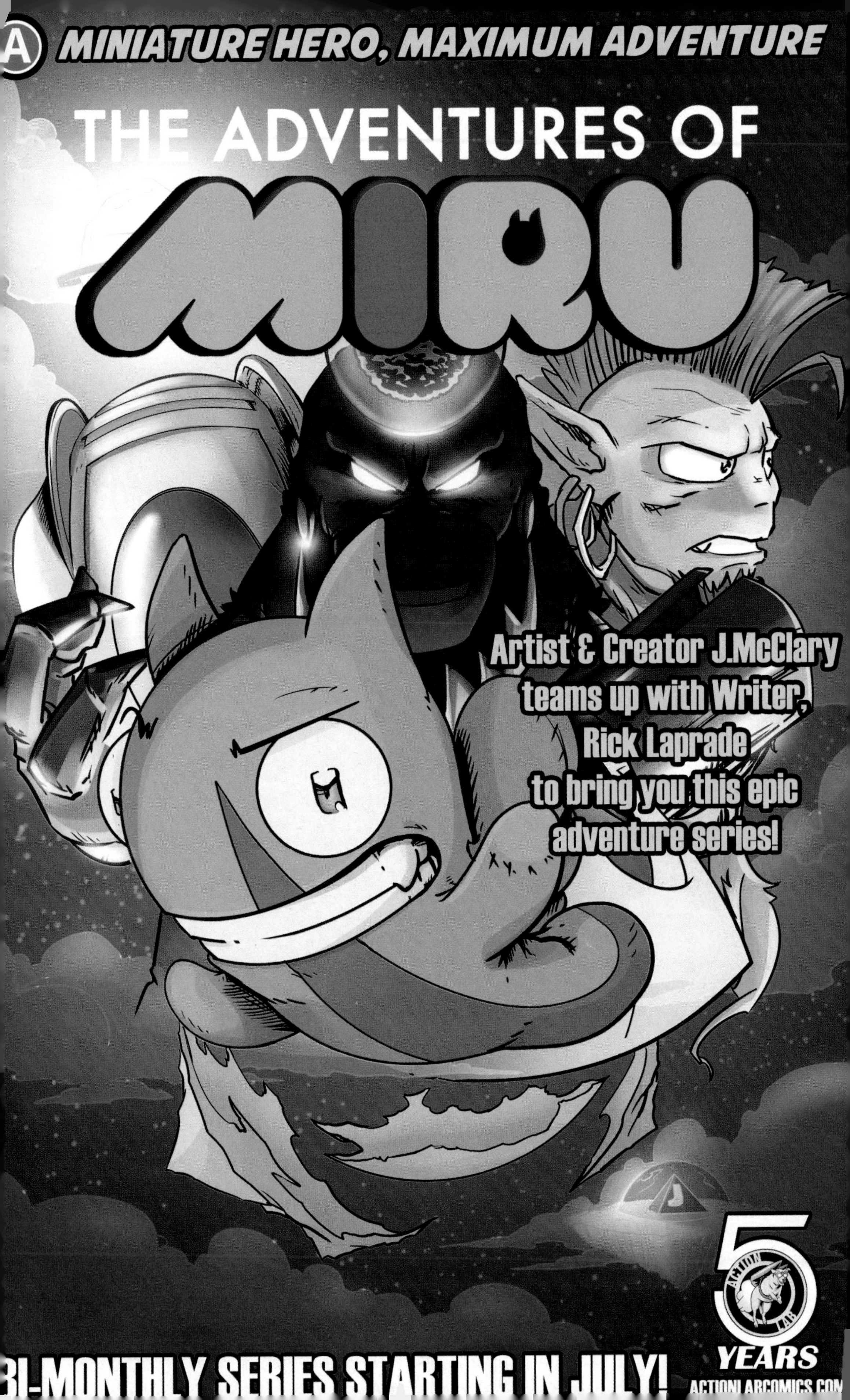
MINIATURE HERO, MAXIMUM ADVENTURE
THE ADVENTURES OF
MIRU
Artist & Creator J.McClary teams up with Writer, Rick Laprade to bring you this epic adventure series!
5 YEARS
ACTION LAB
BI-MONTHLY SERIES STARTING IN JULY!
ACTIONLABCOMICS.COM

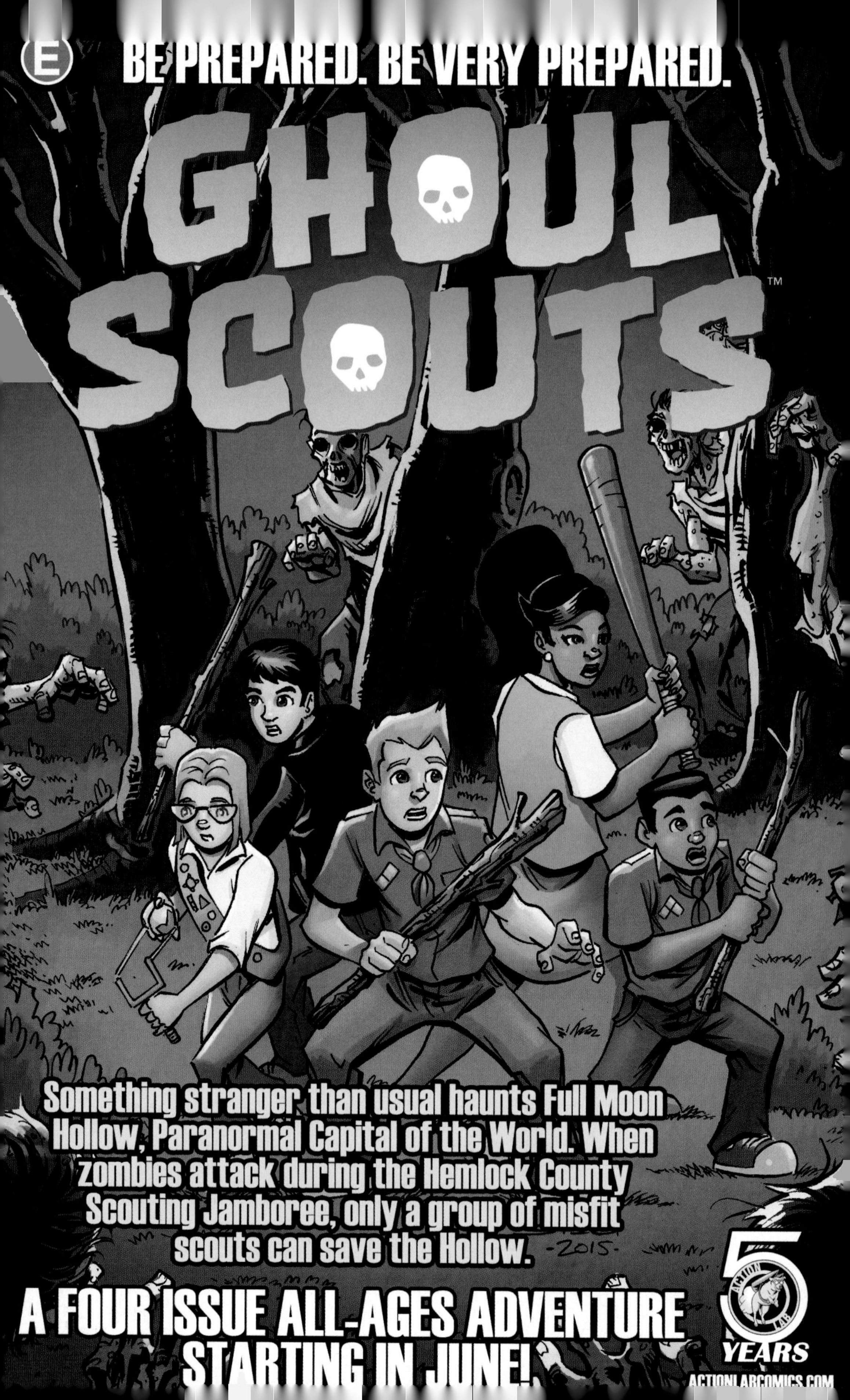
BE PREPARED. BE VERY PREPARED.
GHOUL SCOUTS™
Something stranger than usual haunts Full Moon Hollow, Paranormal Capital of the World. When zombies attack during the Hemlock County Scouting Jamboree, only a group of misfit scouts can save the Hollow.
A FOUR ISSUE ALL-AGES ADVENTURE STARTING IN JUNE!
5 YEARS
ACTIONLABCOMICS.COM

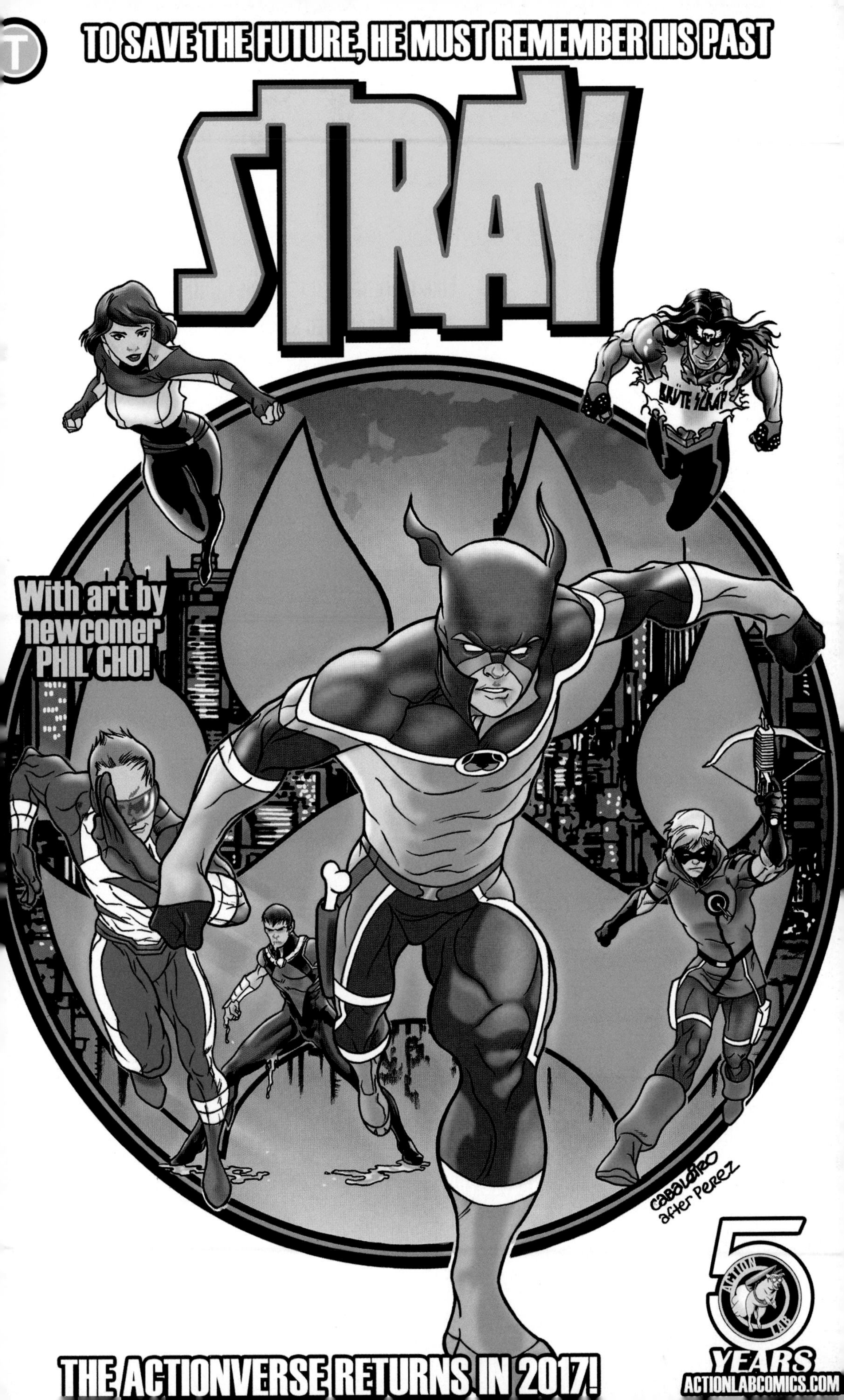
TO SAVE THE FUTURE, HE MUST REMEMBER HIS PAST
STRAY
With art by newcomer PHIL CHO!
CABALLERO after PEREZ
5 YEARS
ACTIONLABCOMICS.COM
THE ACTIONVERSE RETURNS IN 2017!

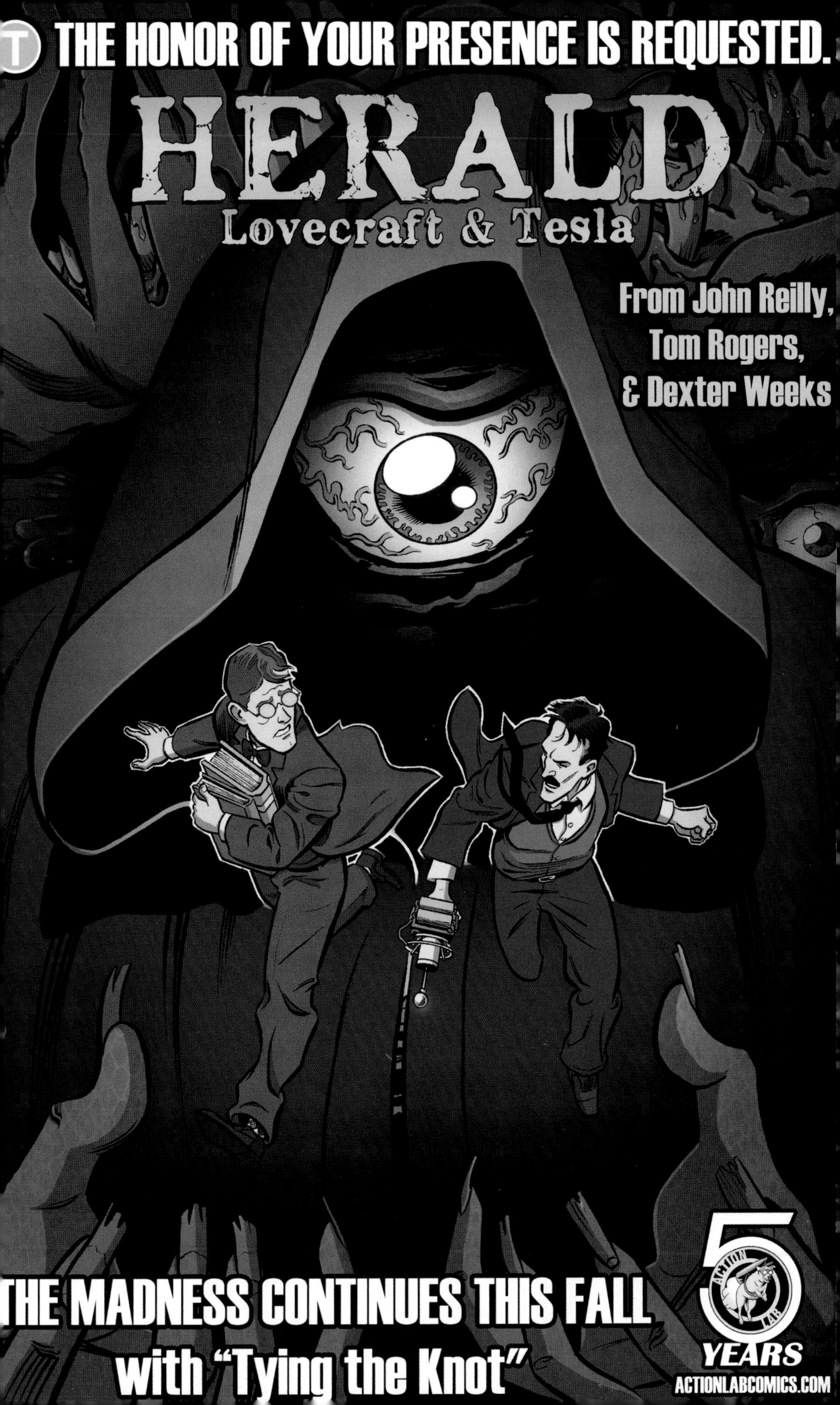
THE HONOR OF YOUR PRESENCE IS REQUESTED.
HERALD
Lovecraft & Tesla
From John Reilly,
Tom Rogers,
& Dexter Weeks
THE MADNESS CONTINUES THIS FALL
with "Tying the Knot"
5 YEARS
ACTIONLABCOMICS.COM

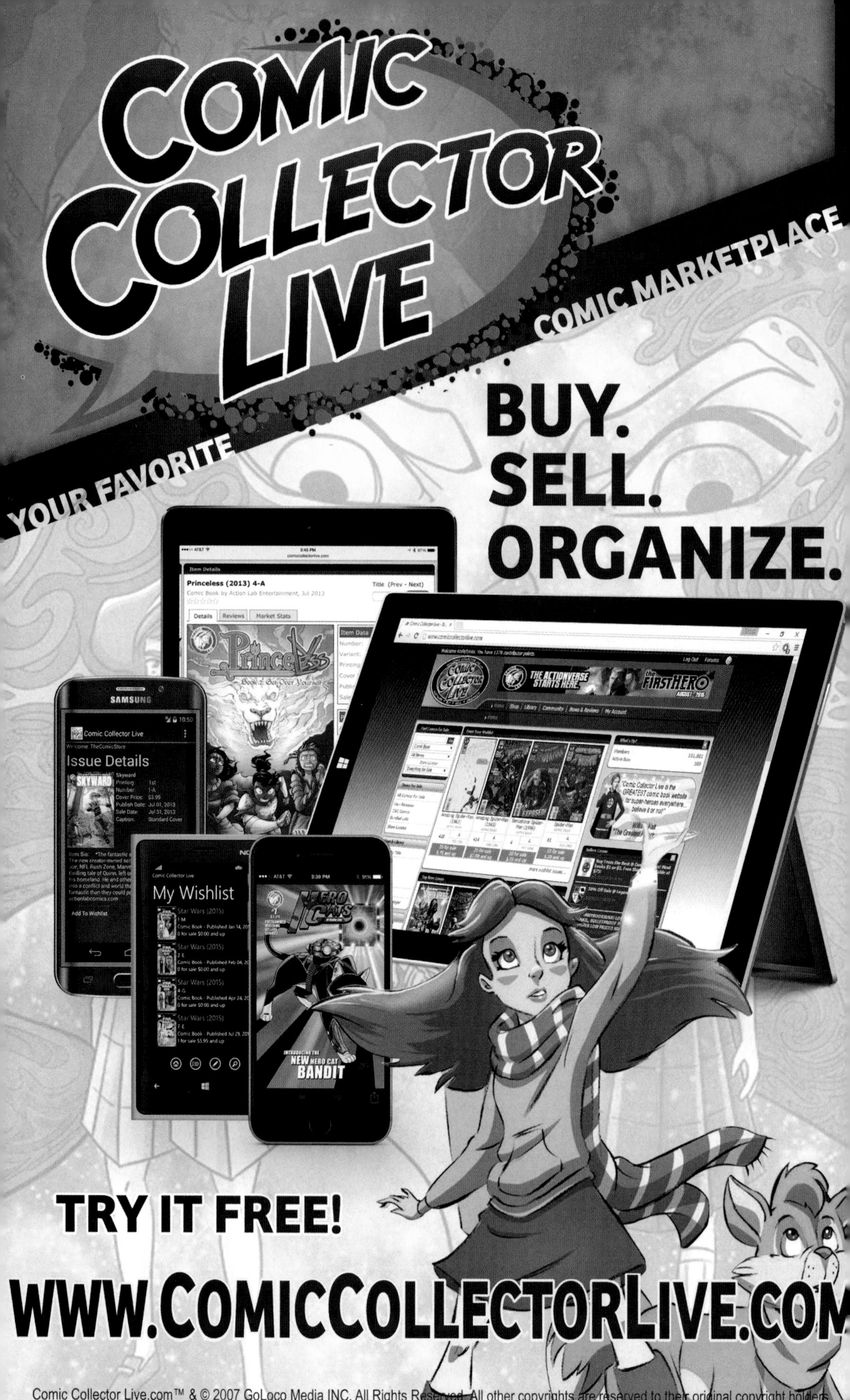
COMIC COLLECTOR LIVE
YOUR FAVORITE COMIC MARKETPLACE
BUY.
SELL.
ORGANIZE.
TRY IT FREE!
WWW.COMICCOLLECTORLIVE.COM

# Meet the new class!

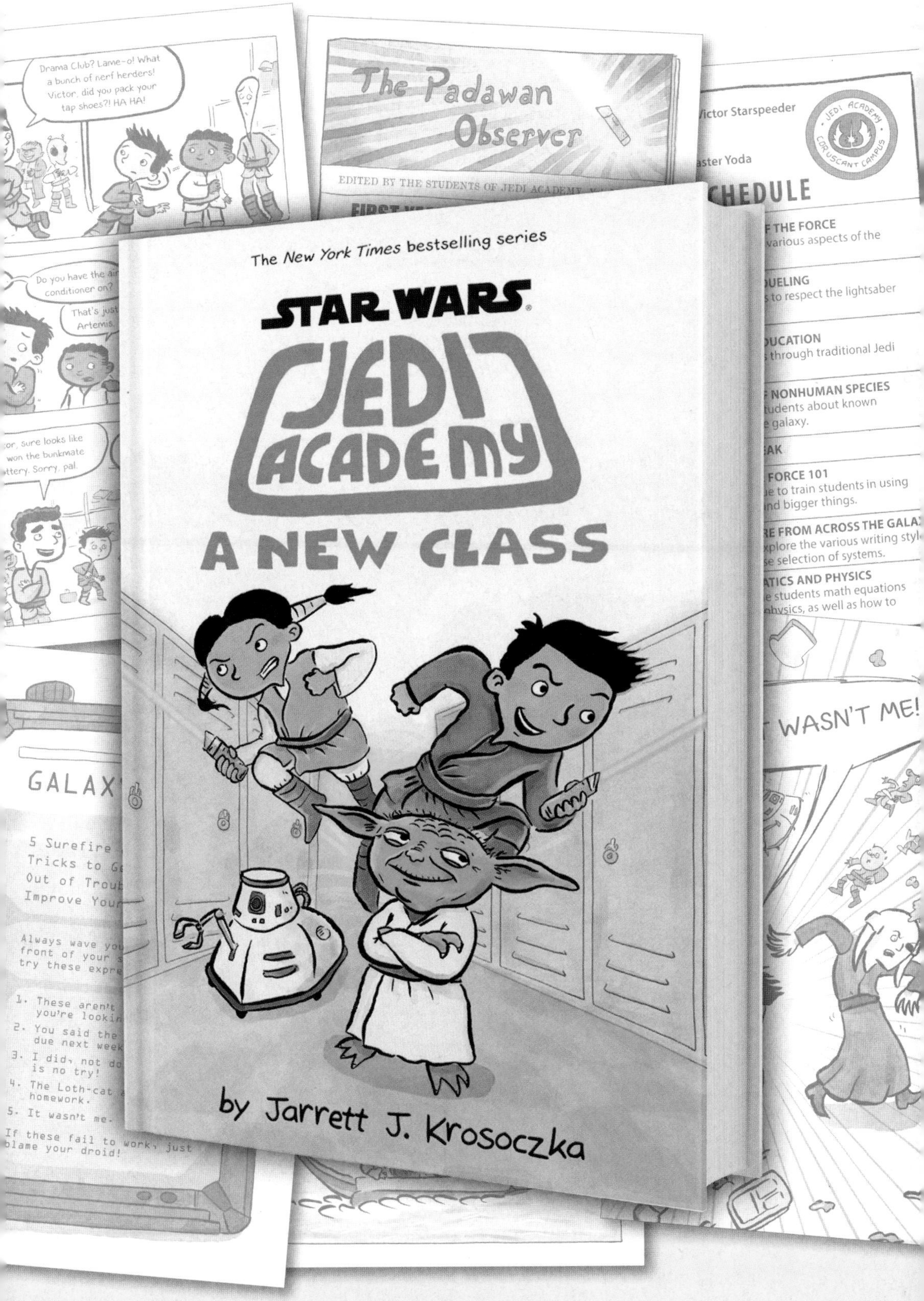
Drama Club? Lame-o! What a bunch of nerf herders! Victor, did you pack your tap shoes?! HA HA!
The Padawan Observer
EDITED BY THE STUDENTS OF JEDI ACADEMY
Victor Starspeeder
aster Yoda
CHEDULE
F THE FORCE
various aspects of the
UELING
to respect the lightsaber
UCATION
through traditional Jedi
NONHUMAN SPECIES
tudents about known
e galaxy.
AK
FORCE 101
e to train students in using
nd bigger things.
RE FROM ACROSS THE GALA
xplore the various writing styl
e selection of systems.
ATICS AND PHYSICS
e students math equations
physics, as well as how to
Do you have the air conditioner on?
That's just Artemis.
or, sure looks like won the bunkmate ttery. Sorry, pal.
The New York Times bestselling series
STAR WARS
JEDI ACADEMY
A NEW CLASS
by Jarrett J. Krosoczka
GALAX
5 Surefire
Tricks to G
Out of Troub
Improve Your
Always wave yo
front of your
try these expre
1. These aren't
you're lookin
2. You said the
due next week
3. I did, not do
is no try!
4. The Loth-cat a
homework.
5. It wasn't me.
If these fail to work, just
blame your droid!
WASN'T ME!

I THOUGHT I WOULD BE ON THE COVER TOO!

Mony The Dinosaur - Action Lab
www.actionlabcomics.com
00111
7 02382 69143 1

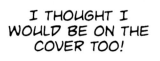

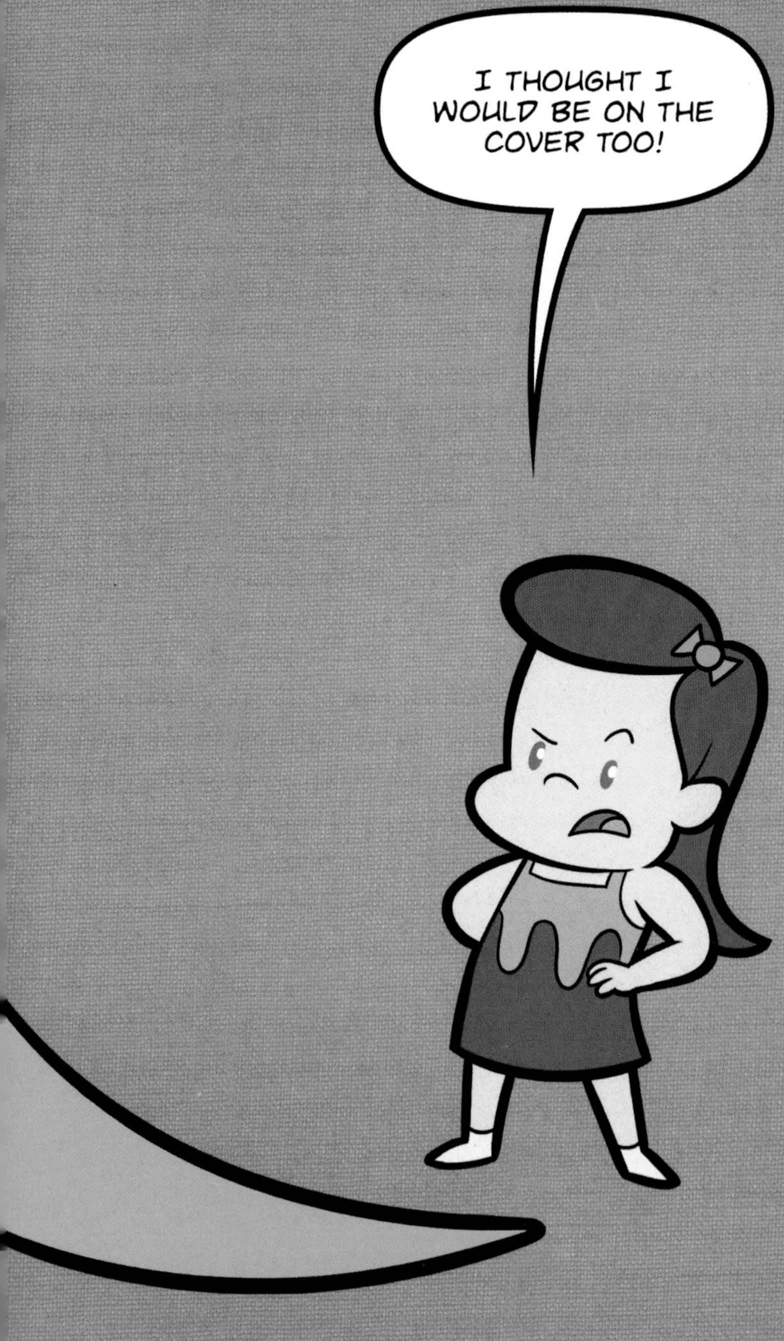

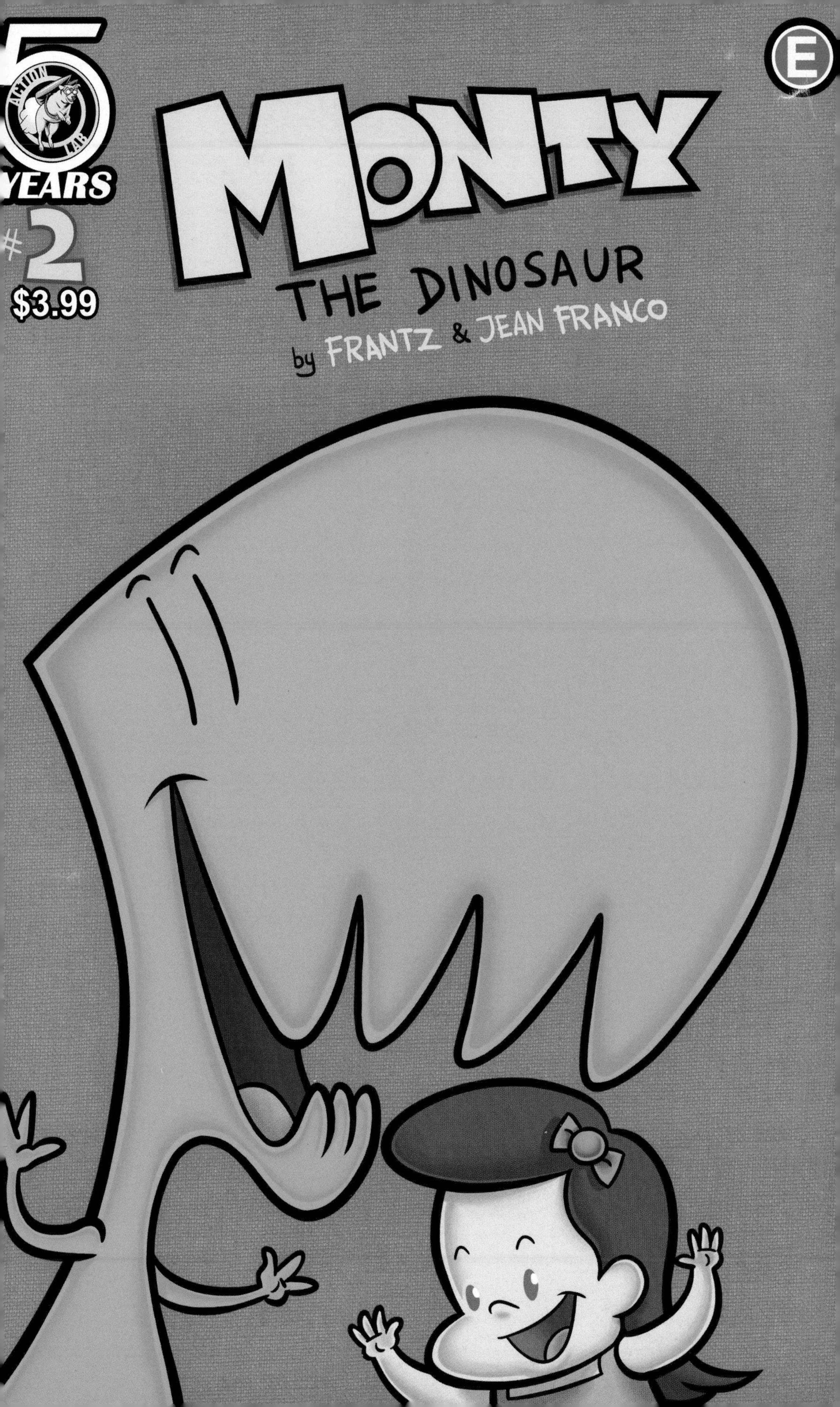

5 YEARS
ACTION LAB
#2
$3.99
E
MONTY
THE DINOSAUR
by FRANTZ & JEAN FRANCO

# MONTY
## THE DINOSAUR
-ISSUE TWO-

Written by:
**Bob Frantz**
@bfrantz19

Art by:
**Jean Franco**
facebook.com/jeanfrancodg

Edited By:
**Mike Exner III**
@mikeexnerIII

Inspiration:
**Sophie and Bobby Frantz**

**Bryan Seaton: Publisher • Dave Dwonch: President • Shawn Gabborin: Editor In Chief**
**Jason Martin: Publisher-Danger Zone • Jamal Igle: Vice-President of Marketing**
**Jim Dietz: Social Media Director • Nicole DAndria: Editor • Chad Cicconi: Lord of the Flies**
**Colleen Boyd: Submissions Editor.**

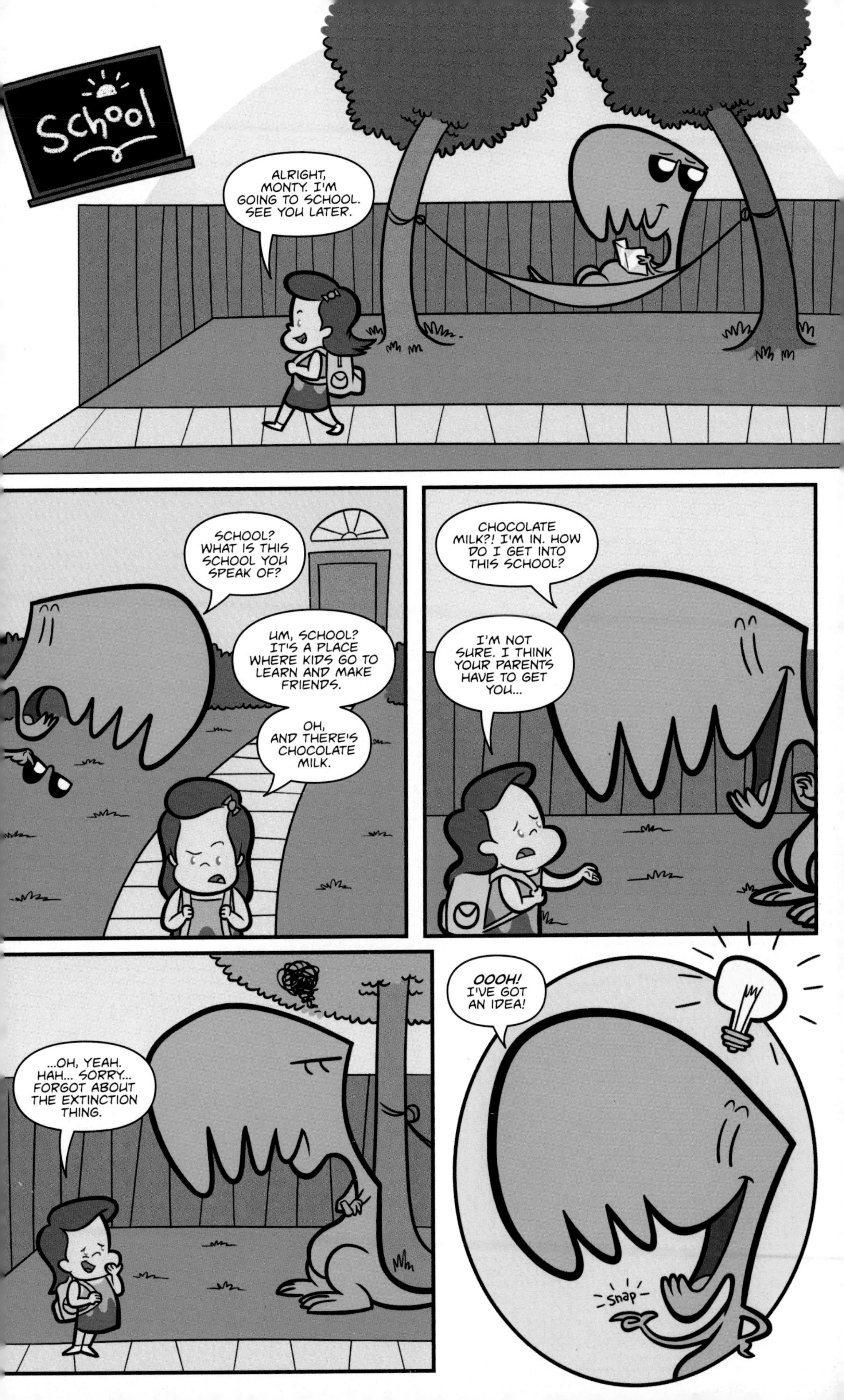
School
ALRIGHT, MONTY. I'M GOING TO SCHOOL. SEE YOU LATER.
SCHOOL? WHAT IS THIS SCHOOL YOU SPEAK OF?
UM, SCHOOL? IT'S A PLACE WHERE KIDS GO TO LEARN AND MAKE FRIENDS.
OH, AND THERE'S CHOCOLATE MILK.
CHOCOLATE MILK?! I'M IN. HOW DO I GET INTO THIS SCHOOL?
I'M NOT SURE. I THINK YOUR PARENTS HAVE TO GET YOU...
...OH, YEAH. HAH... SORRY... FORGOT ABOUT THE EXTINCTION THING.
OOOH! I'VE GOT AN IDEA!
snap

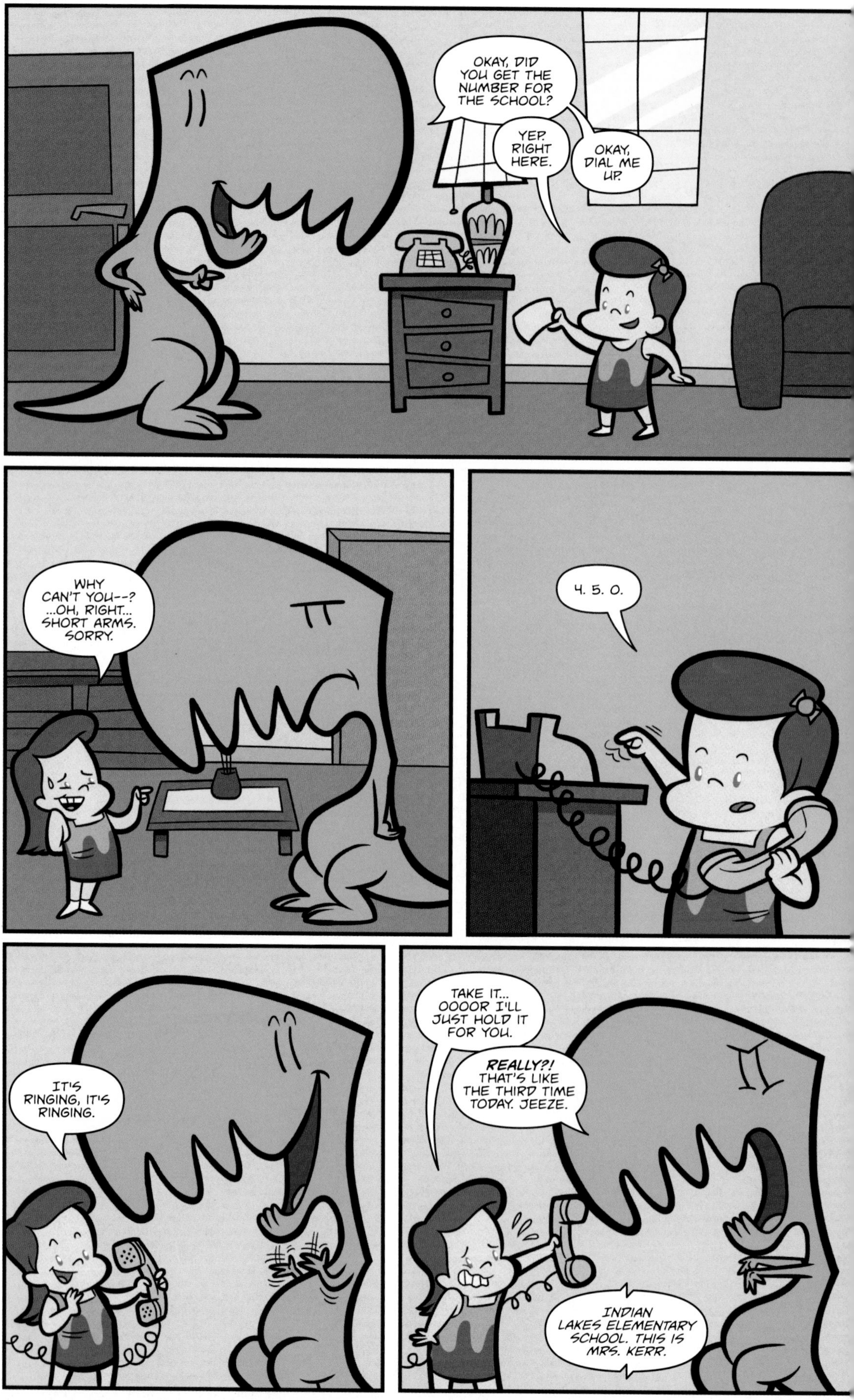
OKAY, DID YOU GET THE NUMBER FOR THE SCHOOL?
YEP. RIGHT HERE.
OKAY, DIAL ME UP.
WHY CAN'T YOU--? ...OH, RIGHT... SHORT ARMS. SORRY.
4. 5. 0.
IT'S RINGING, IT'S RINGING.
TAKE IT... OOOOR I'LL JUST HOLD IT FOR YOU.
REALLY?! THAT'S LIKE THE THIRD TIME TODAY. JEEZE.
INDIAN LAKES ELEMENTARY SCHOOL. THIS IS MRS. KERR.

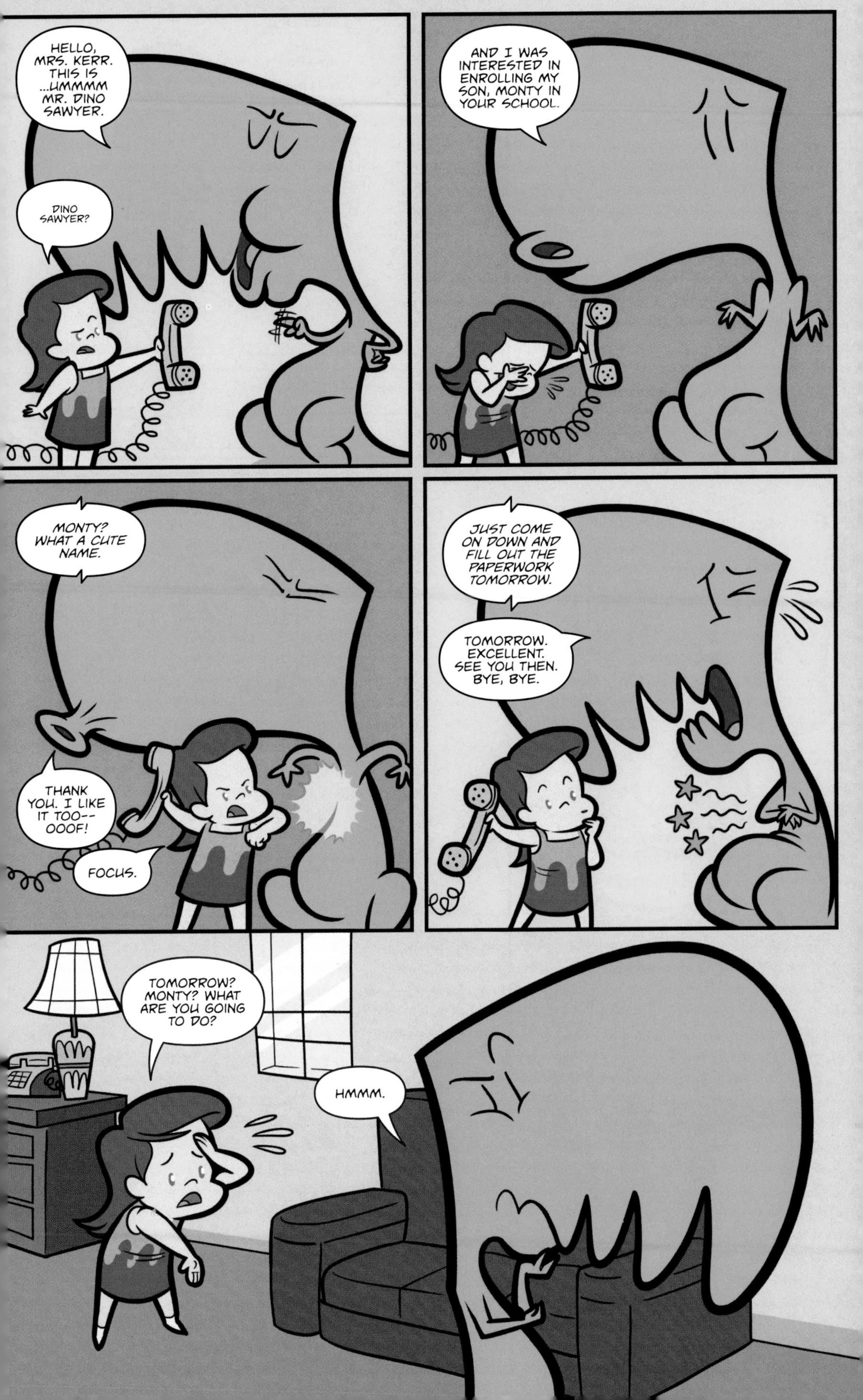
HELLO, MRS. KERR. THIS IS ...UMMMM MR. DINO SAWYER.
DINO SAWYER?
AND I WAS INTERESTED IN ENROLLING MY SON, MONTY IN YOUR SCHOOL.
MONTY? WHAT A CUTE NAME.
THANK YOU. I LIKE IT TOO-- OOOF!
FOCUS.
JUST COME ON DOWN AND FILL OUT THE PAPERWORK TOMORROW.
TOMORROW. EXCELLENT. SEE YOU THEN. BYE, BYE.
TOMORROW? MONTY? WHAT ARE YOU GOING TO DO?
HMMM.

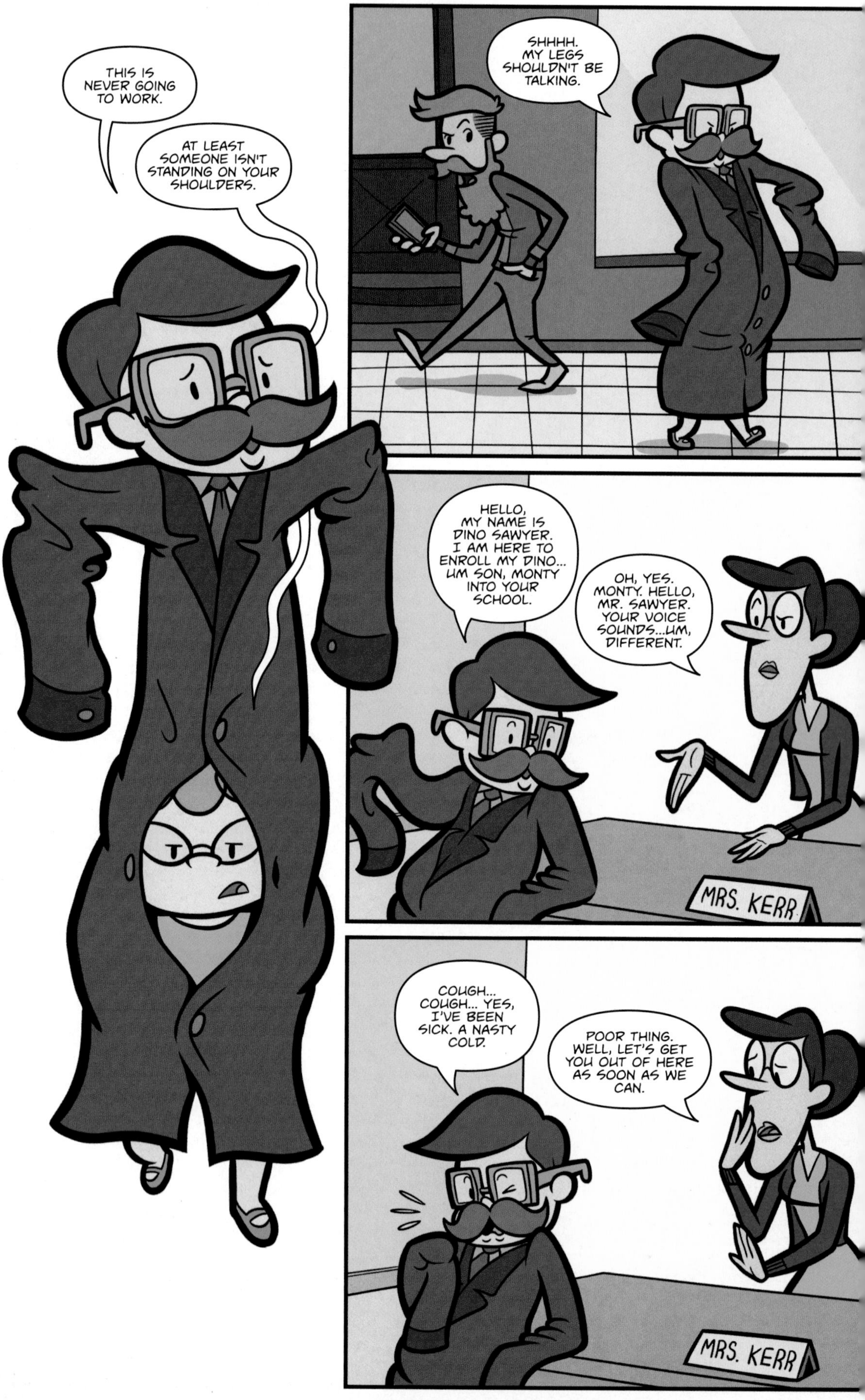
THIS IS NEVER GOING TO WORK.
AT LEAST SOMEONE ISN'T STANDING ON YOUR SHOULDERS.
SHHHH. MY LEGS SHOULDN'T BE TALKING.
HELLO, MY NAME IS DINO SAWYER. I AM HERE TO ENROLL MY DINO... UM SON, MONTY INTO YOUR SCHOOL.
OH, YES. MONTY. HELLO, MR. SAWYER. YOUR VOICE SOUNDS...UM, DIFFERENT.
MRS. KERR
COUGH... COUGH... YES, I'VE BEEN SICK. A NASTY COLD.
POOR THING. WELL, LET'S GET YOU OUT OF HERE AS SOON AS WE CAN.
MRS. KERR

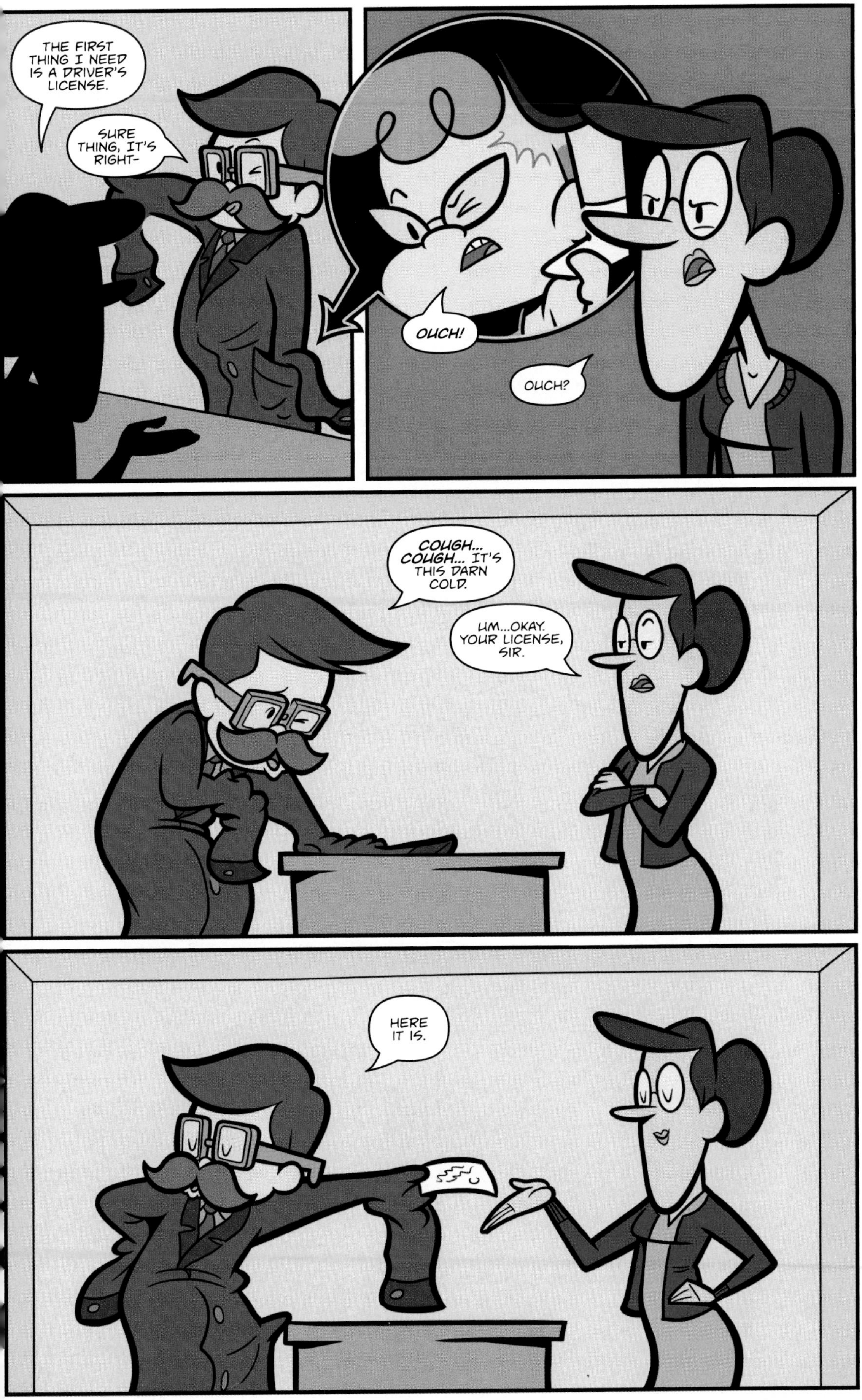
THE FIRST THING I NEED IS A DRIVER'S LICENSE.
SURE THING, IT'S RIGHT-
OUCH!
OUCH?
COUGH... COUGH... IT'S THIS DARN COLD.
UM...OKAY. YOUR LICENSE, SIR.
HERE IT IS.

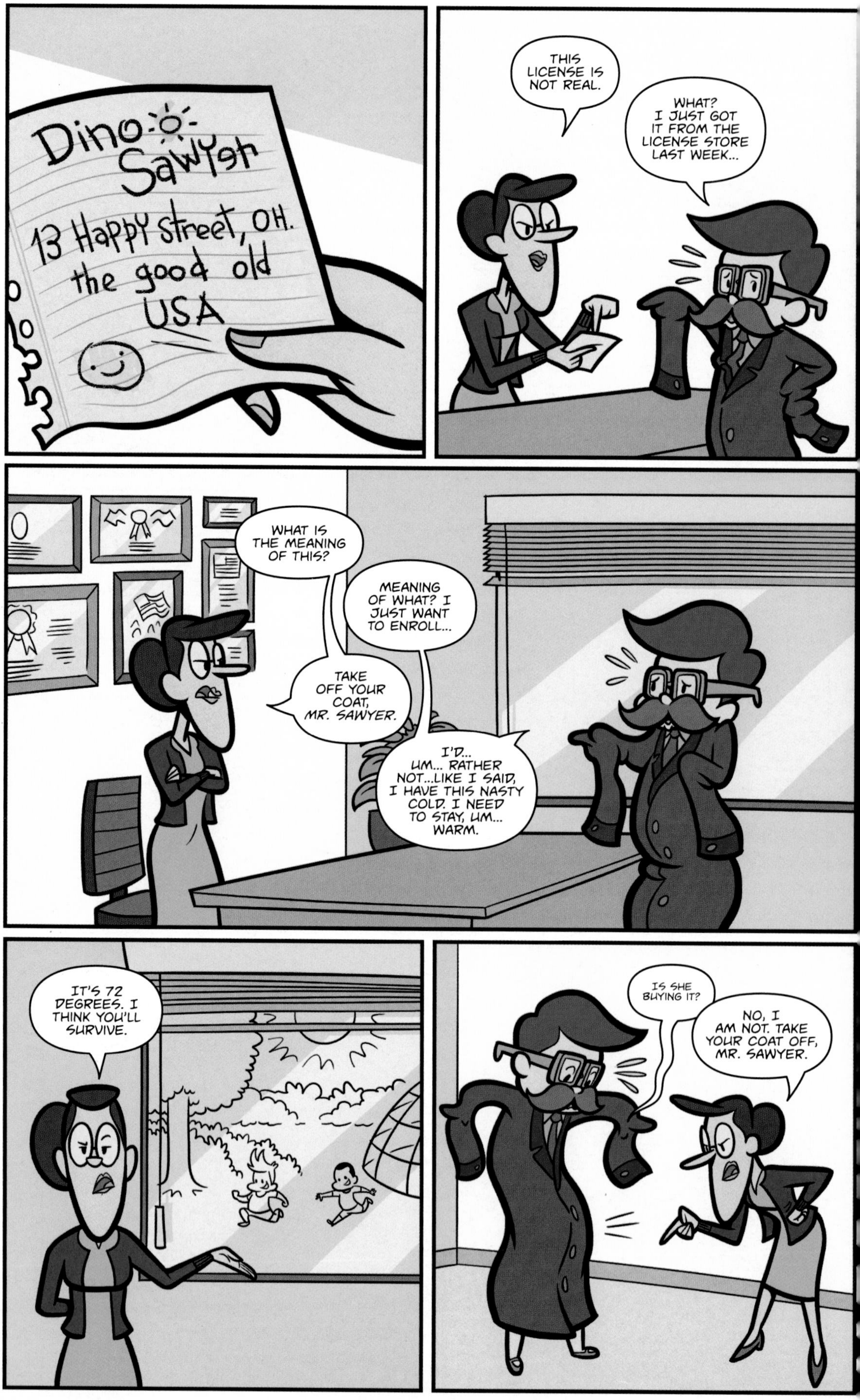

Dino Sawyer
13 Happy street, OH.
the good old
USA
THIS LICENSE IS NOT REAL.
WHAT? I JUST GOT IT FROM THE LICENSE STORE LAST WEEK...
WHAT IS THE MEANING OF THIS?
MEANING OF WHAT? I JUST WANT TO ENROLL...
TAKE OFF YOUR COAT, MR. SAWYER.
I'D... UM... RATHER NOT...LIKE I SAID, I HAVE THIS NASTY COLD. I NEED TO STAY, UM... WARM.
IT'S 72 DEGREES. I THINK YOU'LL SURVIVE.
IS SHE BUYING IT?
NO, I AM NOT. TAKE YOUR COAT OFF, MR. SAWYER.

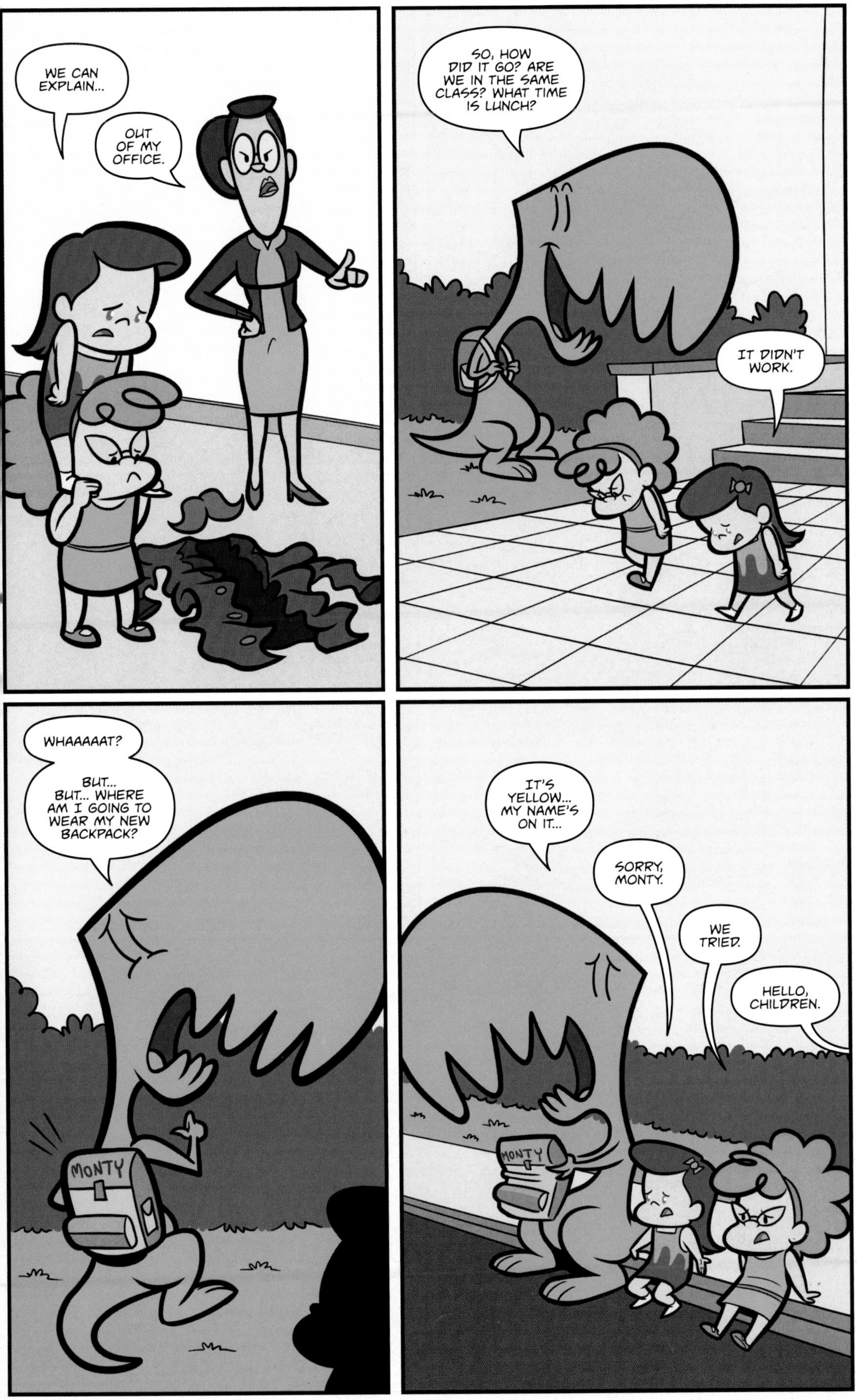
WE CAN EXPLAIN...
OUT OF MY OFFICE.
SO, HOW DID IT GO? ARE WE IN THE SAME CLASS? WHAT TIME IS LUNCH?
IT DIDN'T WORK.
WHAAAAAT?
BUT... BUT... WHERE AM I GOING TO WEAR MY NEW BACKPACK?
MONTY
IT'S YELLOW... MY NAME'S ON IT...
SORRY, MONTY.
WE TRIED.
HELLO, CHILDREN.
MONTY

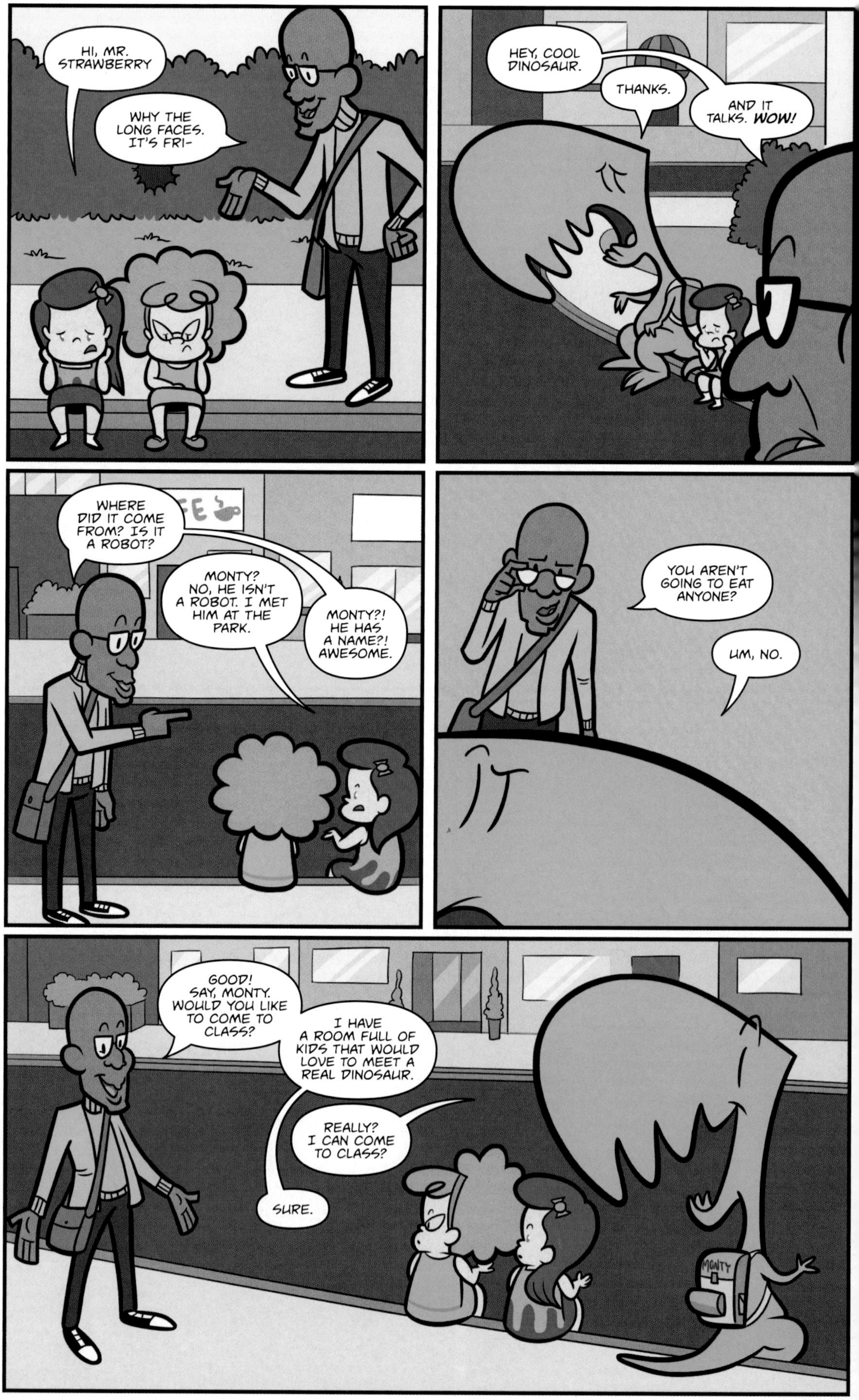

HI, MR. STRAWBERRY
WHY THE LONG FACES. IT'S FRI-
HEY, COOL DINOSAUR.
THANKS.
AND IT TALKS. WOW!
WHERE DID IT COME FROM? IS IT A ROBOT?
MONTY? NO, HE ISN'T A ROBOT. I MET HIM AT THE PARK.
MONTY?! HE HAS A NAME?! AWESOME.
YOU AREN'T GOING TO EAT ANYONE?
UM, NO.
GOOD! SAY, MONTY. WOULD YOU LIKE TO COME TO CLASS?
I HAVE A ROOM FULL OF KIDS THAT WOULD LOVE TO MEET A REAL DINOSAUR.
REALLY? I CAN COME TO CLASS?
SURE.
MONTY

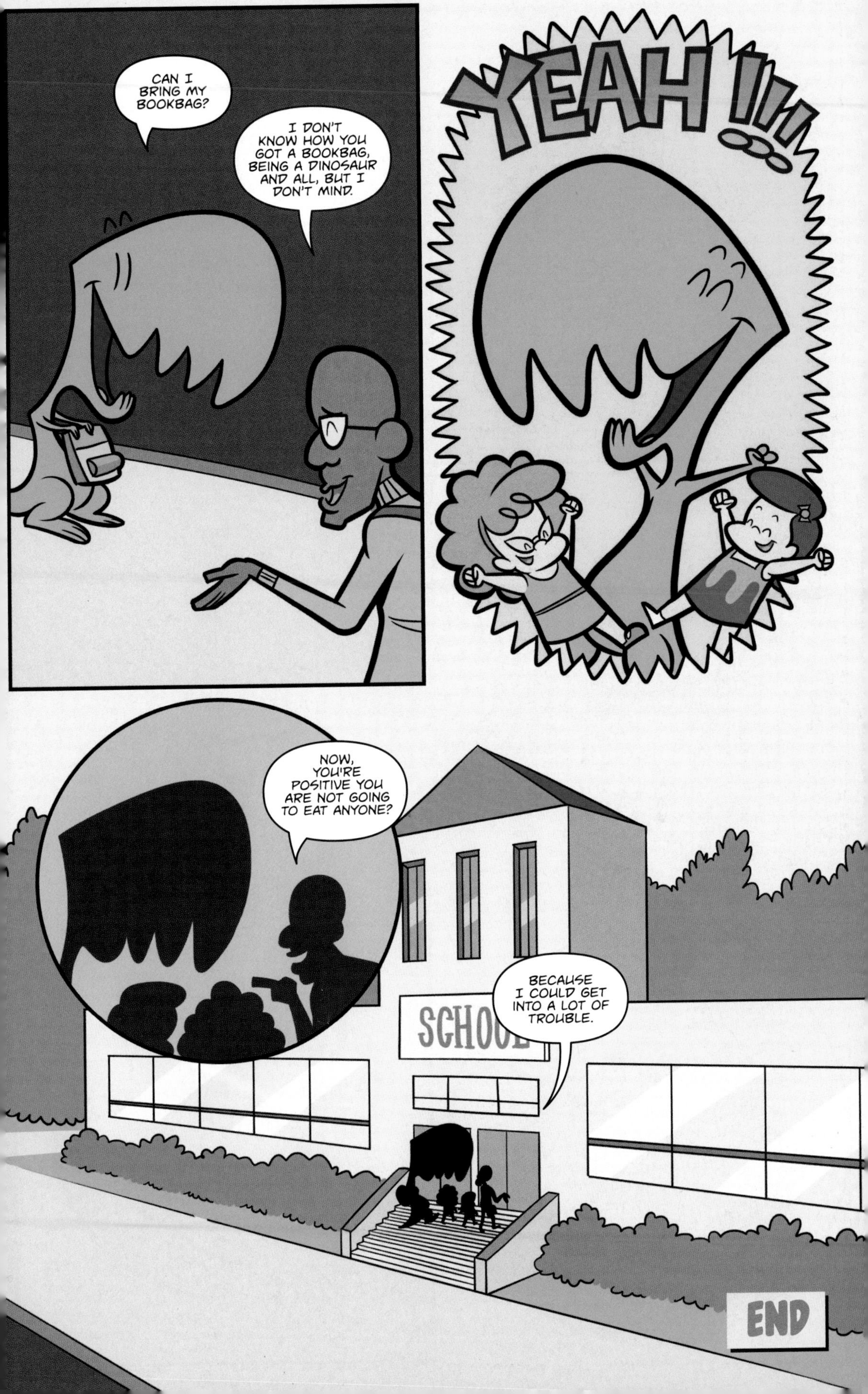

CAN I BRING MY BOOKBAG?
I DON'T KNOW HOW YOU GOT A BOOKBAG, BEING A DINOSAUR AND ALL, BUT I DON'T MIND.
YEAH!!!
NOW, YOU'RE POSITIVE YOU ARE NOT GOING TO EAT ANYONE?
BECAUSE I COULD GET INTO A LOT OF TROUBLE.
SCHOOL
END

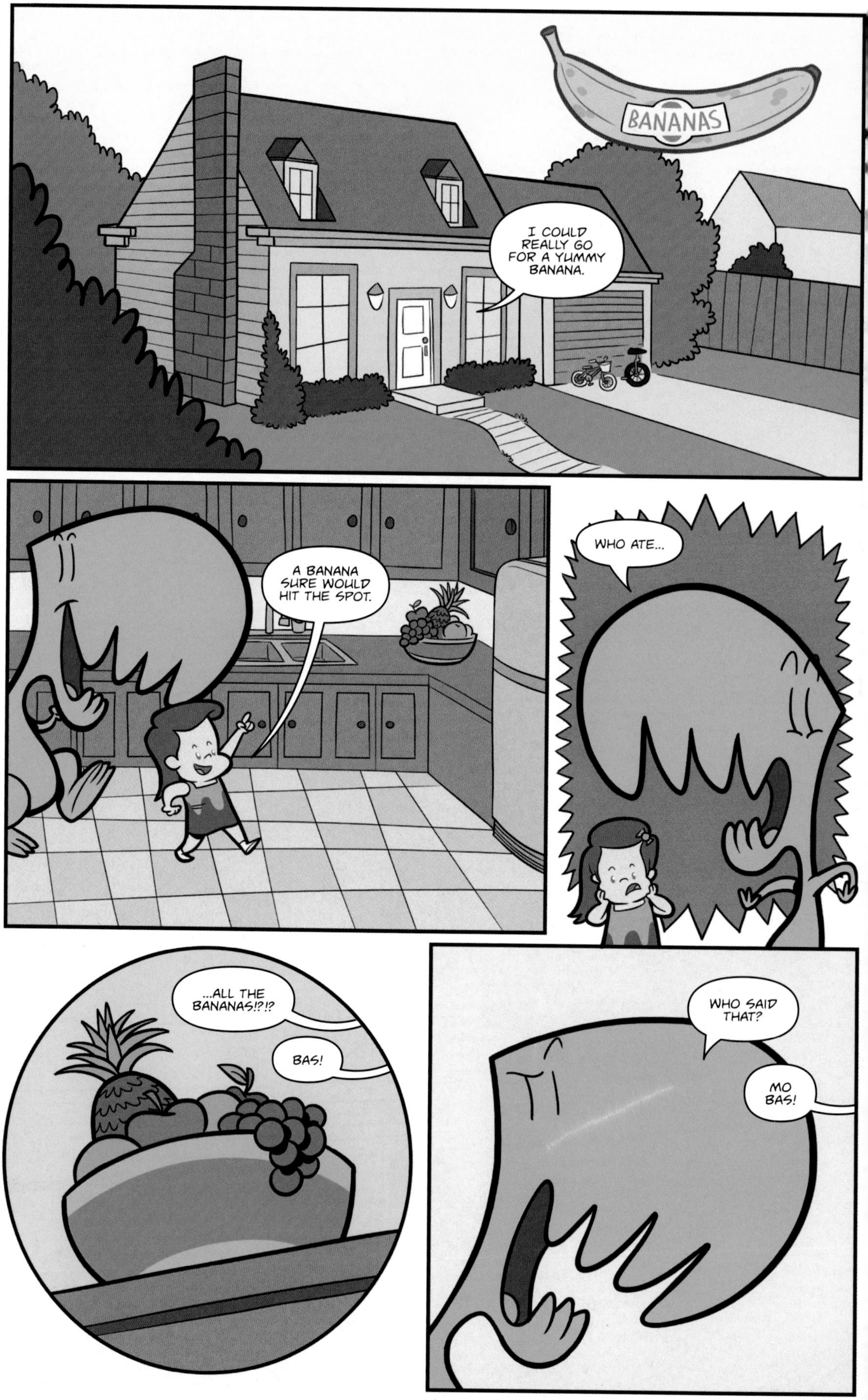
BANANAS
I COULD REALLY GO FOR A YUMMY BANANA.
A BANANA SURE WOULD HIT THE SPOT.
WHO ATE...
...ALL THE BANANAS!?!?
BAS!
WHO SAID THAT?
MO BAS!

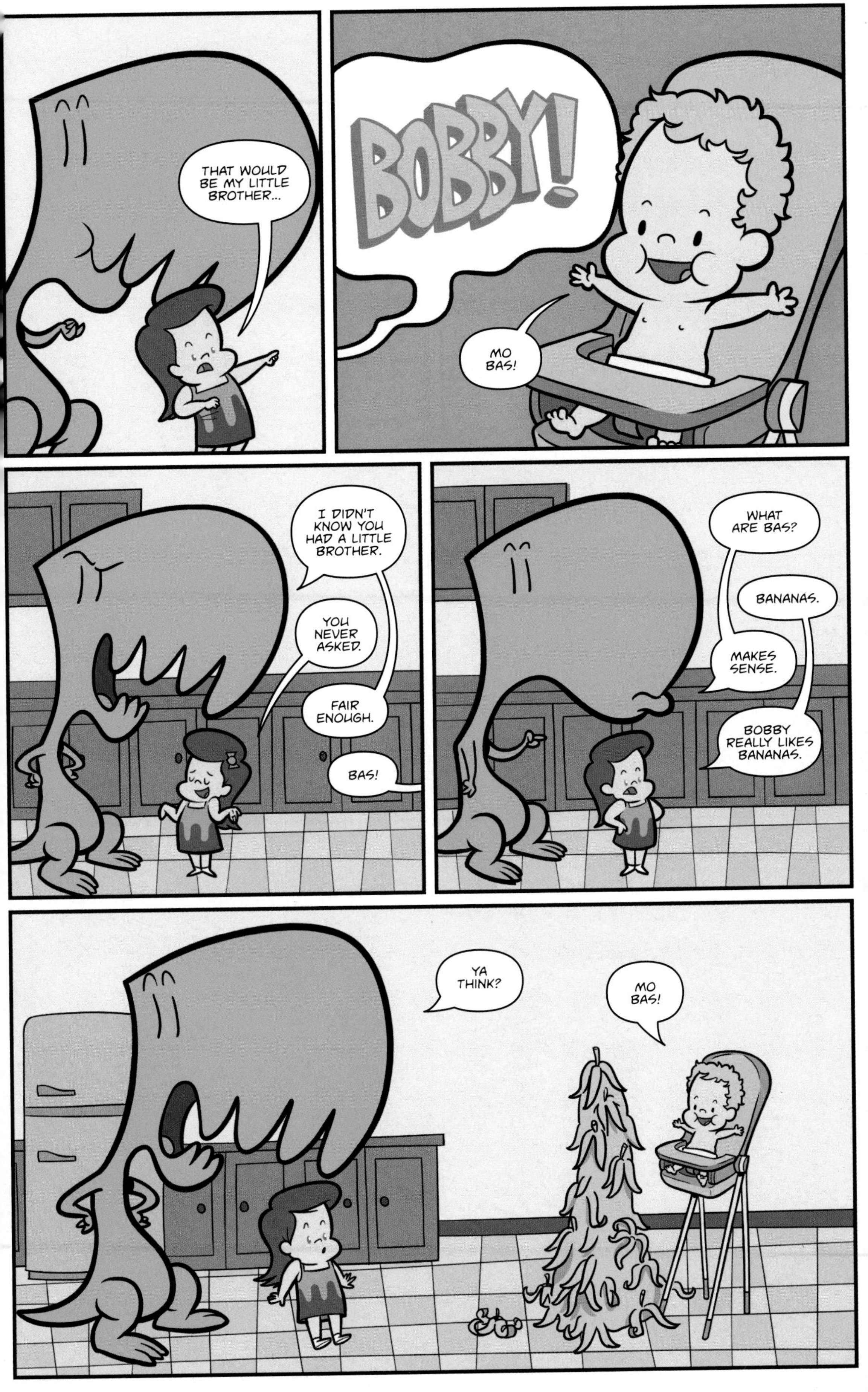
THAT WOULD BE MY LITTLE BROTHER...
BOBBY!
MO BAS!
I DIDN'T KNOW YOU HAD A LITTLE BROTHER.
YOU NEVER ASKED.
FAIR ENOUGH.
BAS!
WHAT ARE BAS?
BANANAS.
MAKES SENSE.
BOBBY REALLY LIKES BANANAS.
YA THINK?
MO BAS!

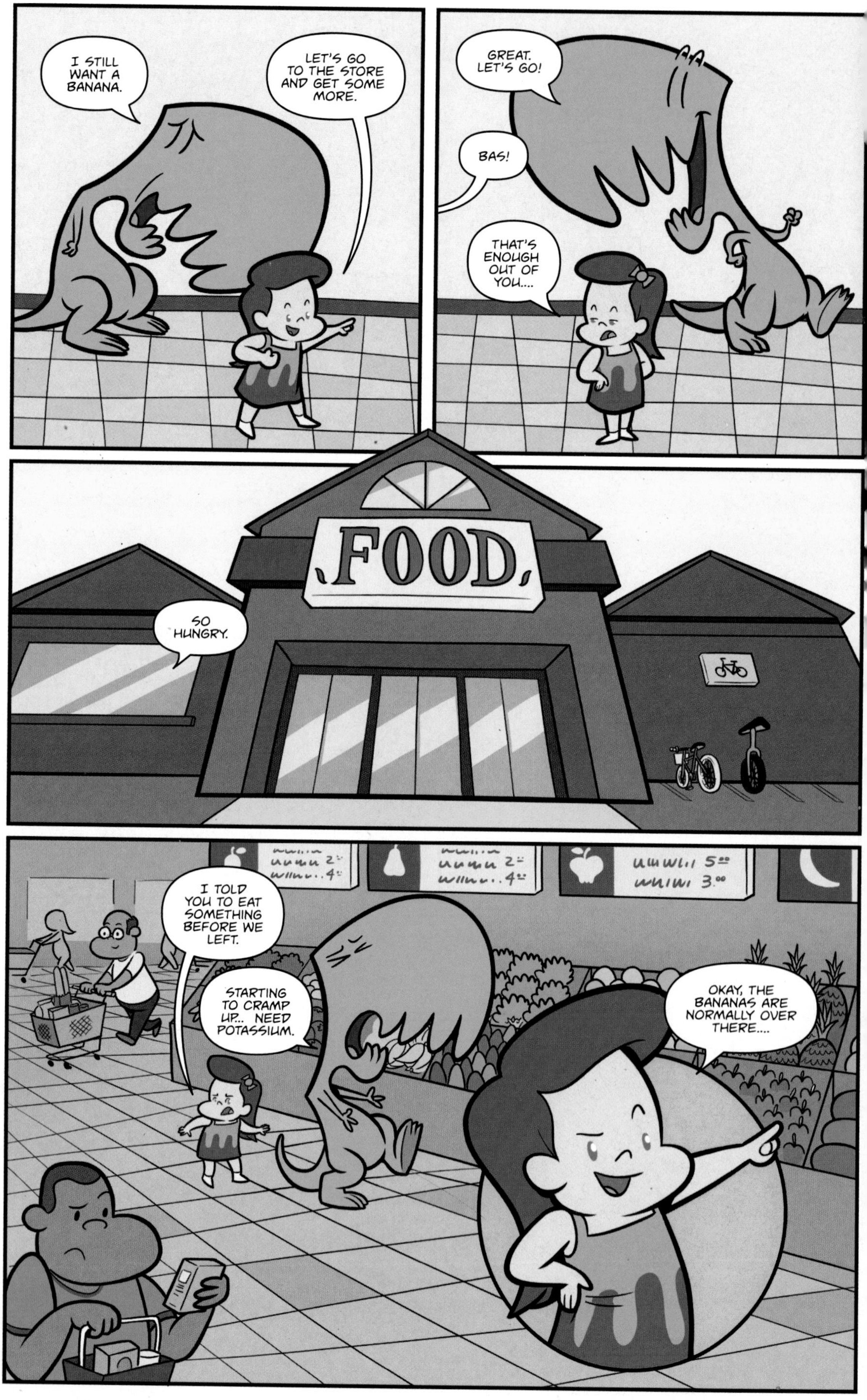

I STILL WANT A BANANA.
LET'S GO TO THE STORE AND GET SOME MORE.
GREAT. LET'S GO!
BAS!
THAT'S ENOUGH OUT OF YOU....
FOOD
SO HUNGRY.
I TOLD YOU TO EAT SOMETHING BEFORE WE LEFT.
STARTING TO CRAMP UP... NEED POTASSIUM.
OKAY, THE BANANAS ARE NORMALLY OVER THERE....

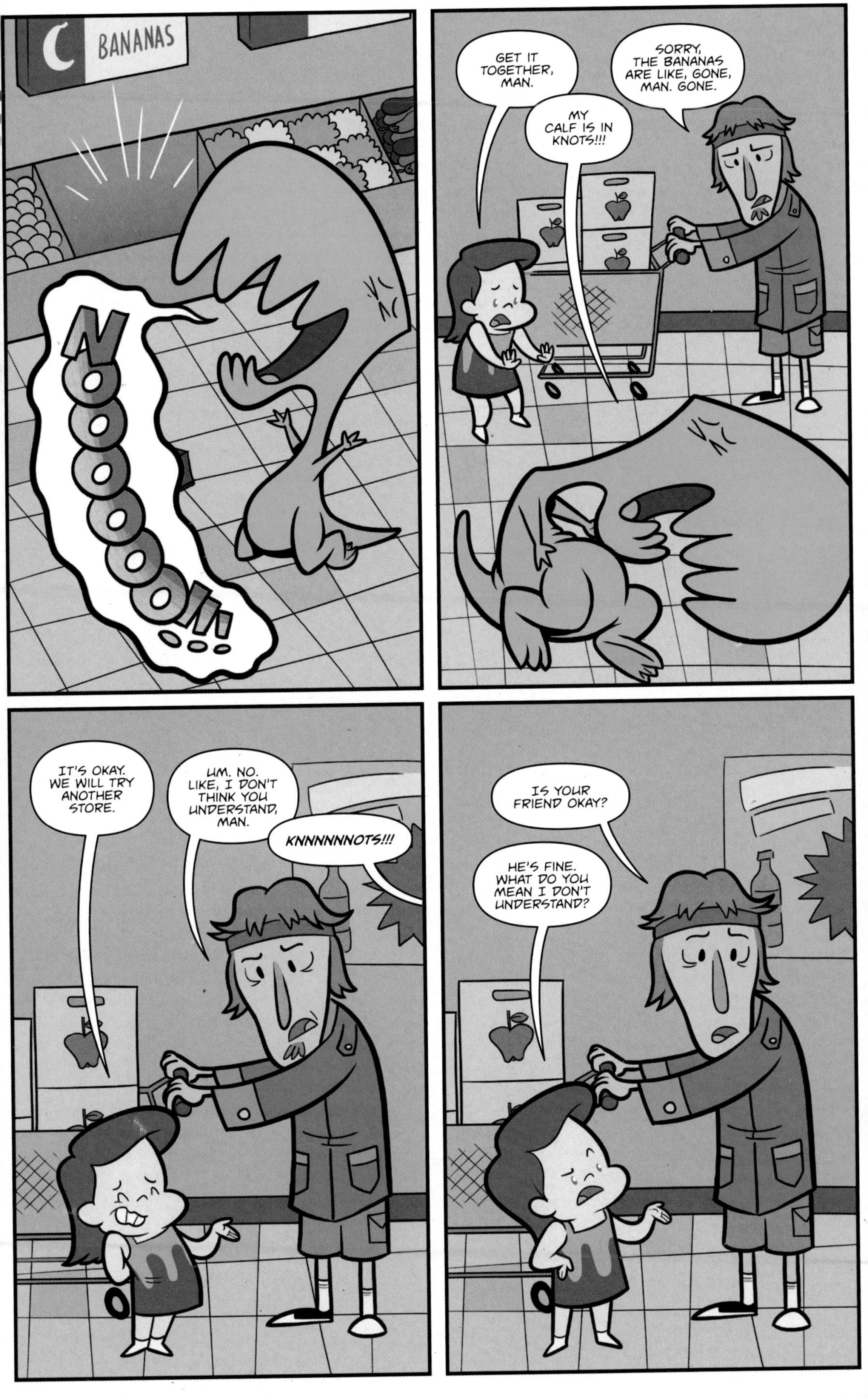
BANANAS
NOOOOOOOH!!...
GET IT TOGETHER, MAN.
SORRY, THE BANANAS ARE LIKE, GONE, MAN. GONE.
MY CALF IS IN KNOTS!!!
IT'S OKAY. WE WILL TRY ANOTHER STORE.
UM. NO. LIKE, I DON'T THINK YOU UNDERSTAND, MAN.
KNNNNNNOTS!!!
IS YOUR FRIEND OKAY?
HE'S FINE. WHAT DO YOU MEAN I DON'T UNDERSTAND?

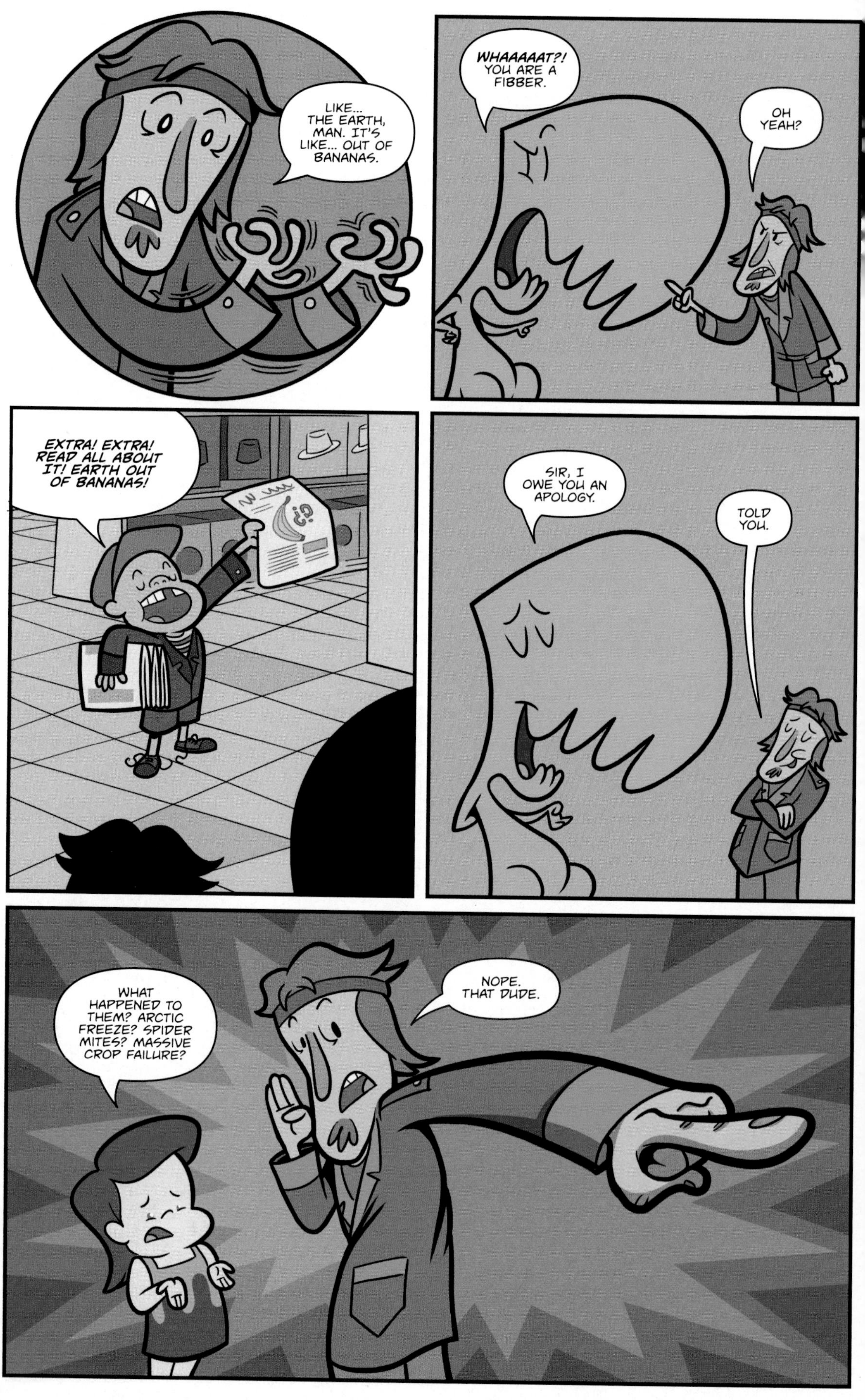
LIKE... THE EARTH, MAN. IT'S LIKE... OUT OF BANANAS.
WHAAAAAT?! YOU ARE A FIBBER.
OH YEAH?
EXTRA! EXTRA! READ ALL ABOUT IT! EARTH OUT OF BANANAS!
SIR, I OWE YOU AN APOLOGY.
TOLD YOU.
WHAT HAPPENED TO THEM? ARCTIC FREEZE? SPIDER MITES? MASSIVE CROP FAILURE?
NOPE. THAT DUDE.

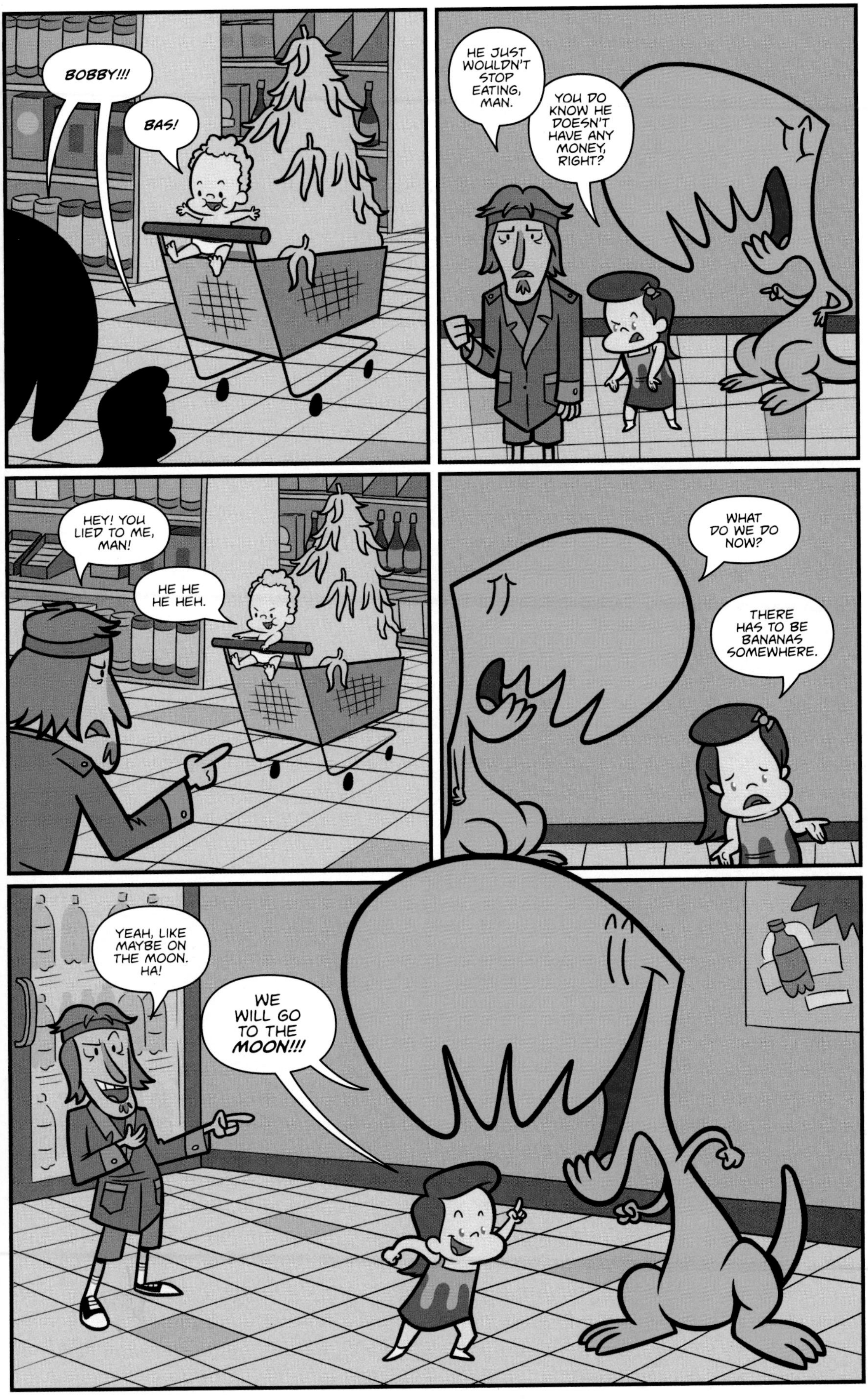
BOBBY!!!
BAS!
HE JUST WOULDN'T STOP EATING, MAN.
YOU DO KNOW HE DOESN'T HAVE ANY MONEY, RIGHT?
HEY! YOU LIED TO ME, MAN!
HE HE HE HEH.
WHAT DO WE DO NOW?
THERE HAS TO BE BANANAS SOMEWHERE.
YEAH, LIKE MAYBE ON THE MOON. HA!
WE WILL GO TO THE MOON!!!

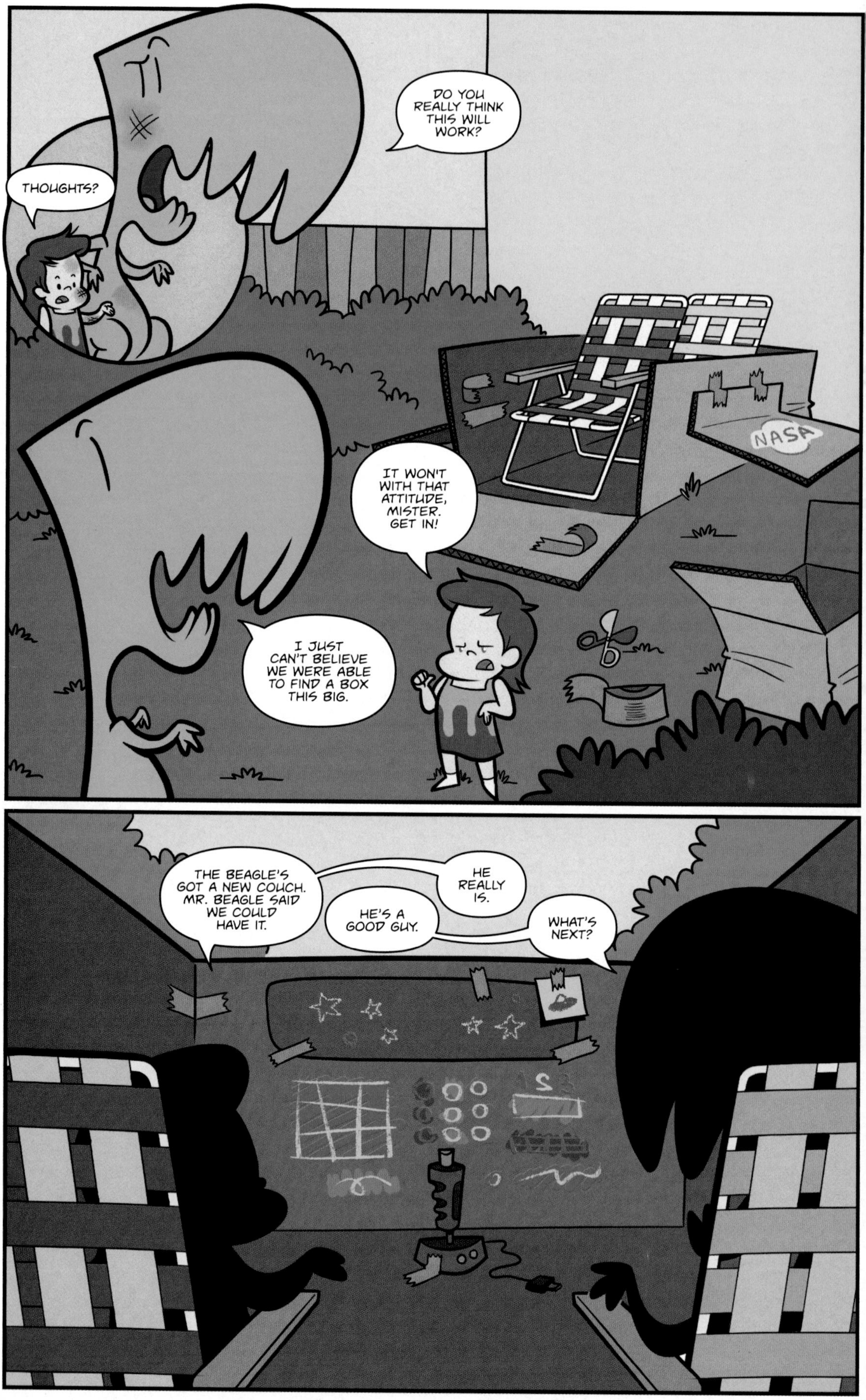
THOUGHTS?
DO YOU REALLY THINK THIS WILL WORK?
IT WON'T WITH THAT ATTITUDE, MISTER. GET IN!
I JUST CAN'T BELIEVE WE WERE ABLE TO FIND A BOX THIS BIG.
NASA
THE BEAGLE'S GOT A NEW COUCH. MR. BEAGLE SAID WE COULD HAVE IT.
HE'S A GOOD GUY.
HE REALLY IS.
WHAT'S NEXT?

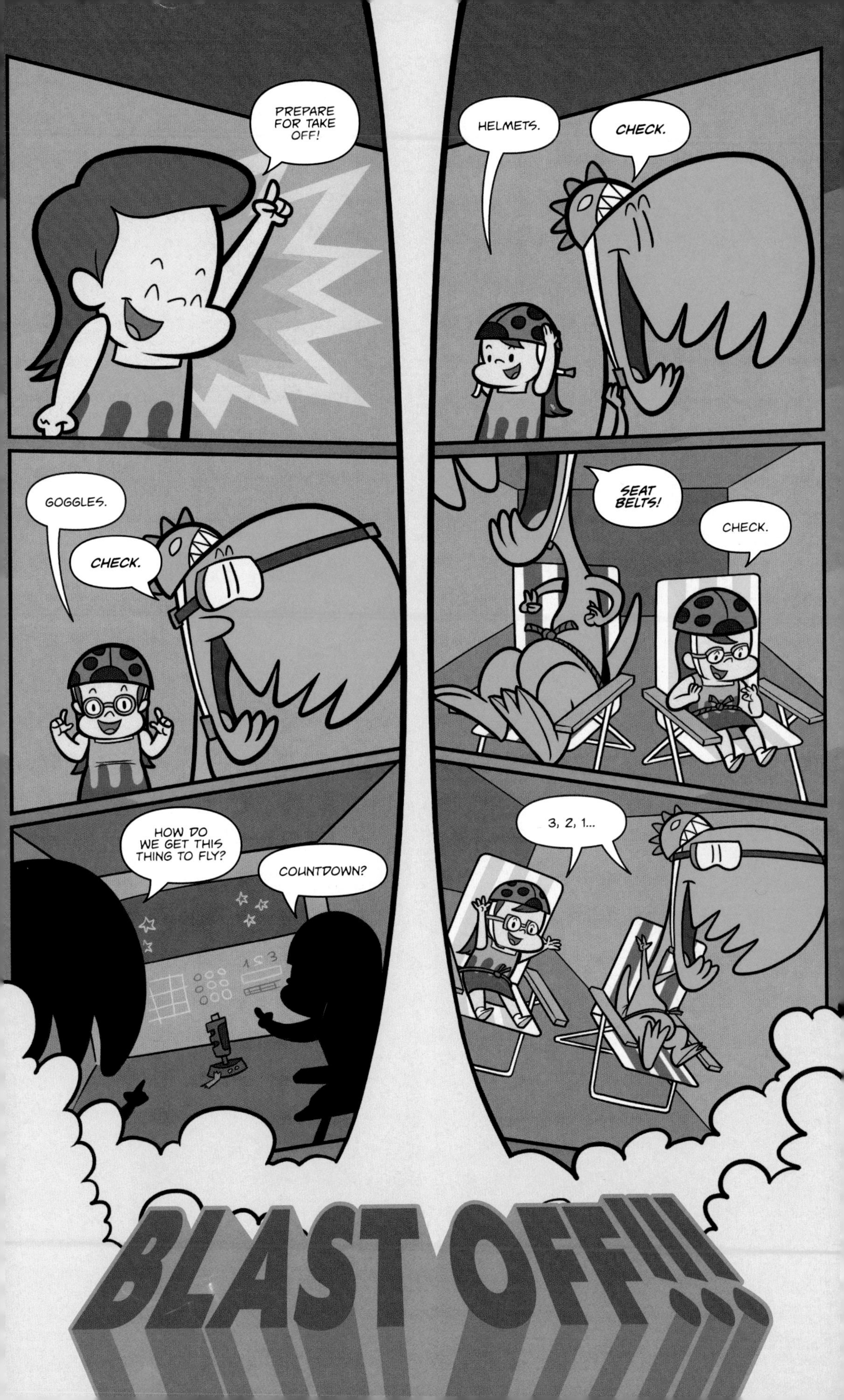
PREPARE FOR TAKE OFF!
HELMETS.
CHECK.
GOGGLES.
CHECK.
SEAT BELTS!
CHECK.
HOW DO WE GET THIS THING TO FLY?
COUNTDOWN?
3, 2, 1...
1 2 3
BLAST OFF!!!

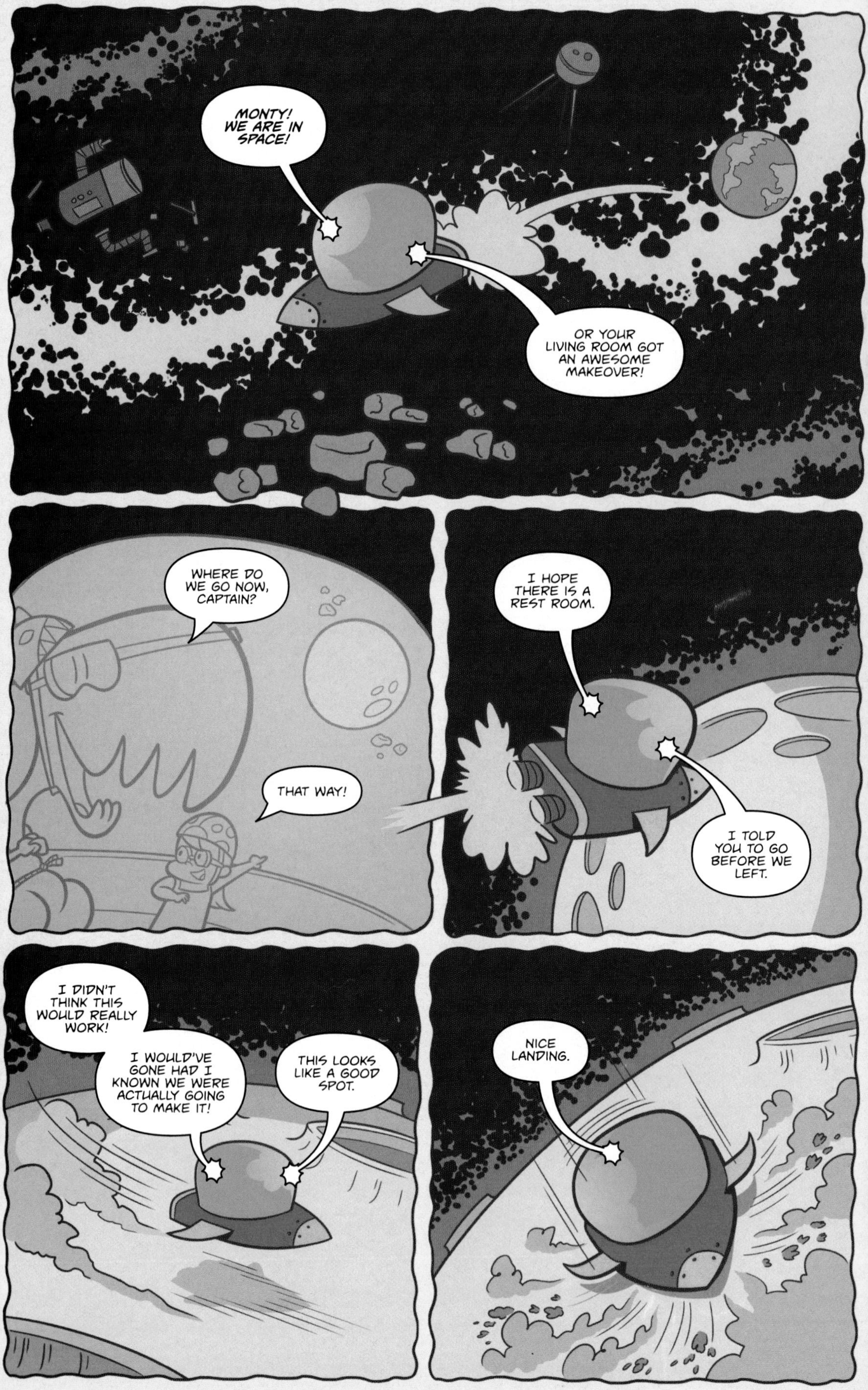
MONTY! WE ARE IN SPACE!
OR YOUR LIVING ROOM GOT AN AWESOME MAKEOVER!
WHERE DO WE GO NOW, CAPTAIN?
THAT WAY!
I HOPE THERE IS A REST ROOM.
I TOLD YOU TO GO BEFORE WE LEFT.
I DIDN'T THINK THIS WOULD REALLY WORK!
I WOULD'VE GONE HAD I KNOWN WE WERE ACTUALLY GOING TO MAKE IT!
THIS LOOKS LIKE A GOOD SPOT.
NICE LANDING.

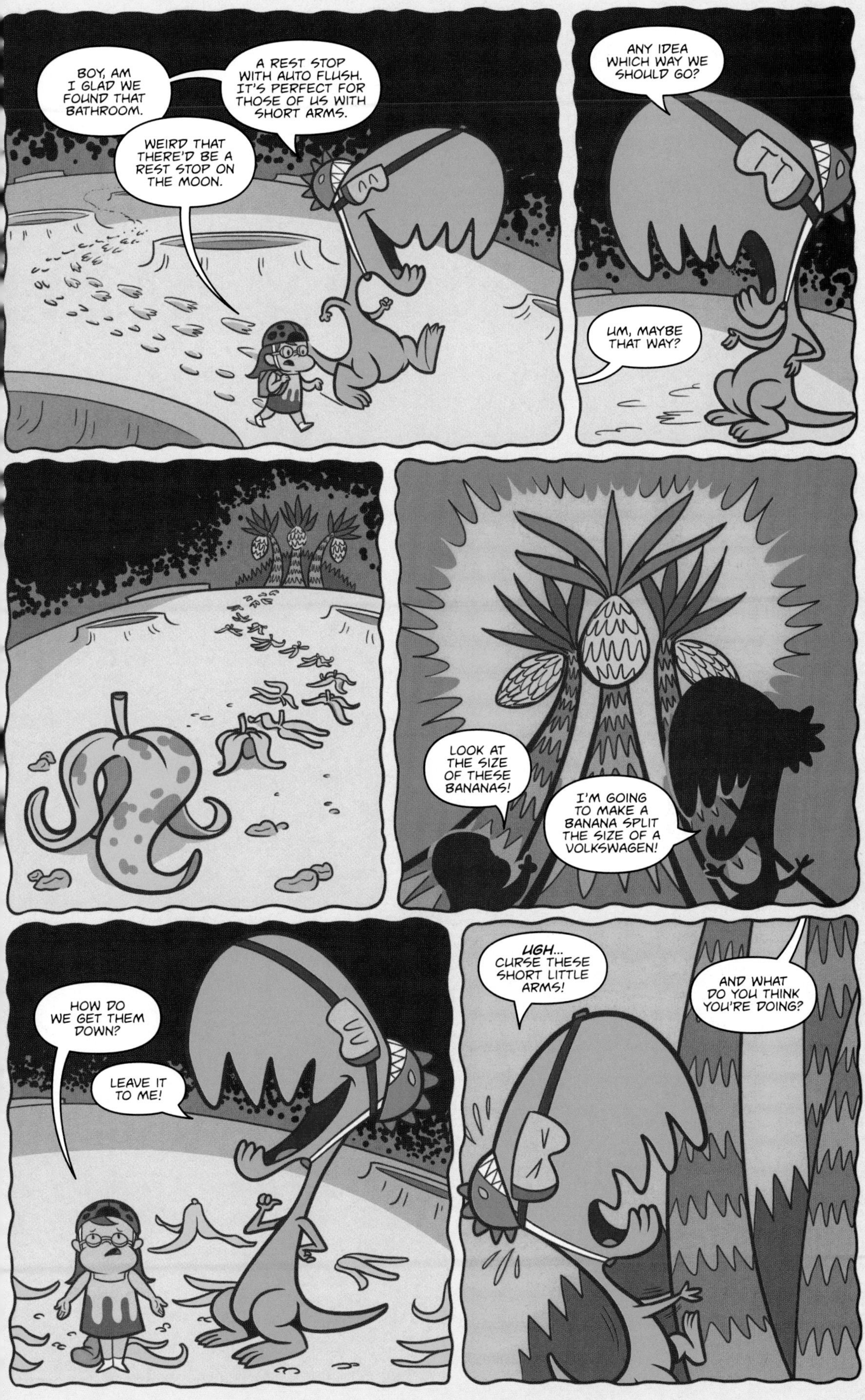
BOY, AM I GLAD WE FOUND THAT BATHROOM.
A REST STOP WITH AUTO FLUSH. IT'S PERFECT FOR THOSE OF US WITH SHORT ARMS.
WEIRD THAT THERE'D BE A REST STOP ON THE MOON.
ANY IDEA WHICH WAY WE SHOULD GO?
UM, MAYBE THAT WAY?
LOOK AT THE SIZE OF THESE BANANAS!
I'M GOING TO MAKE A BANANA SPLIT THE SIZE OF A VOLKSWAGEN!
HOW DO WE GET THEM DOWN?
LEAVE IT TO ME!
UGH... CURSE THESE SHORT LITTLE ARMS!
AND WHAT DO YOU THINK YOU'RE DOING?

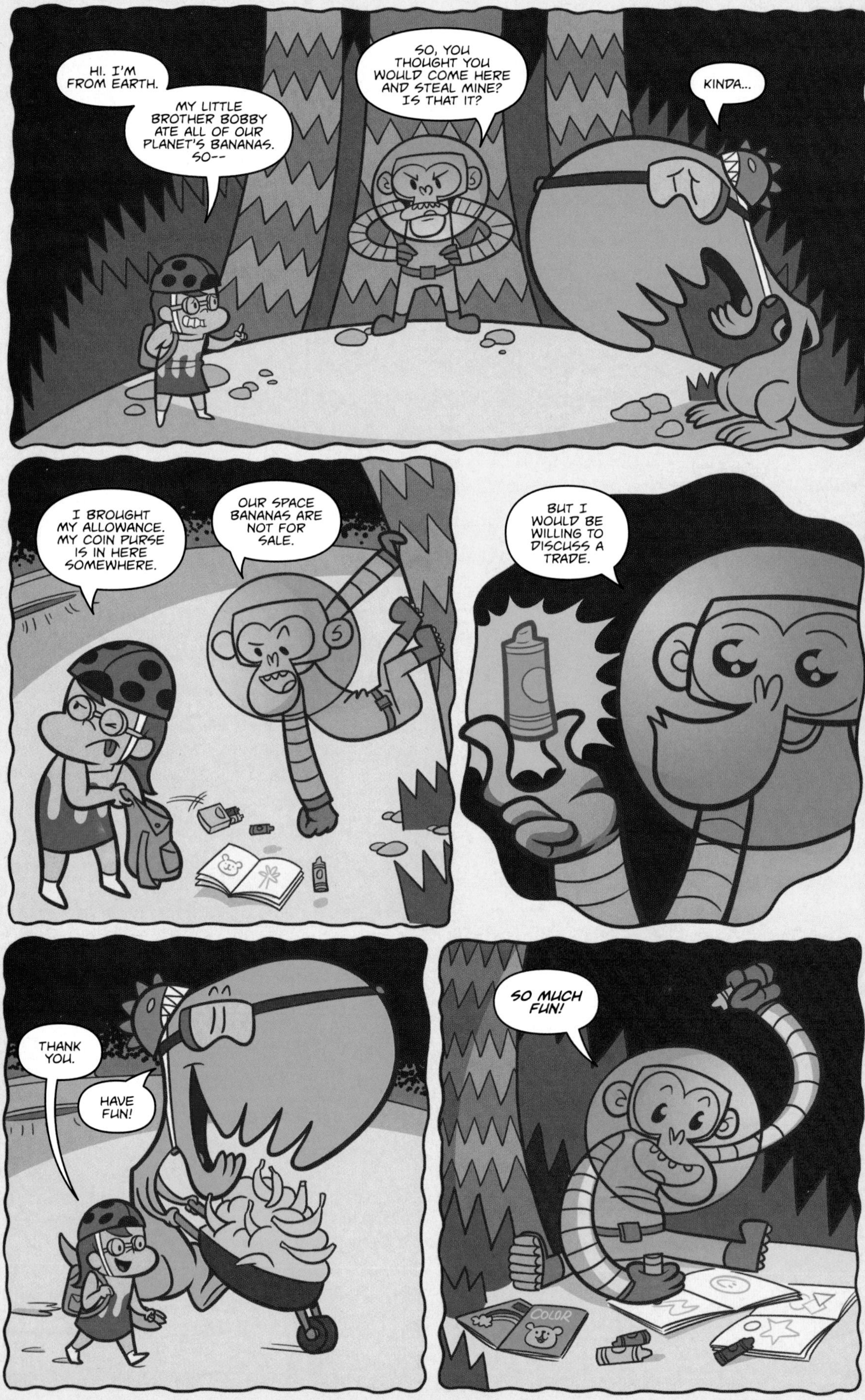
HI. I'M FROM EARTH.
MY LITTLE BROTHER BOBBY ATE ALL OF OUR PLANET'S BANANAS. SO--
SO, YOU THOUGHT YOU WOULD COME HERE AND STEAL MINE? IS THAT IT?
KINDA...
I BROUGHT MY ALLOWANCE. MY COIN PURSE IS IN HERE SOMEWHERE.
OUR SPACE BANANAS ARE NOT FOR SALE.
BUT I WOULD BE WILLING TO DISCUSS A TRADE.
THANK YOU.
HAVE FUN!
SO MUCH FUN!
COLOR

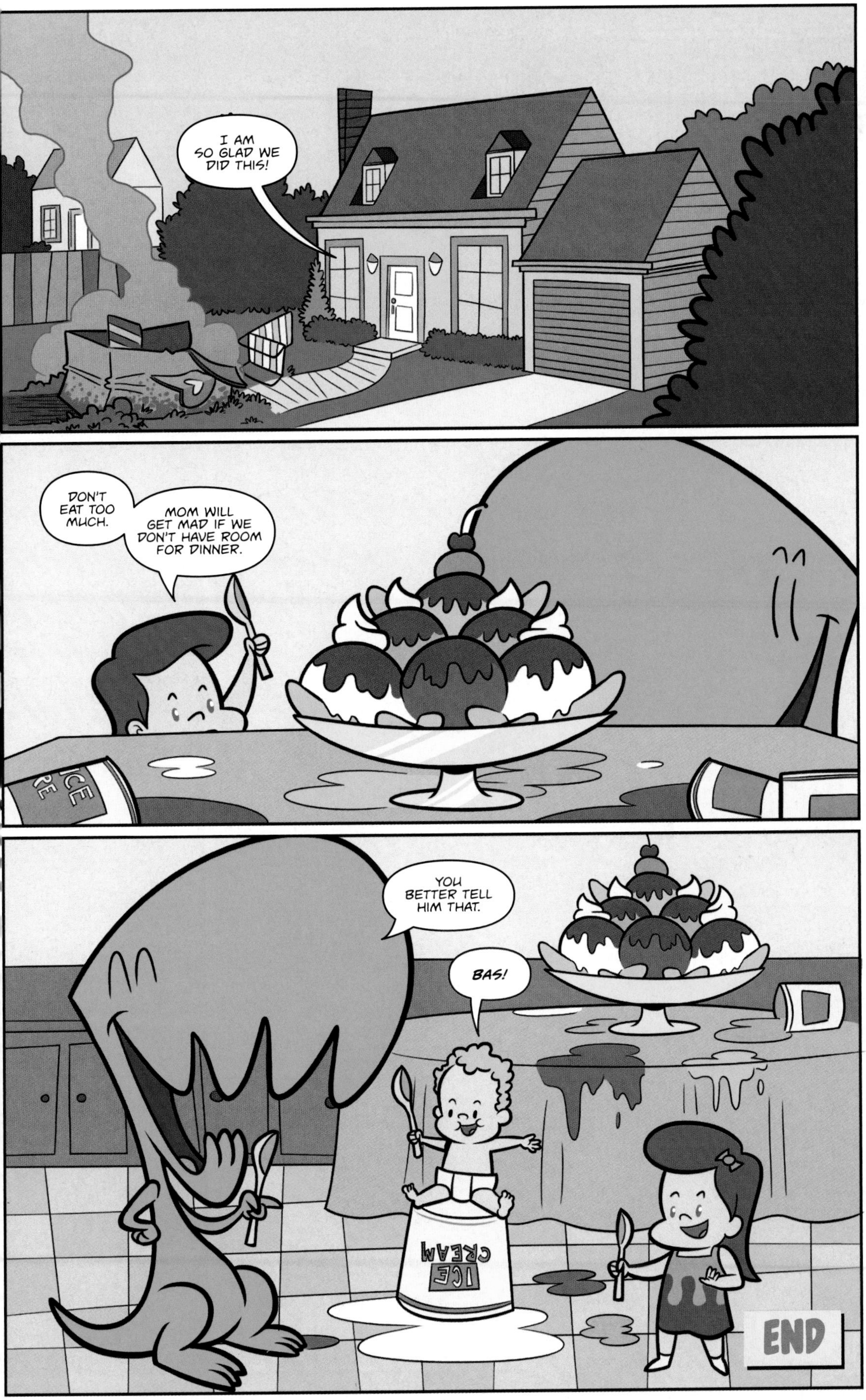
I AM SO GLAD WE DID THIS!
DON'T EAT TOO MUCH.
MOM WILL GET MAD IF WE DON'T HAVE ROOM FOR DINNER.
YOU BETTER TELL HIM THAT.
BAS!
ICE CREAM
END

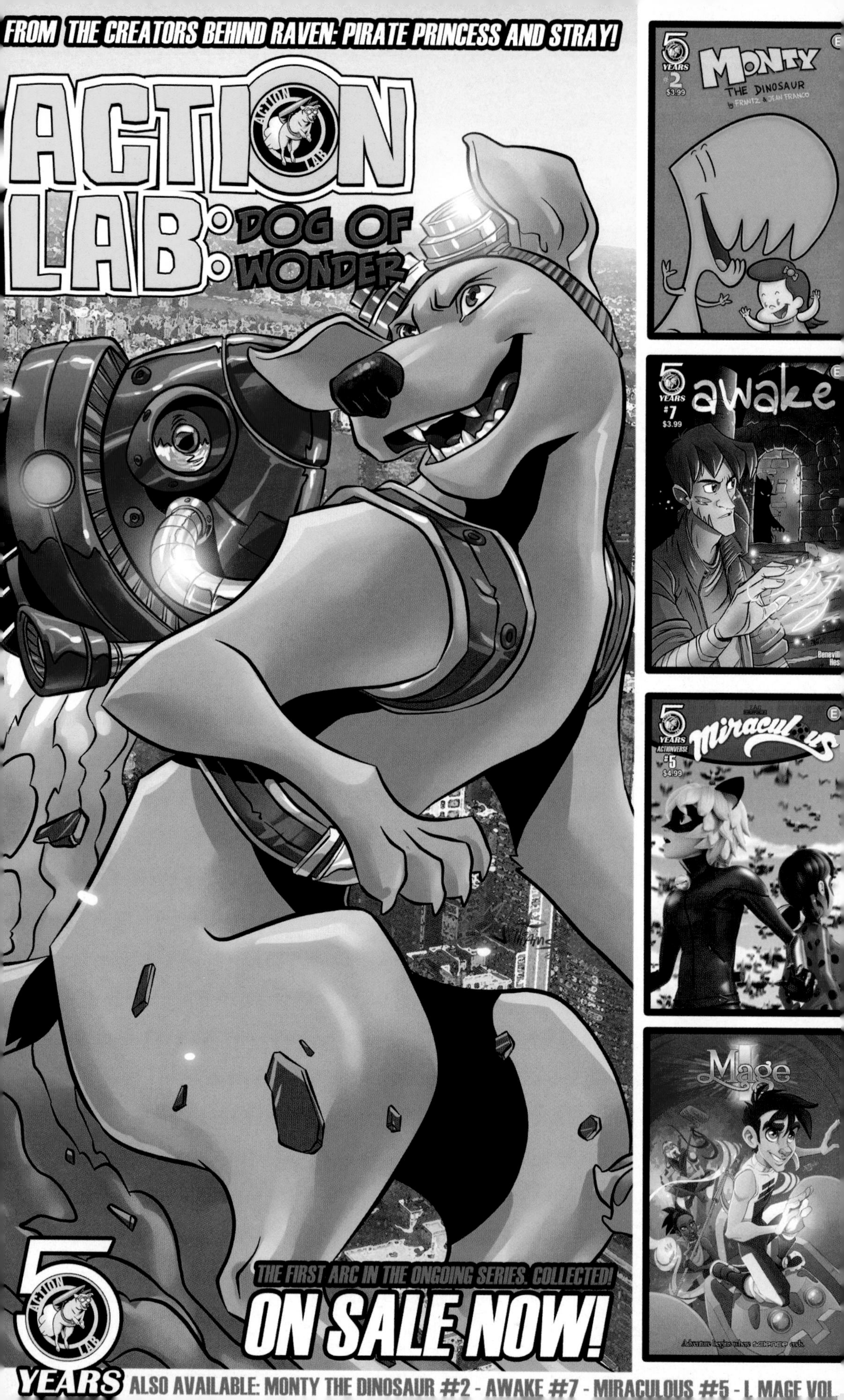
FROM THE CREATORS BEHIND RAVEN: PIRATE PRINCESS AND STRAY!
ACTION LAB: DOG OF WONDER
MONTY THE DINOSAUR
#2 $3.99
by FRANTZ & JEAN FRANCO
awake
#7 $3.99
miraculous
ACTIONVERSE
#5 $4.99
Mage
Adventure begins where science ends
THE FIRST ARC IN THE ONGOING SERIES, COLLECTED!
ON SALE NOW!
5 YEARS
ALSO AVAILABLE: MONTY THE DINOSAUR #2 - AWAKE #7 - MIRACULOUS #5 - L MAGE VOL

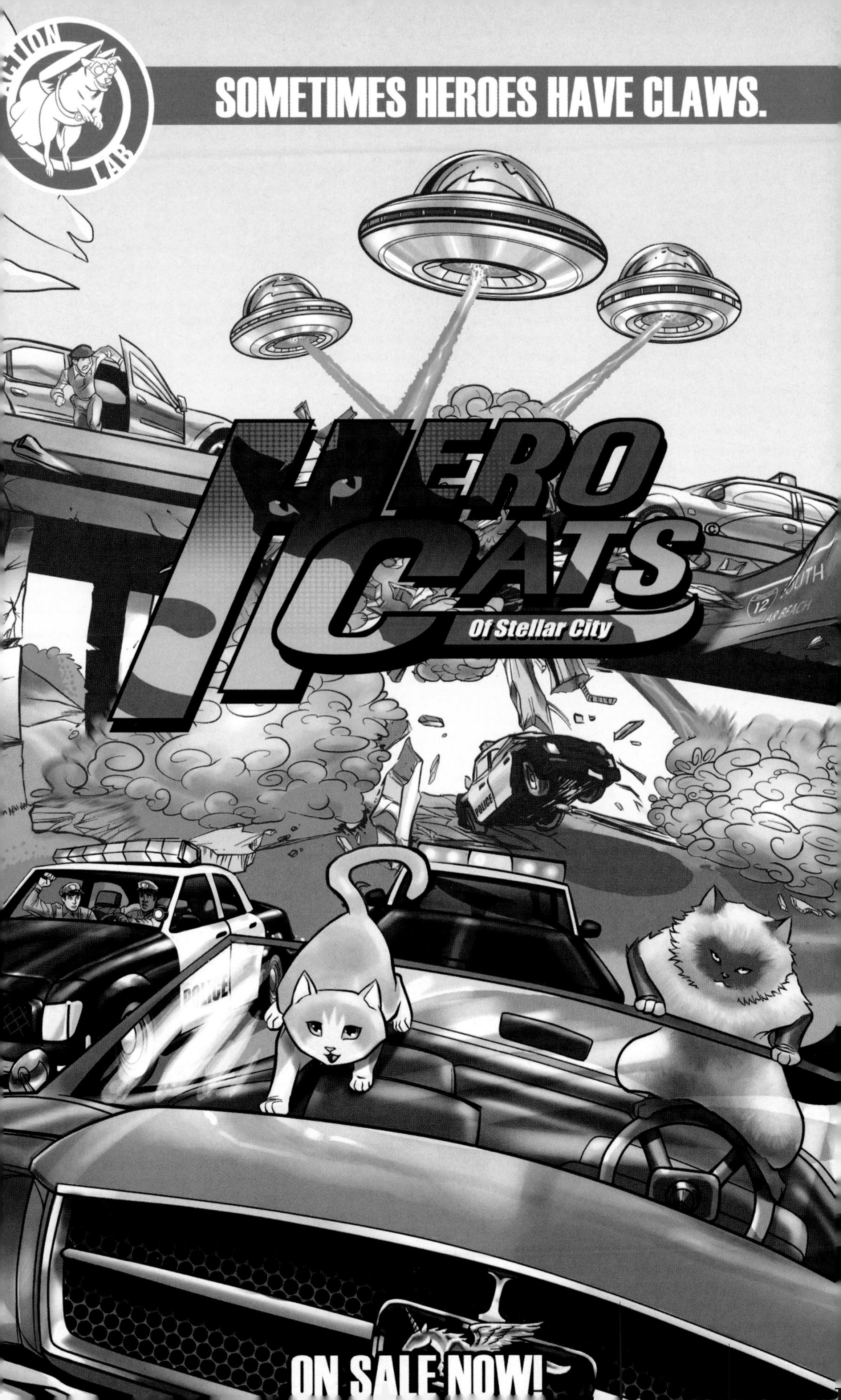
ACTION LAB
SOMETIMES HEROES HAVE CLAWS.
HERO CATS
Of Stellar City
POLICE
POLICE
ON SALE NOW!

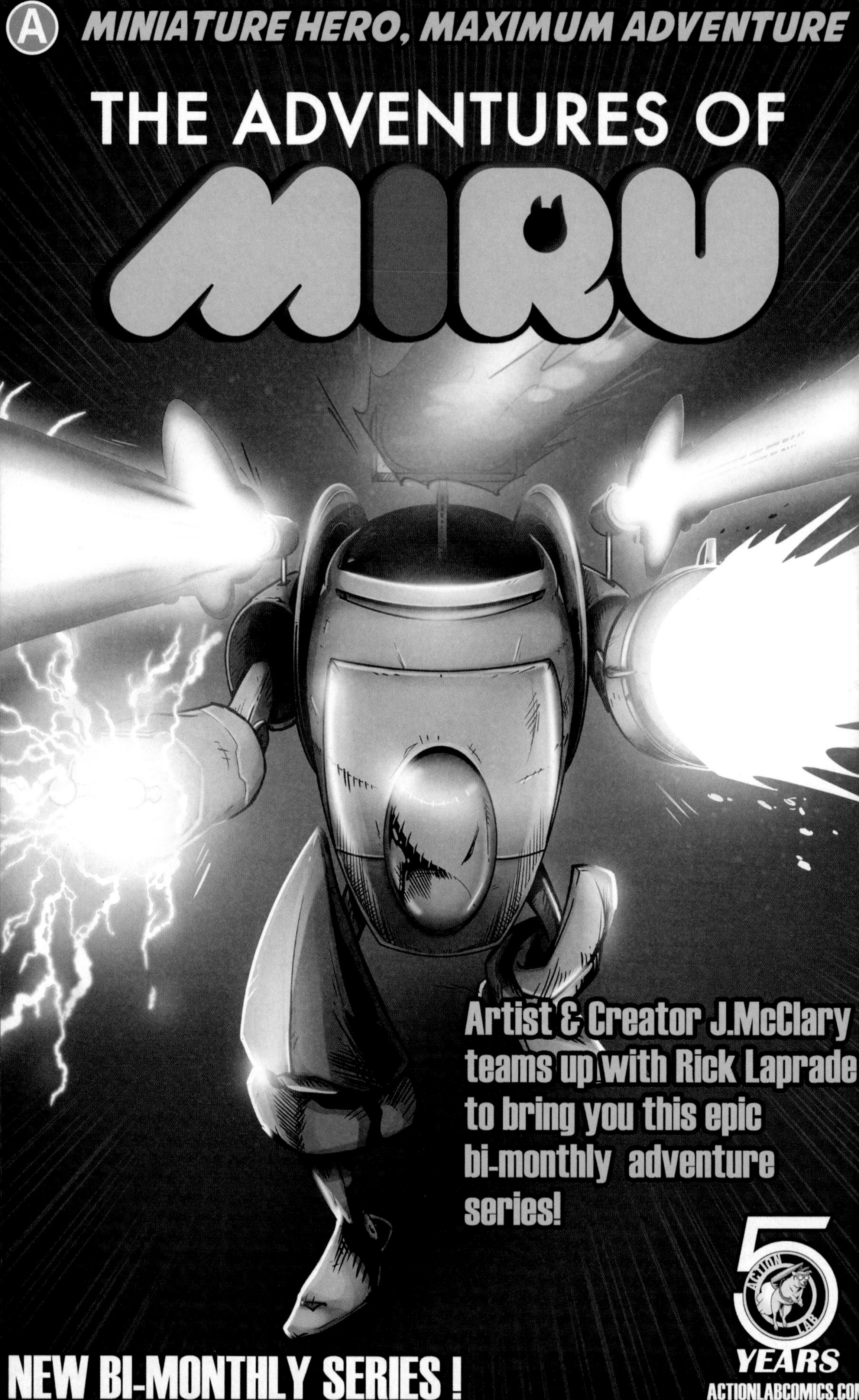
MINIATURE HERO, MAXIMUM ADVENTURE
THE ADVENTURES OF
MIRU
Artist & Creator J.McClary teams up with Rick Laprade to bring you this epic bi-monthly adventure series!
5 YEARS
ACTIONLABCOMICS.CO
NEW BI-MONTHLY SERIES !

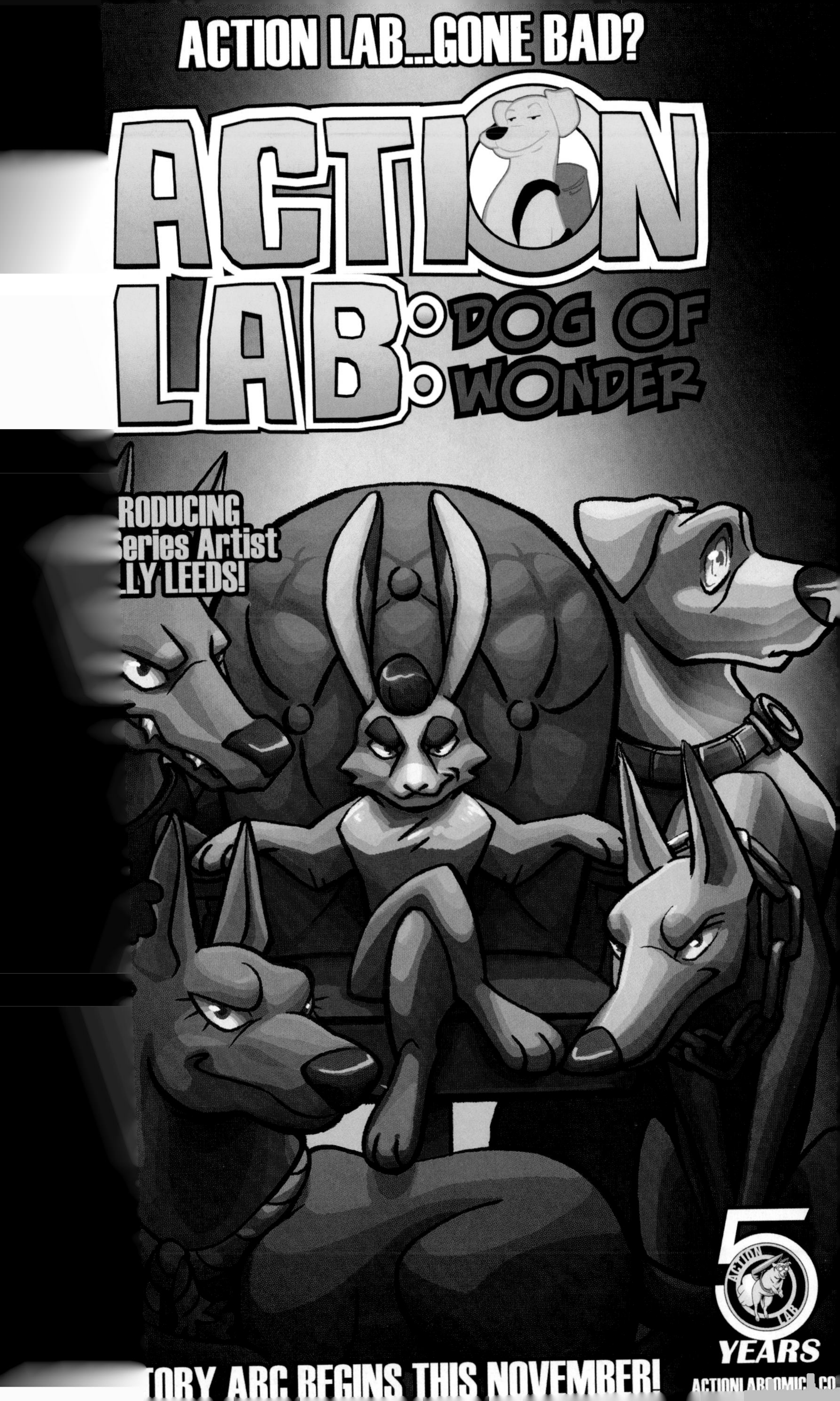

ACTION LAB...GONE BAD?
ACTION LAB: DOG OF WONDER
RODUCING
eries Artist
LLY LEEDS!
5 YEARS
TORY ARC BEGINS THIS NOVEMBER!
ACTIONLABCOMIC CO

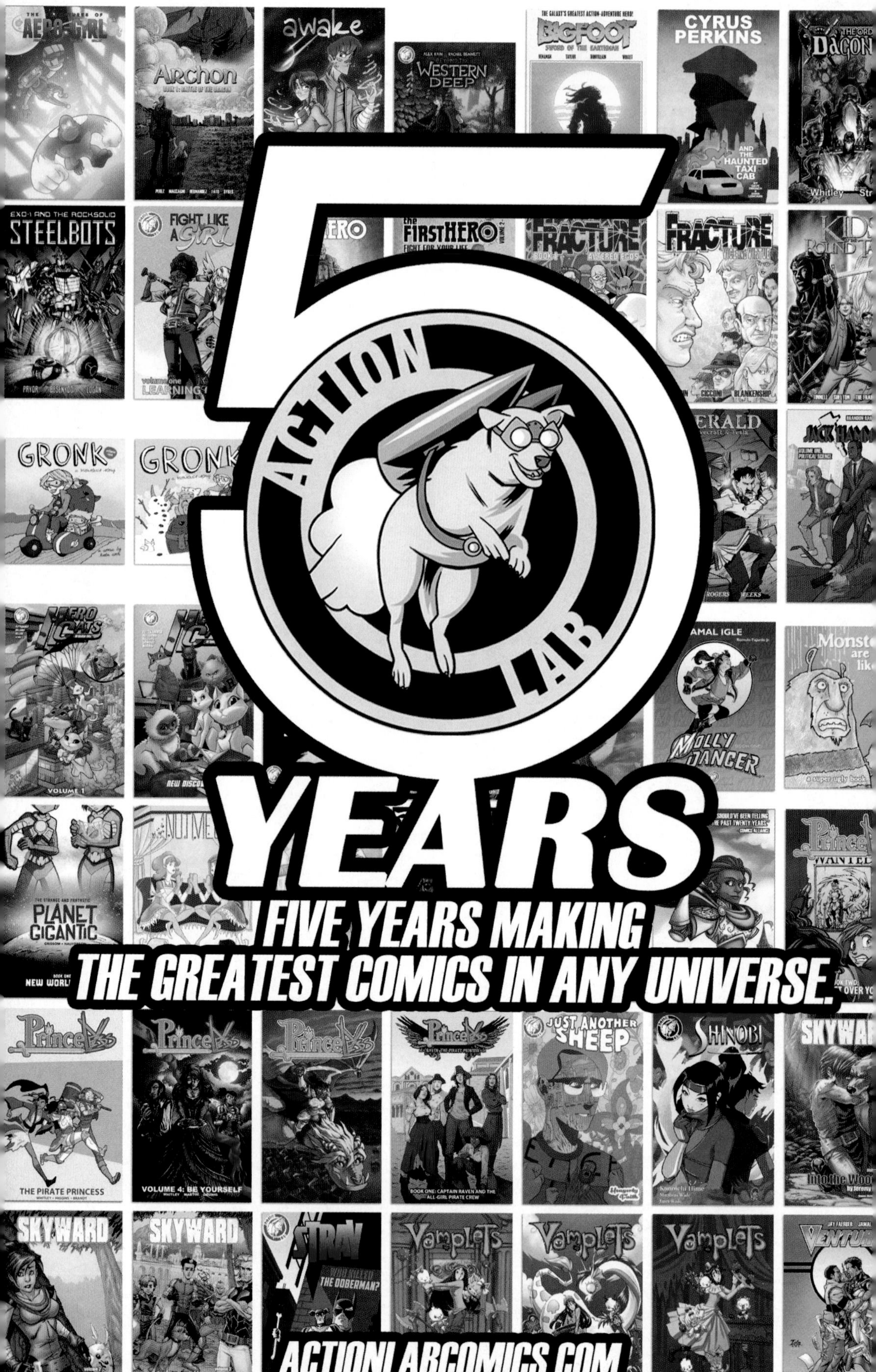
5
ACTION LAB
YEARS
FIVE YEARS MAKING
THE GREATEST COMICS IN ANY UNIVERSE.
ACTIONLABCOMICS.COM

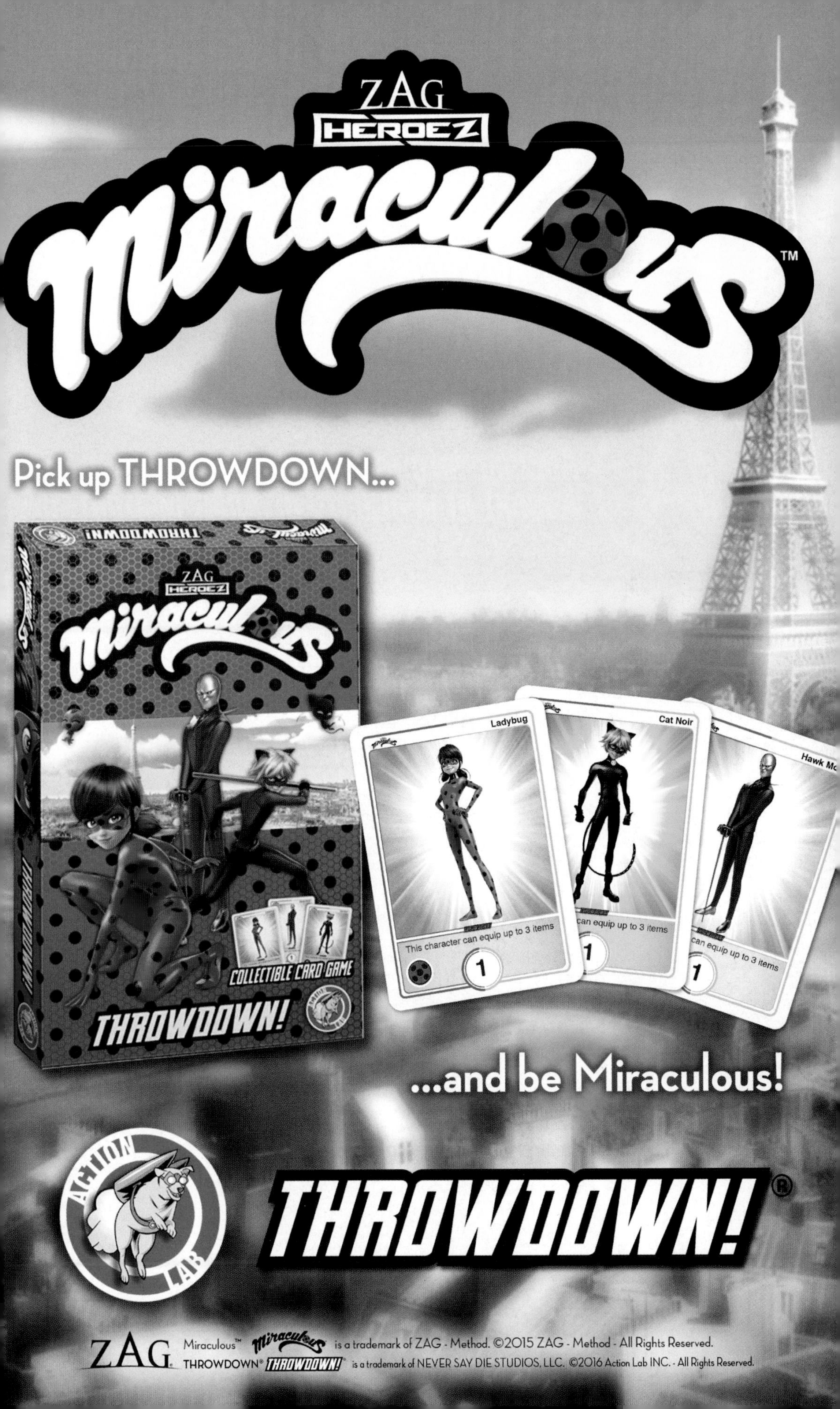

ZAG
HEROEZ
Miraculous™
Pick up THROWDOWN...
Ladybug
This character can equip up to 3 items
Cat Noir
...and be Miraculous!
ACTION LAB
THROWDOWN!®
ZAG Miraculous™ is a trademark of ZAG - Method. ©2015 ZAG - Method - All Rights Reserved.
THROWDOWN® THROWDOWN! is a trademark of NEVER SAY DIE STUDIOS, LLC. ©2016 Action Lab INC. - All Rights Reserved.

# FROM ALL-AGES TO MATURE READERS
# ACTION LAB HAS YOU COVERED.

 **Appropriate for everyone.**

 **Appropriate for age 9 and up. Absent of profanity or adult content.**

 **Suggested for 12 and Up. Comics with this rating are comparable to a PG-13 movie rating. Recommended for our teen and young adult readers.**

 **Appropriate for older teens. Similar to Teen, but featuring more mature themes and/or more graphic imagery.**

 **Contains extreme violence and some nudity. Basically the Rated-R of comics.**

## FIND YOUR NEW FAVORITE COMICS.

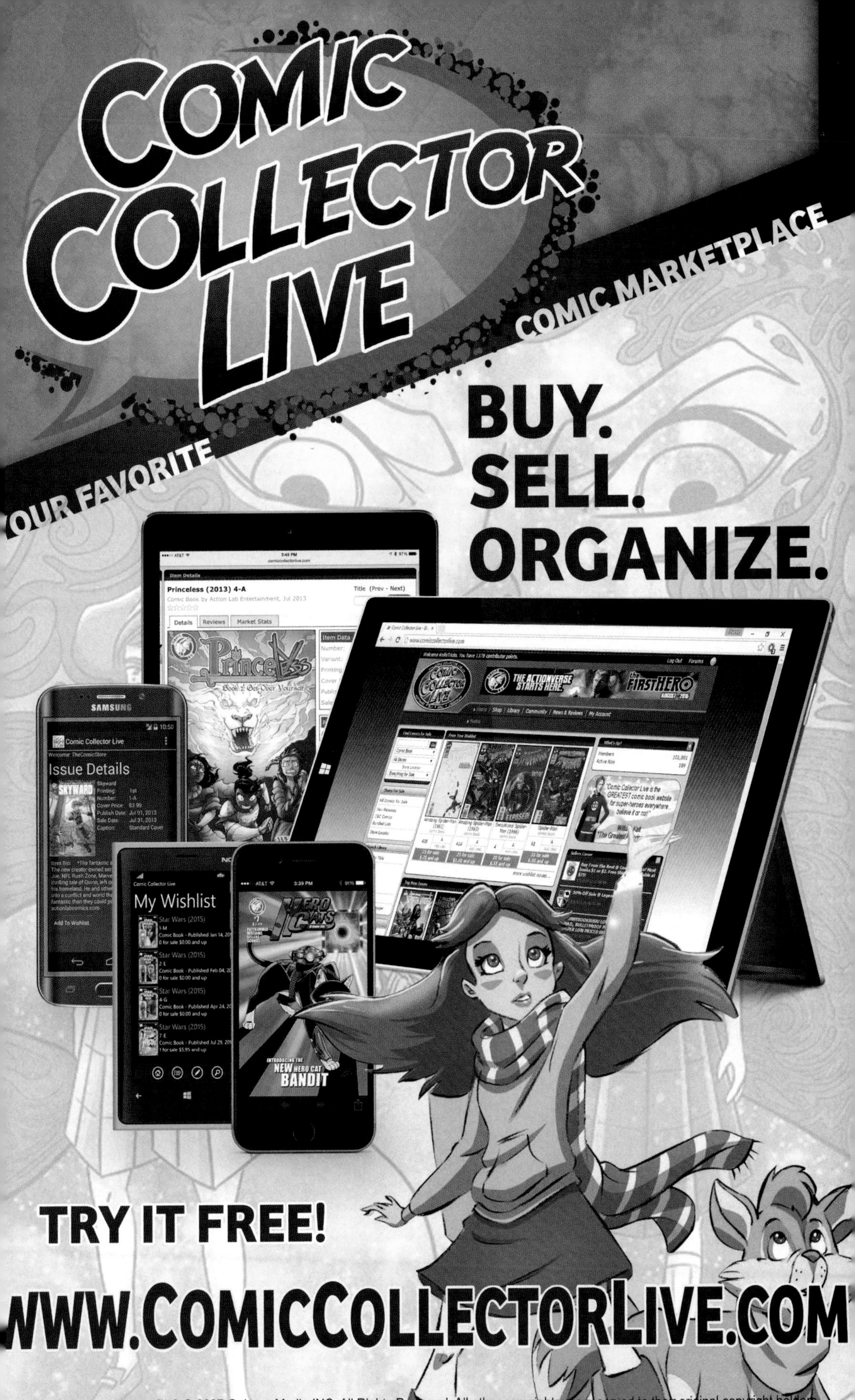
COMIC COLLECTOR LIVE
OUR FAVORITE COMIC MARKETPLACE
BUY.
SELL.
ORGANIZE.
TRY IT FREE!
WWW.COMICCOLLECTORLIVE.COM

**READ MORE NOW**

**ACTIONLABCOMICS.COM**

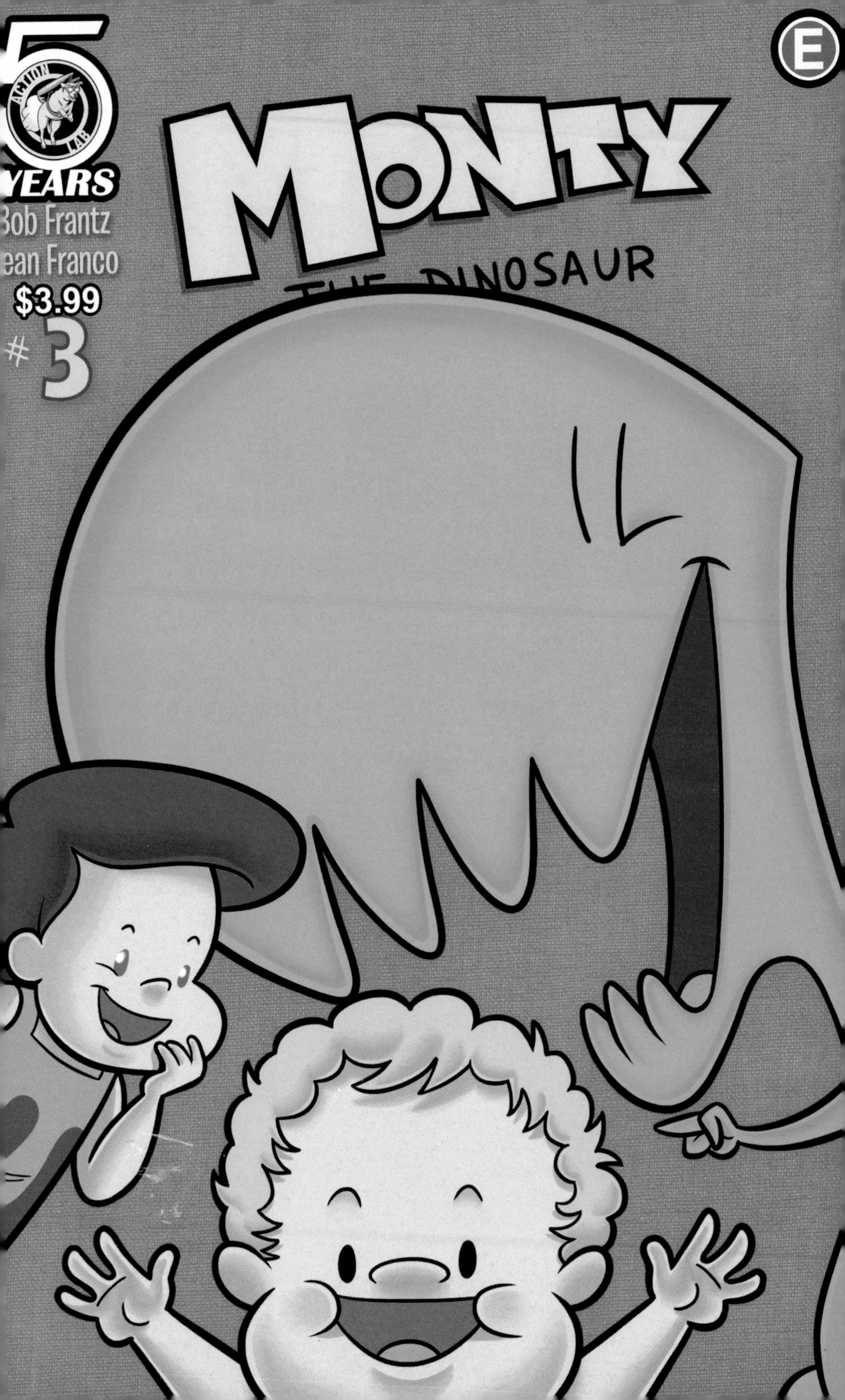

5
YEARS
ob Frantz
ean Franco
$3.99
# 3
E
MONTY
DINOSAUR

# MONTY
## THE DINOSAUR
-ISSUE THREE-

Written by:
**Bob Frantz**
@bfrantz19

Art by:
**Jean Franco**
facebook.com/jeanfrancodg

Variant cover by:
**Jamie Cosley**

Edited By:
**Mike Exner III**
@mikeexnerIII

Inspiration:
**Sophie and Bobby Frantz**

Bryan Seaton: Publisher • Dave Dwonch: President • Shawn Gabborin: Editor In Chief
Jason Martin: Publisher-Danger Zone • Jamal Igle: Vice-President of Marketing
Jim Dietz: Social Media Director • Nicole DAndria: Editor • Chad Cicconi: Lord of the Flies
Colleen Boyd: Submissions Editor.

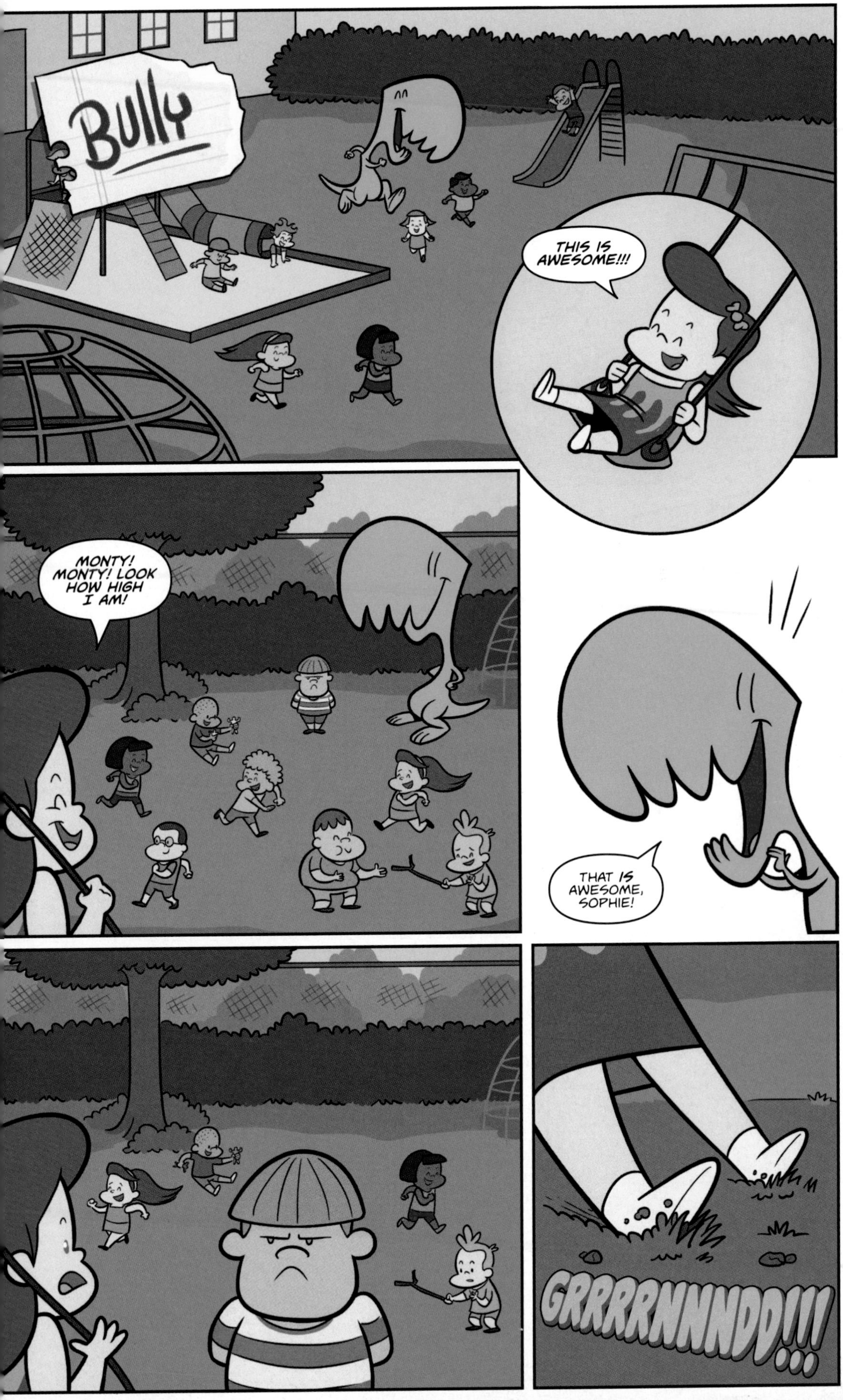

Bully
THIS IS AWESOME!!!
MONTY! MONTY! LOOK HOW HIGH I AM!
THAT IS AWESOME, SOPHIE!
GRRRRNNNDD!!!

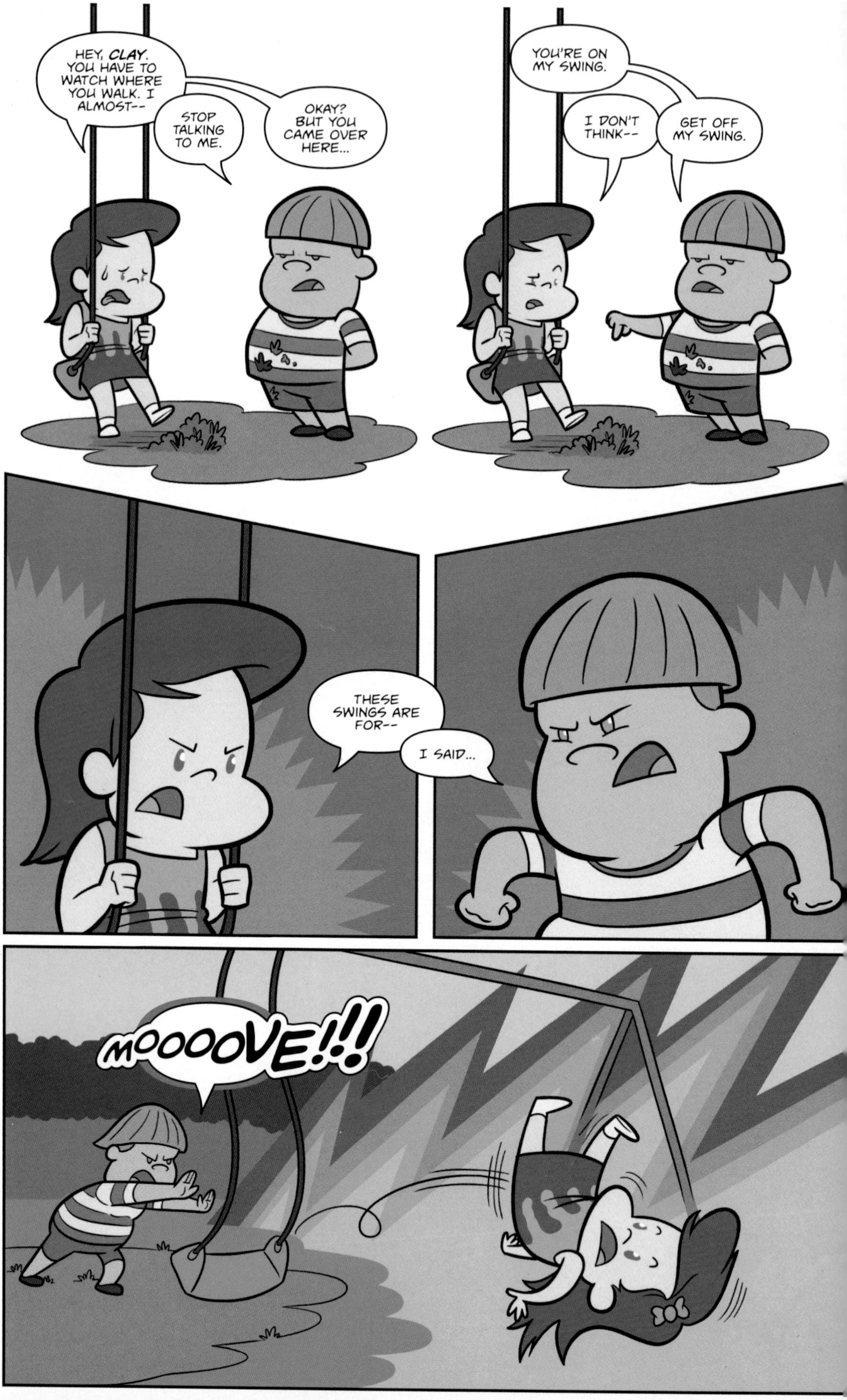
HEY, CLAY. YOU HAVE TO WATCH WHERE YOU WALK. I ALMOST--
STOP TALKING TO ME.
OKAY? BUT YOU CAME OVER HERE...
YOU'RE ON MY SWING.
I DON'T THINK--
GET OFF MY SWING.
THESE SWINGS ARE FOR--
I SAID...
MOOOOVE!!!

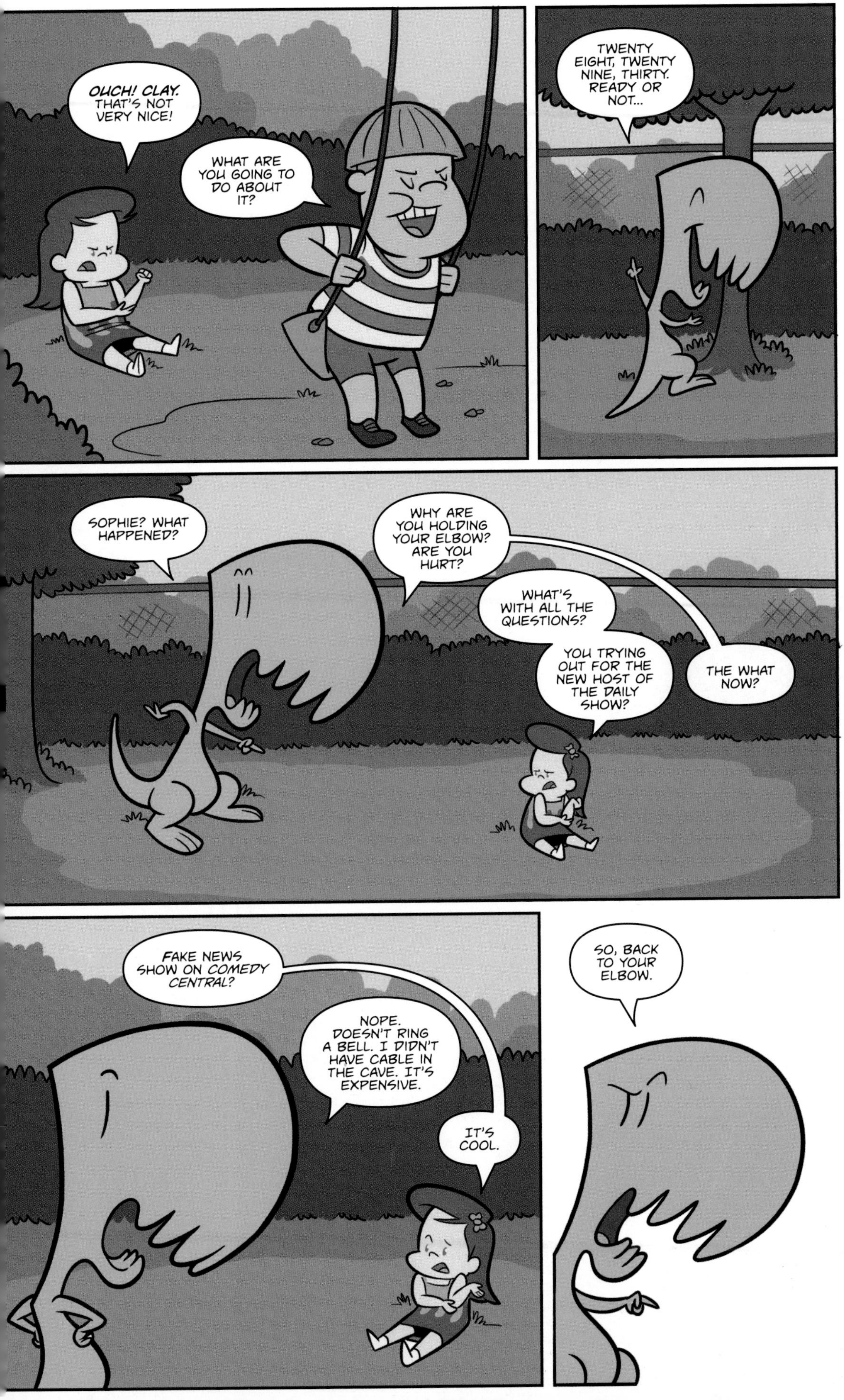
OUCH! CLAY. THAT'S NOT VERY NICE!
WHAT ARE YOU GOING TO DO ABOUT IT?
TWENTY EIGHT, TWENTY NINE, THIRTY. READY OR NOT...
SOPHIE? WHAT HAPPENED?
WHY ARE YOU HOLDING YOUR ELBOW? ARE YOU HURT?
WHAT'S WITH ALL THE QUESTIONS?
YOU TRYING OUT FOR THE NEW HOST OF THE DAILY SHOW?
THE WHAT NOW?
FAKE NEWS SHOW ON COMEDY CENTRAL?
NOPE. DOESN'T RING A BELL. I DIDN'T HAVE CABLE IN THE CAVE. IT'S EXPENSIVE.
IT'S COOL.
SO, BACK TO YOUR ELBOW.

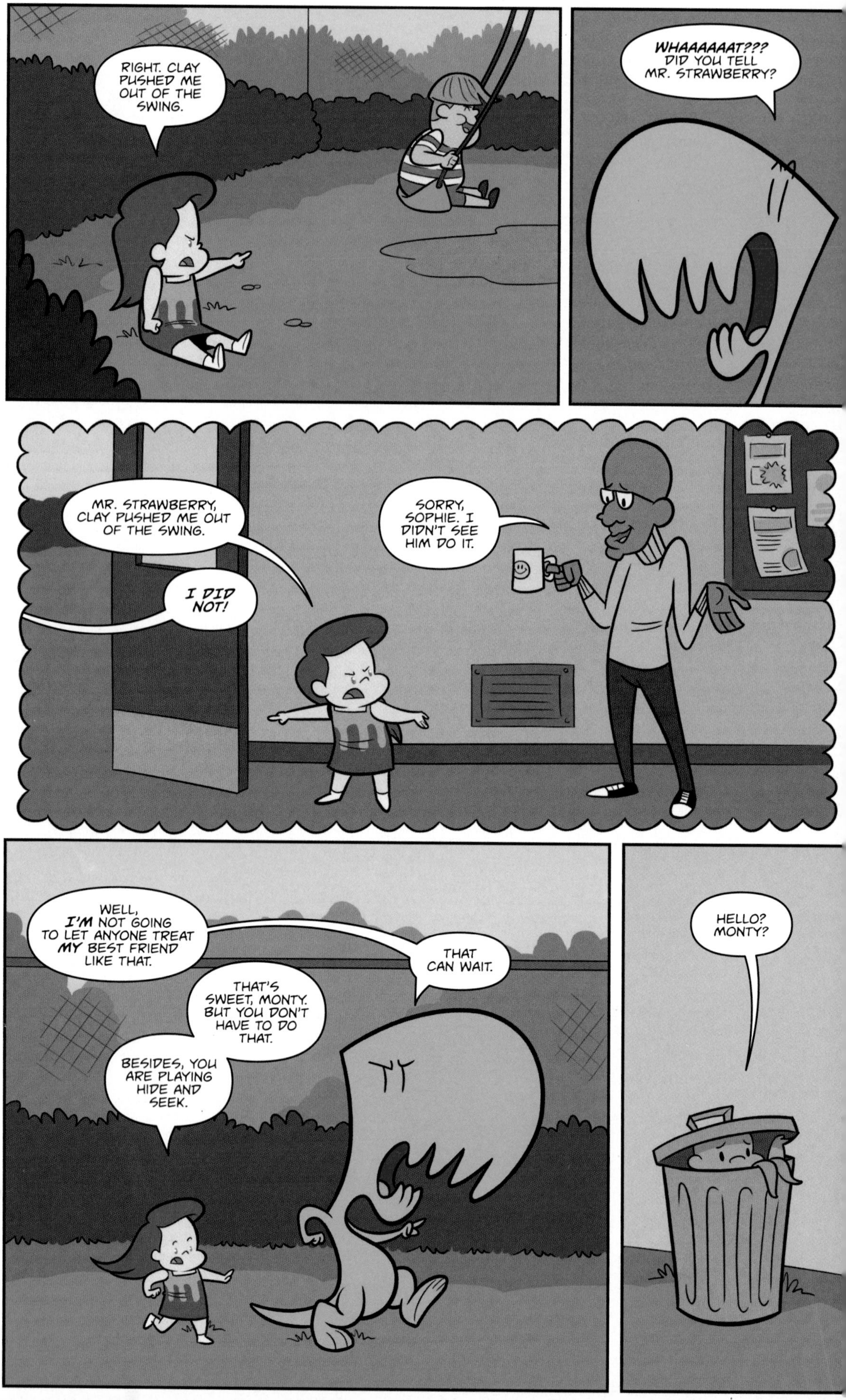
RIGHT. CLAY PUSHED ME OUT OF THE SWING.
WHAAAAAAT??? DID YOU TELL MR. STRAWBERRY?
MR. STRAWBERRY, CLAY PUSHED ME OUT OF THE SWING.
I DID NOT!
SORRY, SOPHIE. I DIDN'T SEE HIM DO IT.
WELL, I'M NOT GOING TO LET ANYONE TREAT MY BEST FRIEND LIKE THAT.
THAT CAN WAIT.
THAT'S SWEET, MONTY. BUT YOU DON'T HAVE TO DO THAT.
BESIDES, YOU ARE PLAYING HIDE AND SEEK.
HELLO? MONTY?

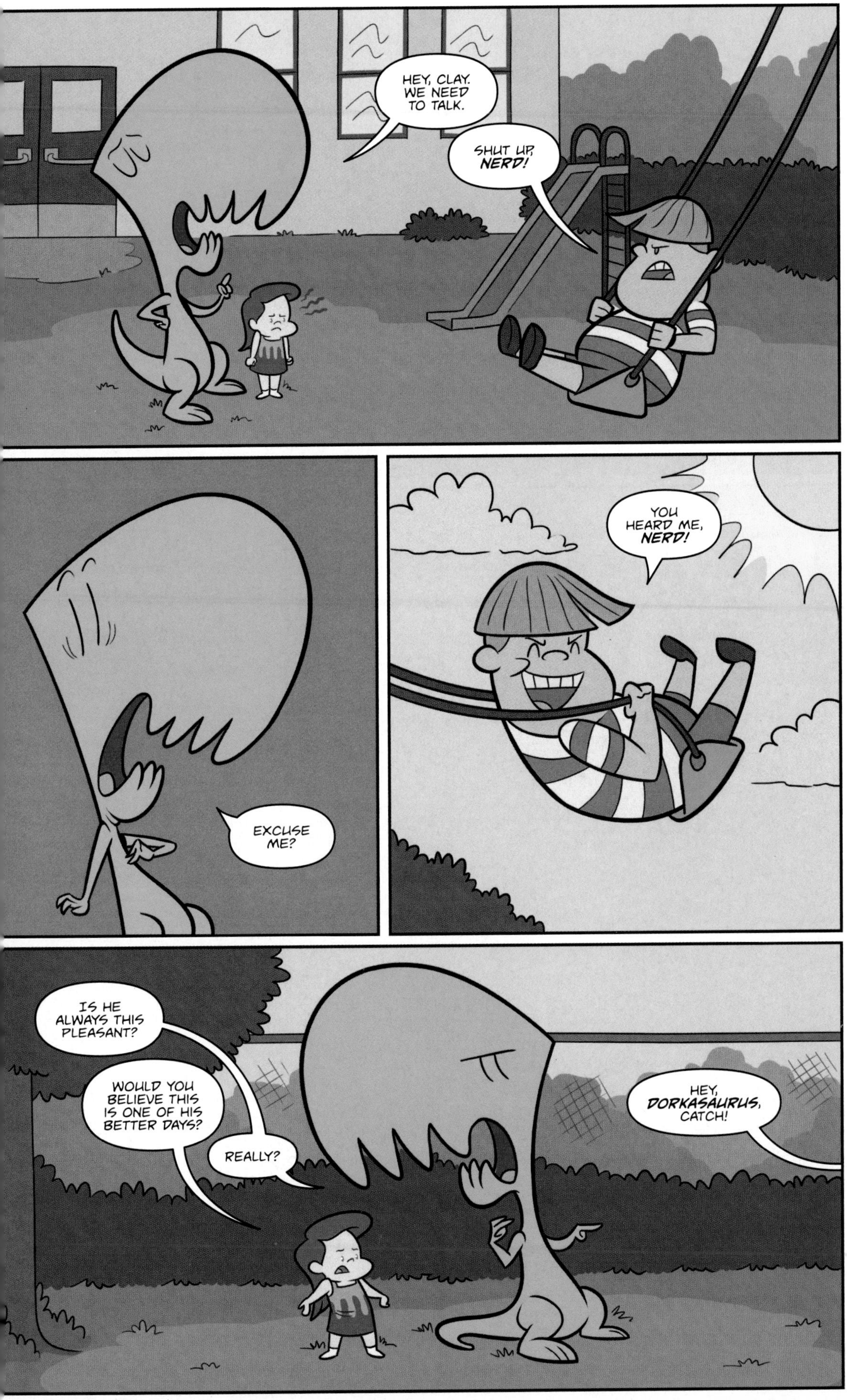
HEY, CLAY. WE NEED TO TALK.
SHUT UP, NERD!
EXCUSE ME?
YOU HEARD ME, NERD!
IS HE ALWAYS THIS PLEASANT?
WOULD YOU BELIEVE THIS IS ONE OF HIS BETTER DAYS?
REALLY?
HEY, DORKASAURUS, CATCH!

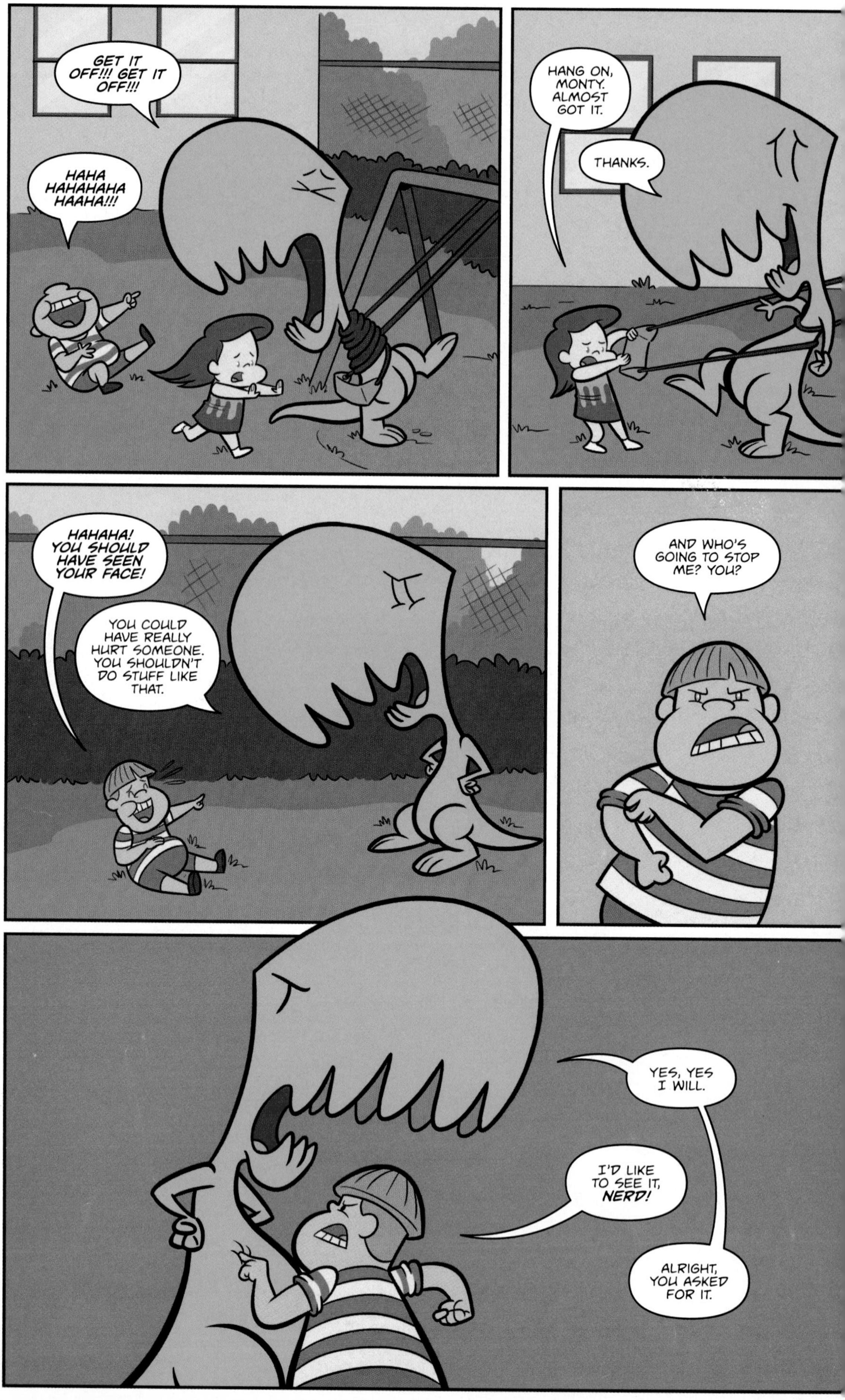
GET IT OFF!!! GET IT OFF!!!
HAHA HAHAHAHA HAAHA!!!
HANG ON, MONTY. ALMOST GOT IT.
THANKS.
HAHAHA! YOU SHOULD HAVE SEEN YOUR FACE!
YOU COULD HAVE REALLY HURT SOMEONE. YOU SHOULDN'T DO STUFF LIKE THAT.
AND WHO'S GOING TO STOP ME? YOU?
YES, YES I WILL.
I'D LIKE TO SEE IT, NERD!
ALRIGHT, YOU ASKED FOR IT.

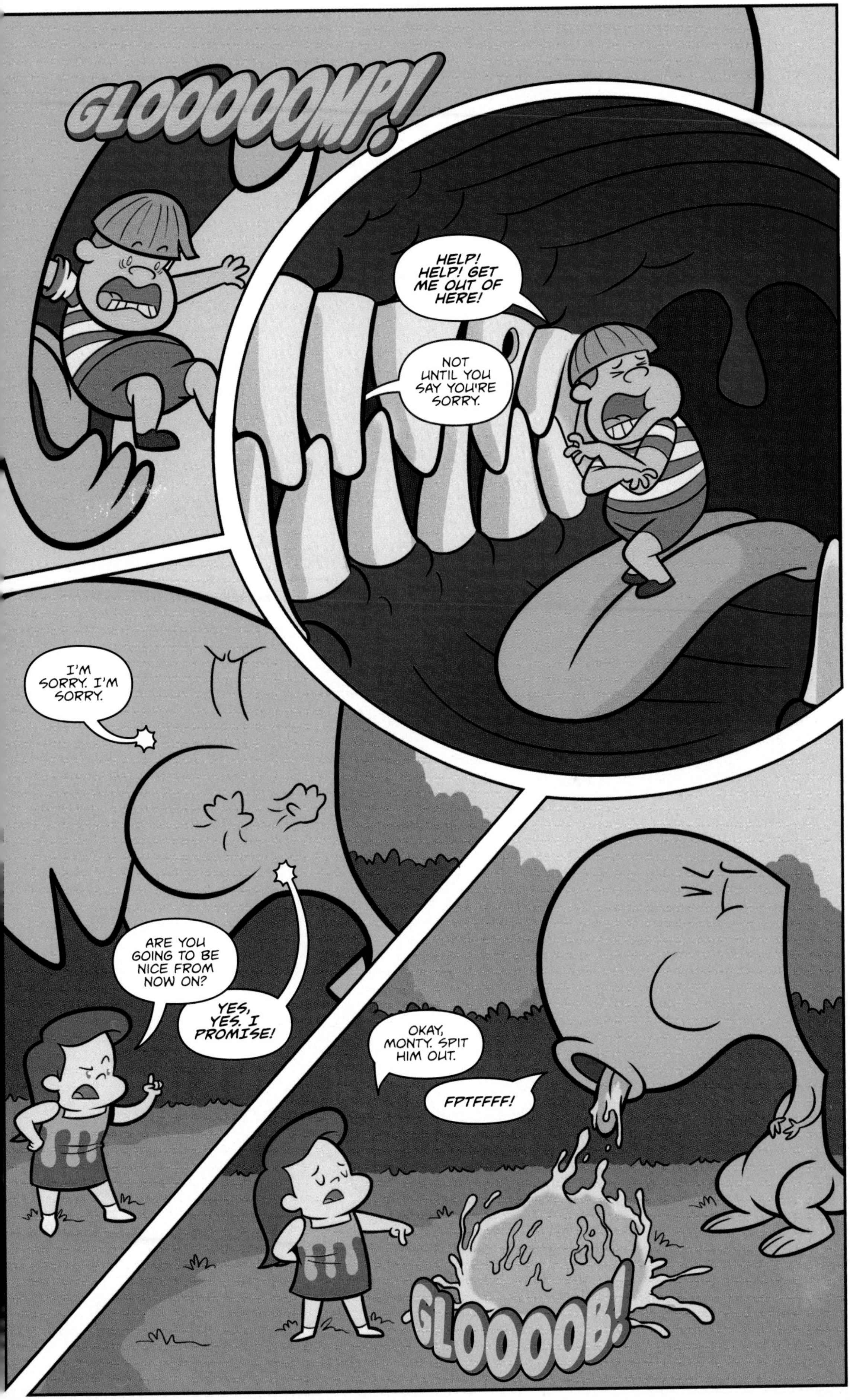
GLOOOOOMP!
HELP! HELP! GET ME OUT OF HERE!
NOT UNTIL YOU SAY YOU'RE SORRY.
I'M SORRY. I'M SORRY.
ARE YOU GOING TO BE NICE FROM NOW ON?
YES, YES. I PROMISE!
OKAY, MONTY. SPIT HIM OUT.
FPTFFFF!
GLOOOOB!

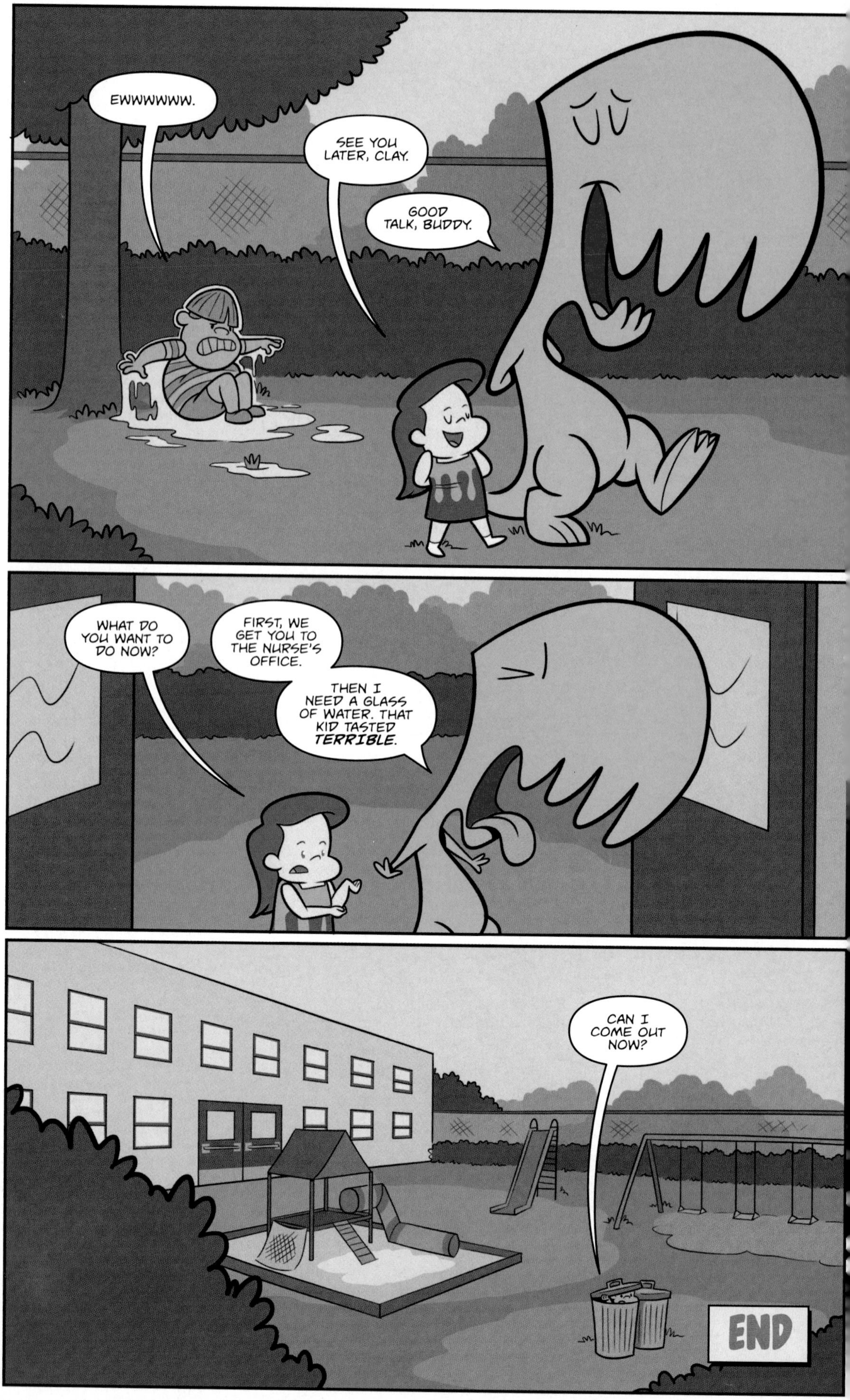
EWWWWWW.
SEE YOU LATER, CLAY.
GOOD TALK, BUDDY.
WHAT DO YOU WANT TO DO NOW?
FIRST, WE GET YOU TO THE NURSE'S OFFICE.
THEN I NEED A GLASS OF WATER. THAT KID TASTED *TERRIBLE*.
CAN I COME OUT NOW?
END

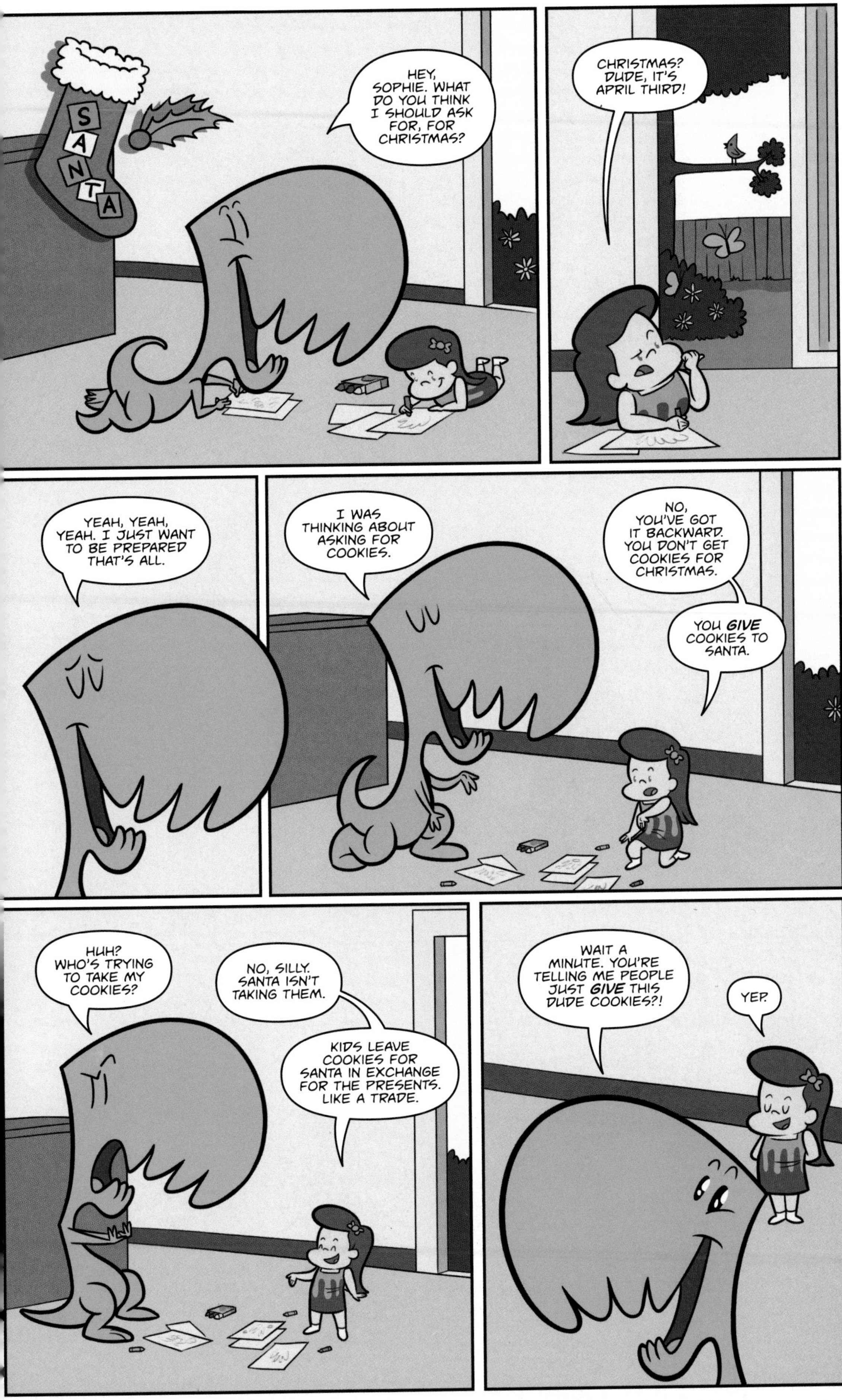

SANTA
HEY, SOPHIE. WHAT DO YOU THINK I SHOULD ASK FOR, FOR CHRISTMAS?
CHRISTMAS? DUDE, IT'S APRIL THIRD!
YEAH, YEAH, YEAH. I JUST WANT TO BE PREPARED THAT'S ALL.
I WAS THINKING ABOUT ASKING FOR COOKIES.
NO, YOU'VE GOT IT BACKWARD. YOU DON'T GET COOKIES FOR CHRISTMAS.
YOU **GIVE** COOKIES TO SANTA.
HUH? WHO'S TRYING TO TAKE MY COOKIES?
NO, SILLY. SANTA ISN'T TAKING THEM.
KIDS LEAVE COOKIES FOR SANTA IN EXCHANGE FOR THE PRESENTS. LIKE A TRADE.
WAIT A MINUTE. YOU'RE TELLING ME PEOPLE JUST **GIVE** THIS DUDE COOKIES?!
YEP.

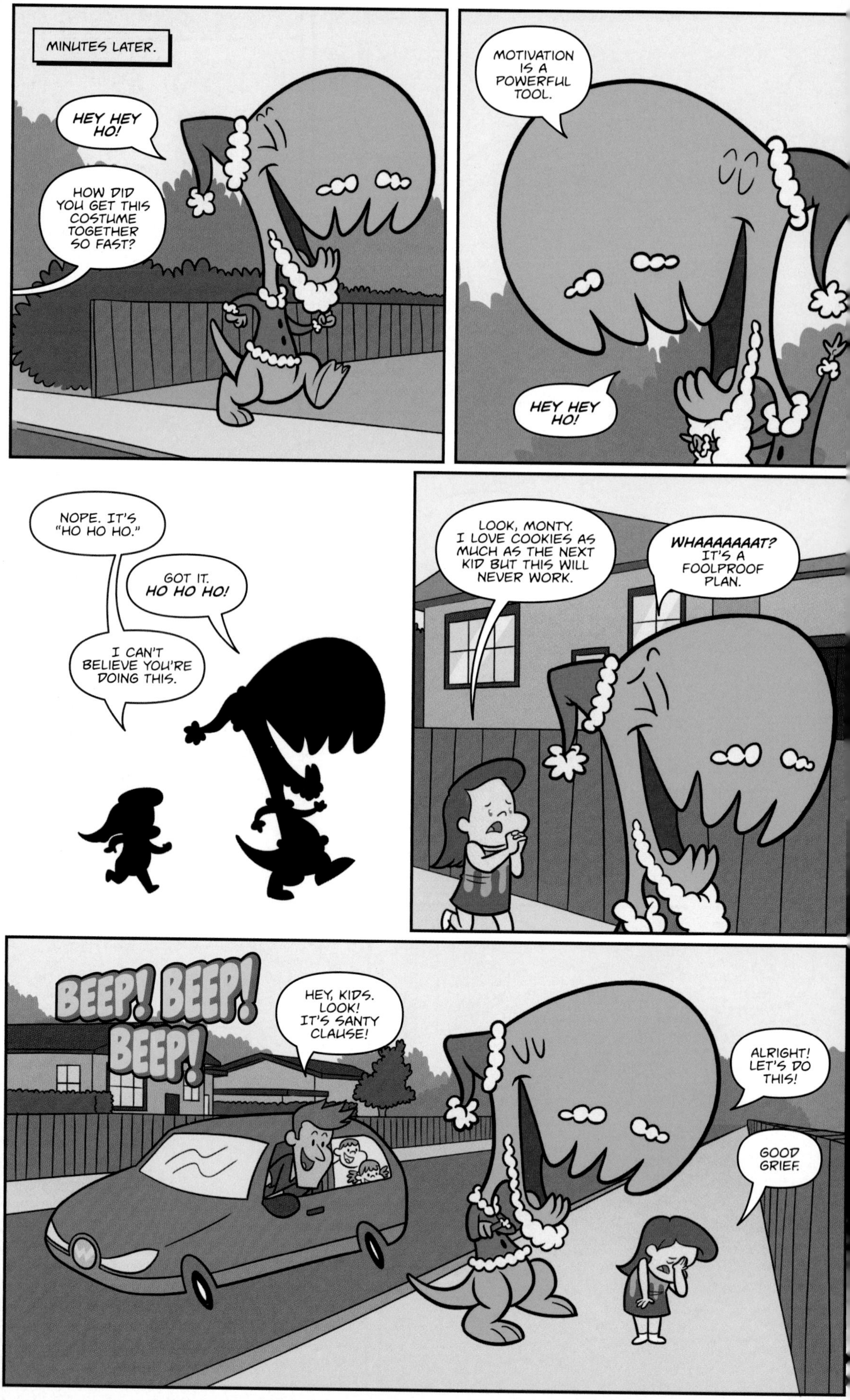

MINUTES LATER.
HEY HEY HO!
HOW DID YOU GET THIS COSTUME TOGETHER SO FAST?
MOTIVATION IS A POWERFUL TOOL.
HEY HEY HO!
NOPE. IT'S "HO HO HO."
GOT IT. HO HO HO!
I CAN'T BELIEVE YOU'RE DOING THIS.
LOOK, MONTY. I LOVE COOKIES AS MUCH AS THE NEXT KID BUT THIS WILL NEVER WORK.
WHAAAAAAAT? IT'S A FOOLPROOF PLAN.
BEEP! BEEP! BEEP!
HEY, KIDS. LOOK! IT'S SANTY CLAUSE!
ALRIGHT! LET'S DO THIS!
GOOD GRIEF.

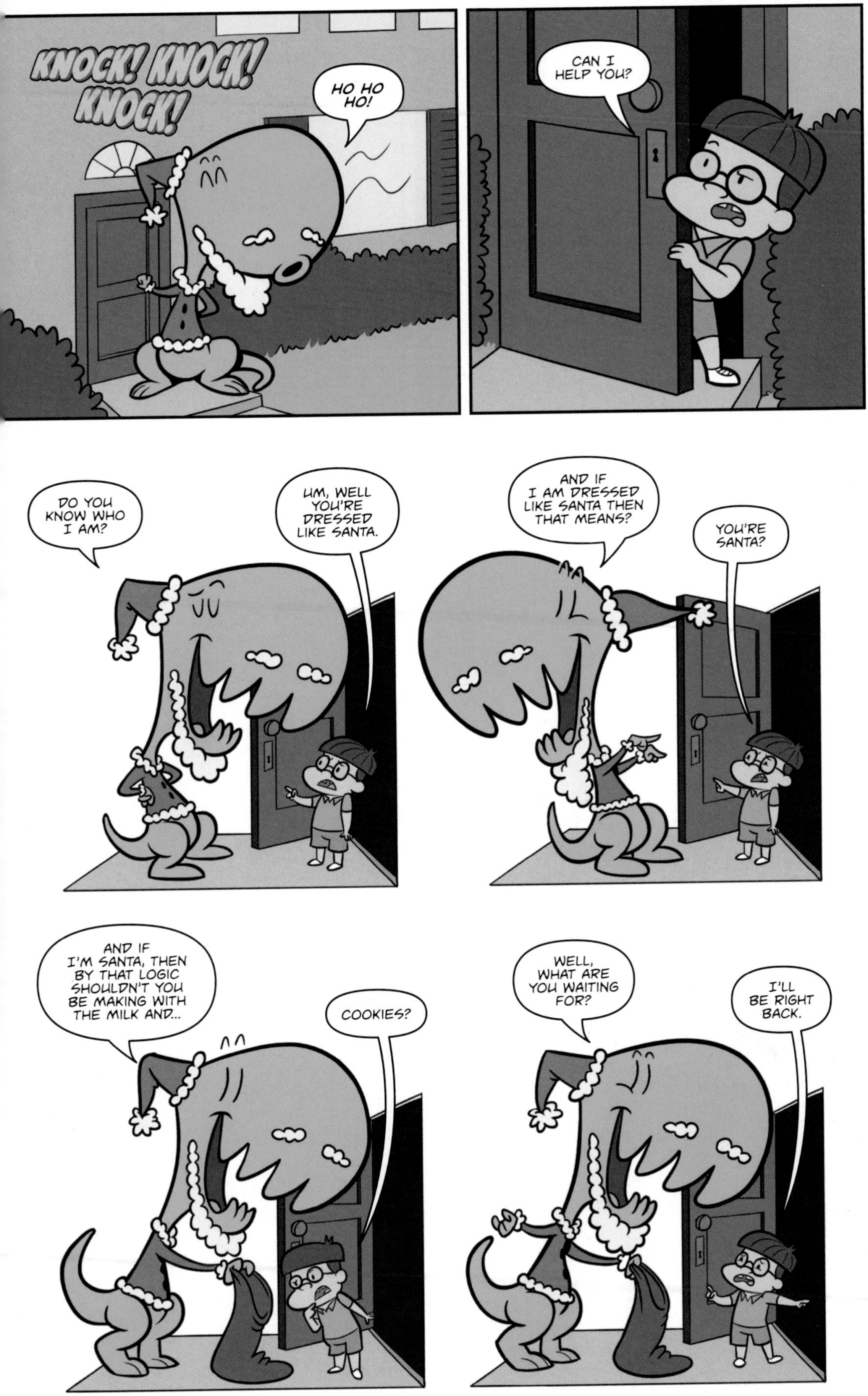
KNOCK! KNOCK! KNOCK!
HO HO HO!
CAN I HELP YOU?
DO YOU KNOW WHO I AM?
UM, WELL YOU'RE DRESSED LIKE SANTA.
AND IF I AM DRESSED LIKE SANTA THEN THAT MEANS?
YOU'RE SANTA?
AND IF I'M SANTA, THEN BY THAT LOGIC SHOULDN'T YOU BE MAKING WITH THE MILK AND...
COOKIES?
WELL, WHAT ARE YOU WAITING FOR?
I'LL BE RIGHT BACK.

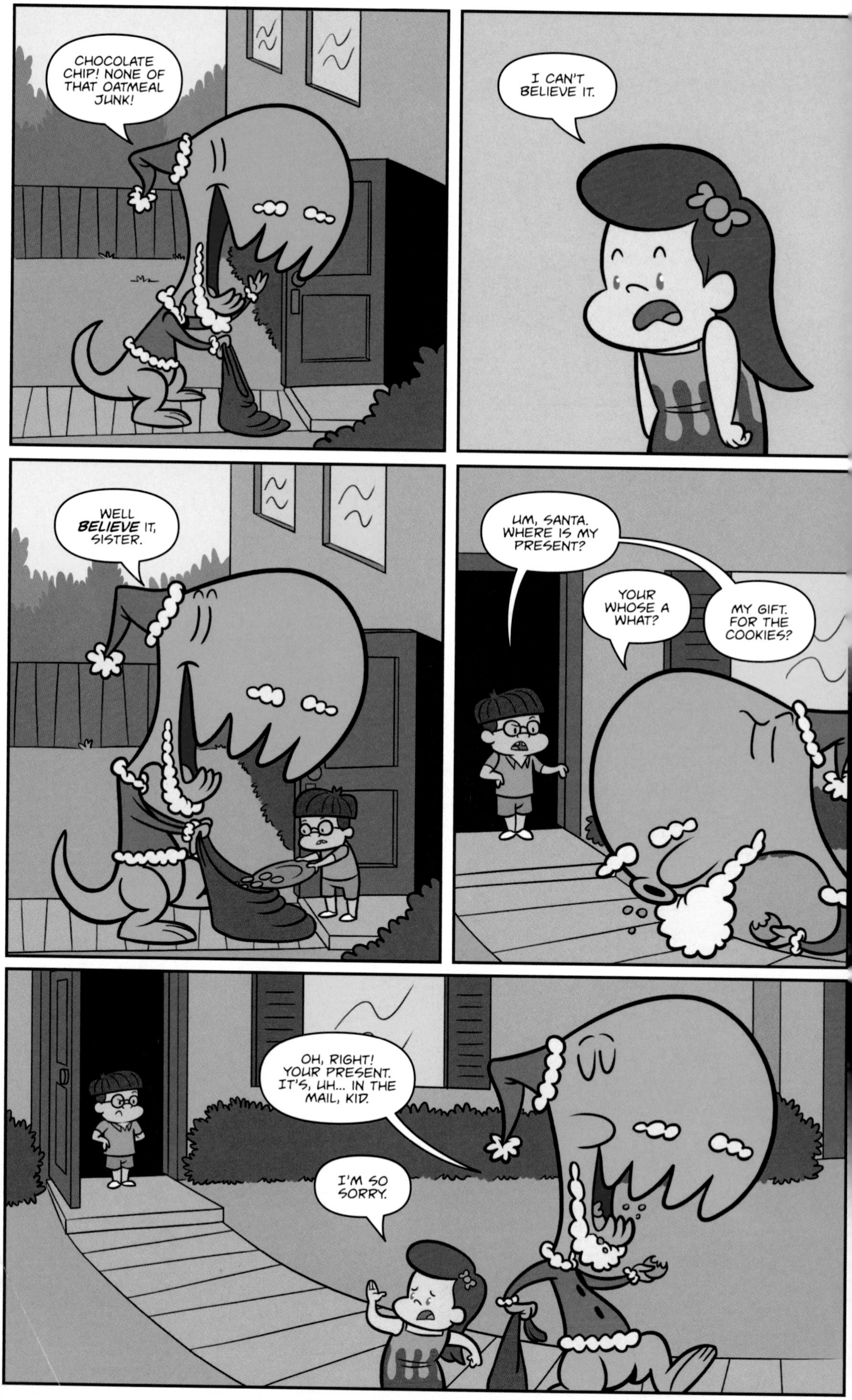
CHOCOLATE CHIP! NONE OF THAT OATMEAL JUNK!
I CAN'T BELIEVE IT.
WELL BELIEVE IT, SISTER.
UM, SANTA. WHERE IS MY PRESENT?
YOUR WHOSE A WHAT?
MY GIFT. FOR THE COOKIES?
OH, RIGHT! YOUR PRESENT. IT'S, UH... IN THE MAIL, KID.
I'M SO SORRY.

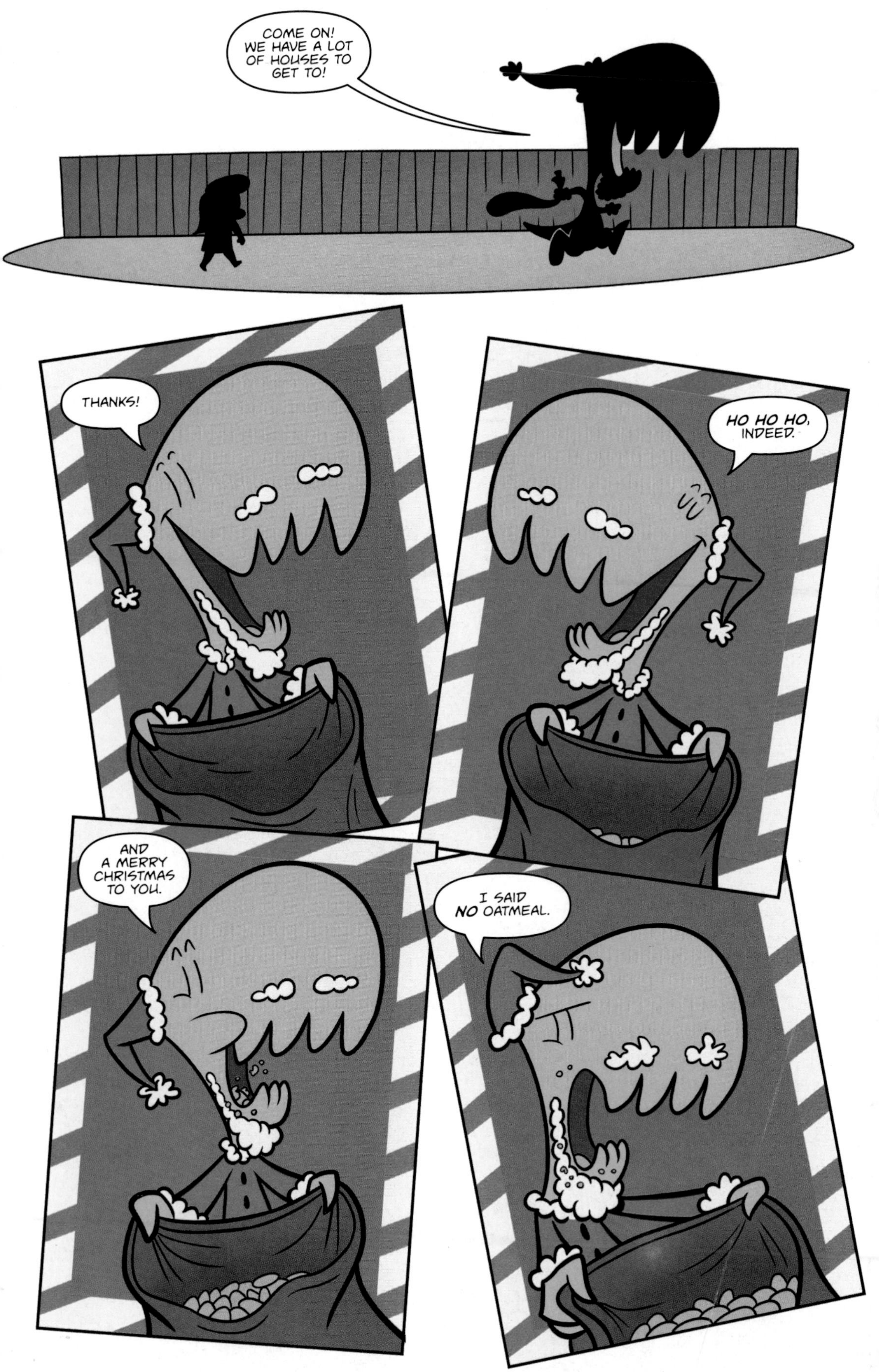
COME ON! WE HAVE A LOT OF HOUSES TO GET TO!
THANKS!
HO HO HO, INDEED.
AND A MERRY CHRISTMAS TO YOU.
I SAID NO OATMEAL.

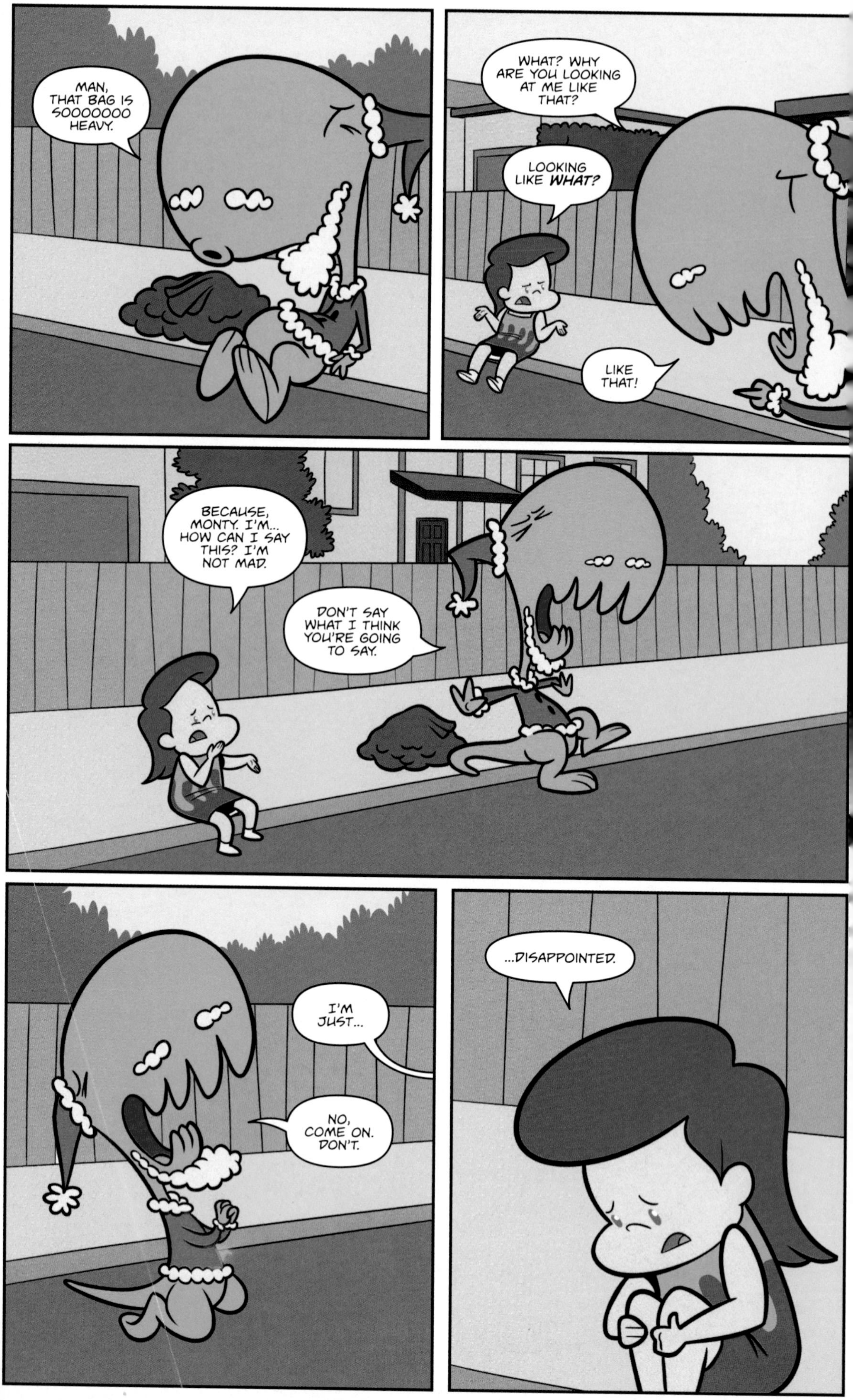
MAN, THAT BAG IS SOOOOOOO HEAVY.
WHAT? WHY ARE YOU LOOKING AT ME LIKE THAT?
LOOKING LIKE **WHAT?**
LIKE THAT!
BECAUSE, MONTY. I'M... HOW CAN I SAY THIS? I'M NOT MAD.
DON'T SAY WHAT I THINK YOU'RE GOING TO SAY.
I'M JUST...
NO, COME ON. DON'T.
...DISAPPOINTED.

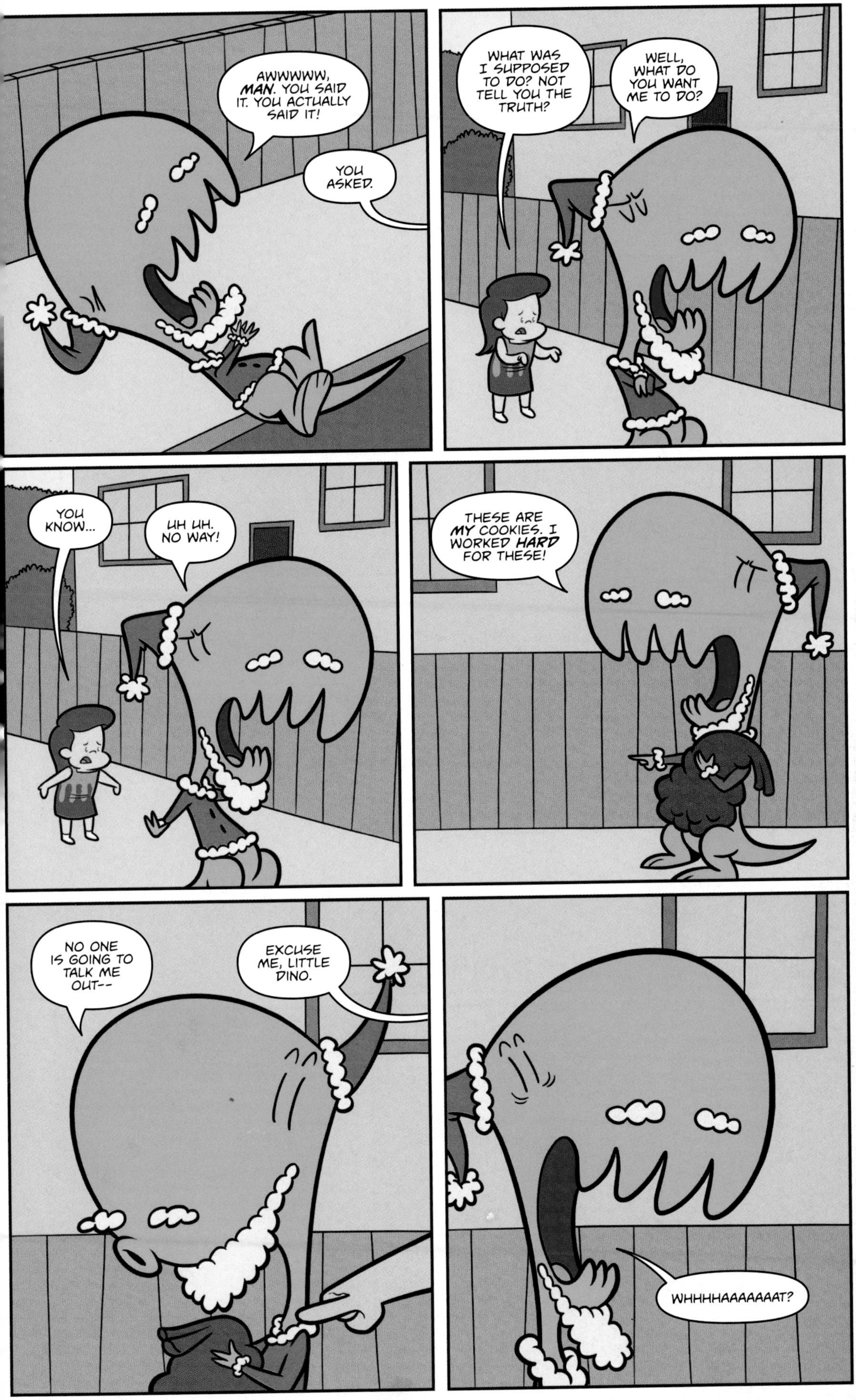
AWWWWW, MAN. YOU SAID IT. YOU ACTUALLY SAID IT!
YOU ASKED.
WHAT WAS I SUPPOSED TO DO? NOT TELL YOU THE TRUTH?
WELL, WHAT DO YOU WANT ME TO DO?
YOU KNOW...
UH UH. NO WAY!
THESE ARE MY COOKIES. I WORKED HARD FOR THESE!
NO ONE IS GOING TO TALK ME OUT--
EXCUSE ME, LITTLE DINO.
WHHHHAAAAAAAT?

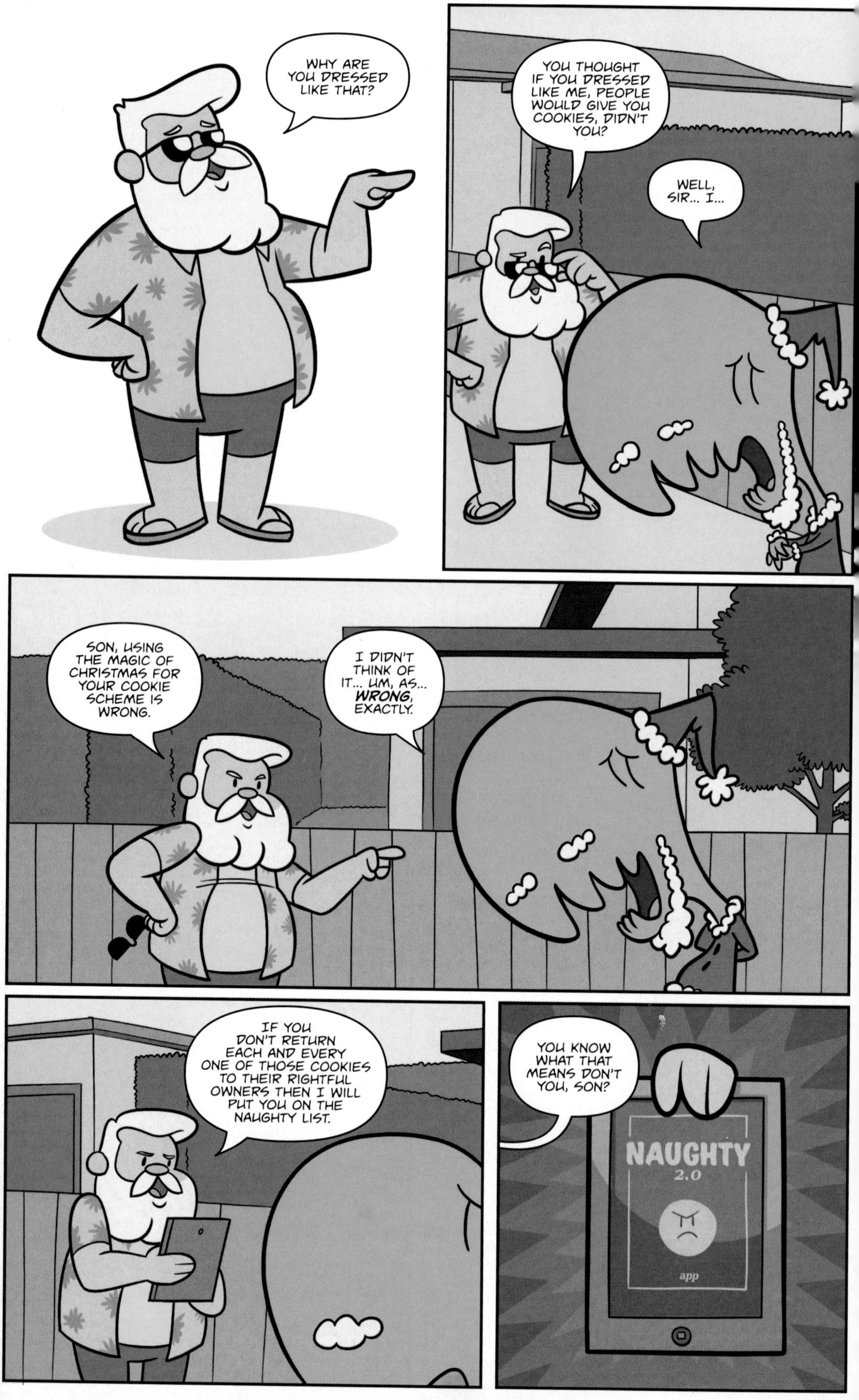
WHY ARE YOU DRESSED LIKE THAT?
YOU THOUGHT IF YOU DRESSED LIKE ME, PEOPLE WOULD GIVE YOU COOKIES, DIDN'T YOU?
WELL, SIR... I...
SON, USING THE MAGIC OF CHRISTMAS FOR YOUR COOKIE SCHEME IS WRONG.
I DIDN'T THINK OF IT... UM, AS... *WRONG*, EXACTLY.
IF YOU DON'T RETURN EACH AND EVERY ONE OF THOSE COOKIES TO THEIR RIGHTFUL OWNERS THEN I WILL PUT YOU ON THE NAUGHTY LIST.
YOU KNOW WHAT THAT MEANS DON'T YOU, SON?
NAUGHTY
2.0
app

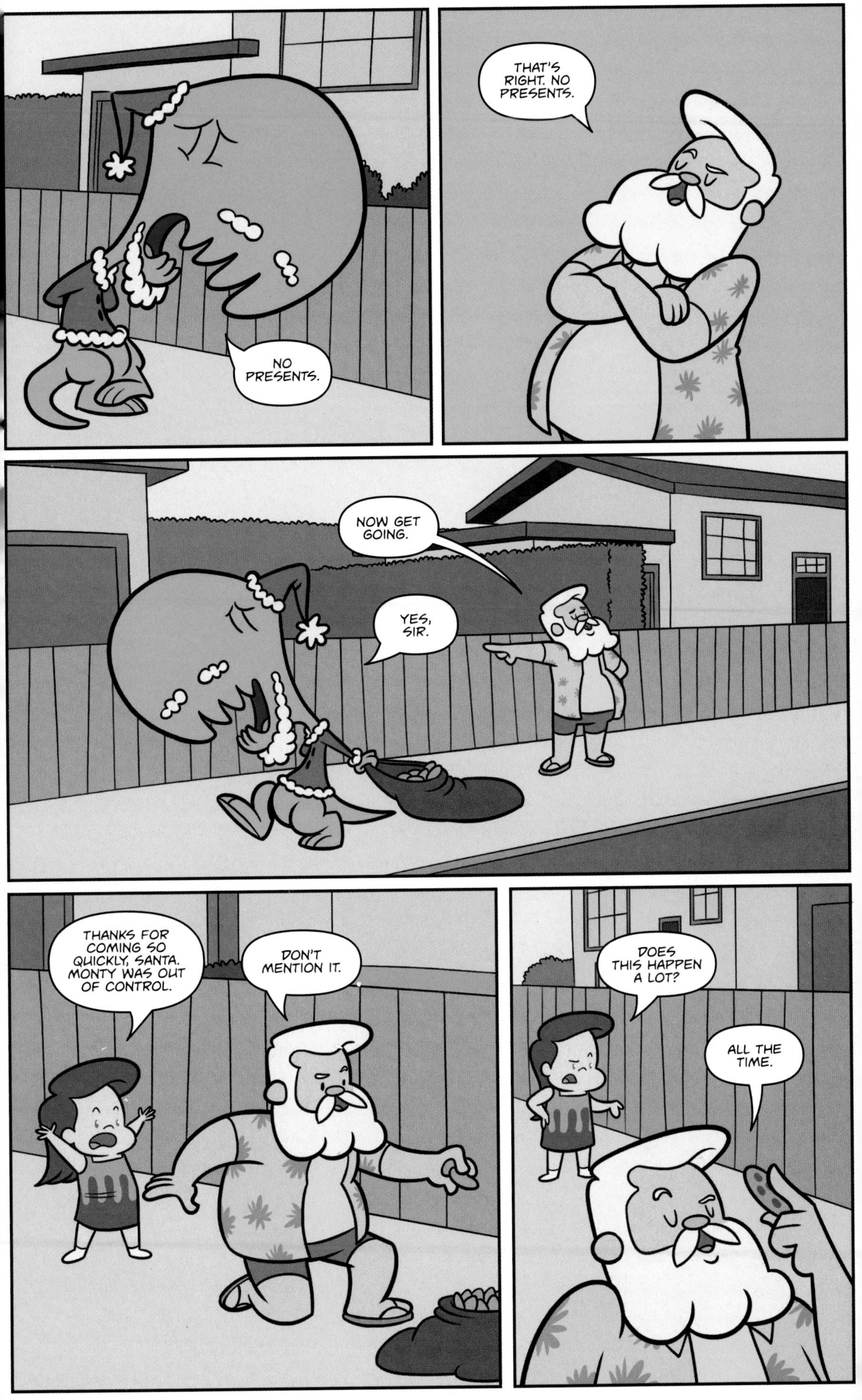
NO PRESENTS.
THAT'S RIGHT. NO PRESENTS.
NOW GET GOING.
YES, SIR.
THANKS FOR COMING SO QUICKLY, SANTA. MONTY WAS OUT OF CONTROL.
DON'T MENTION IT.
DOES THIS HAPPEN A LOT?
ALL THE TIME.

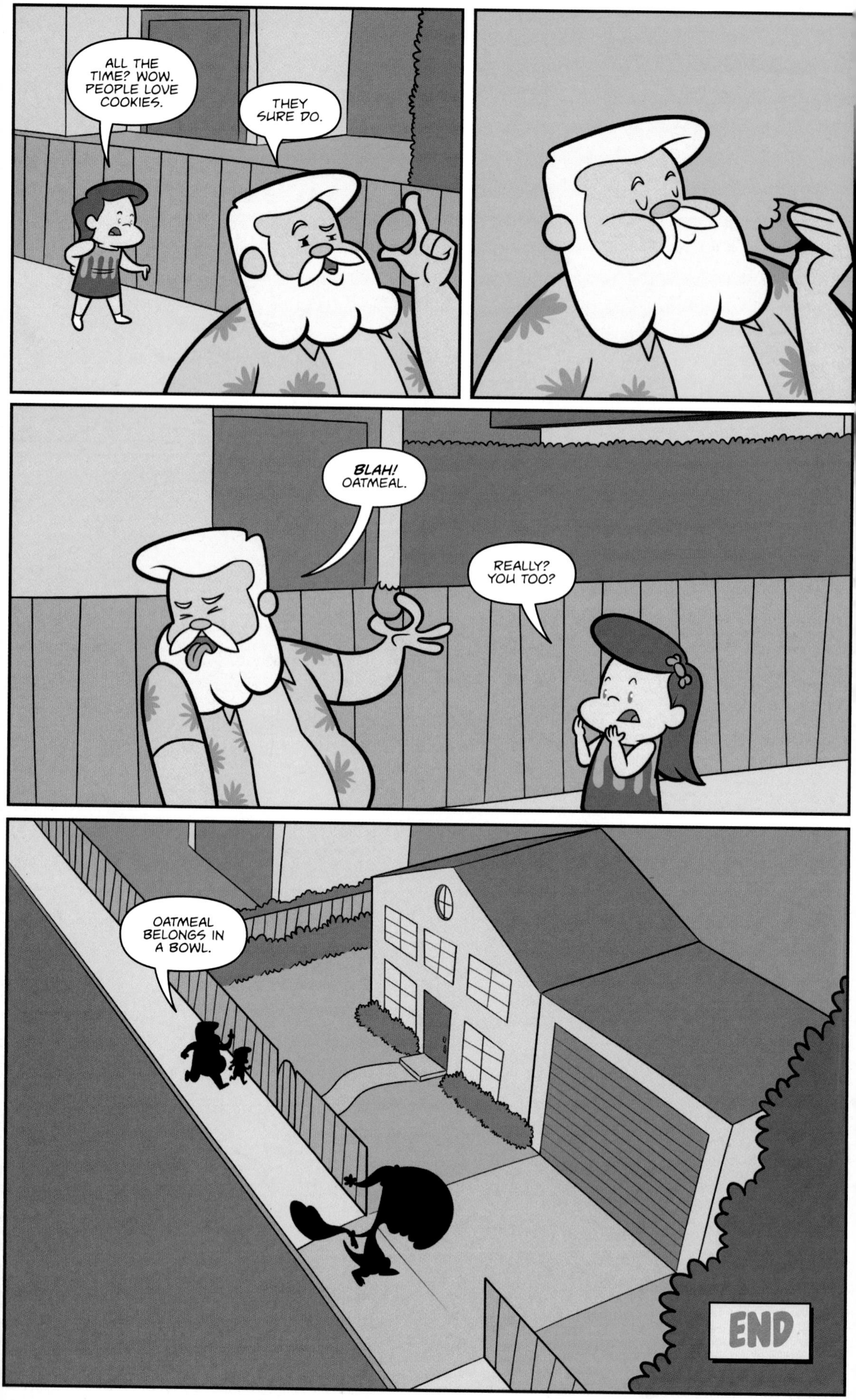
ALL THE TIME? WOW. PEOPLE LOVE COOKIES.
THEY SURE DO.
BLAH! OATMEAL.
REALLY? YOU TOO?
OATMEAL BELONGS IN A BOWL.
END

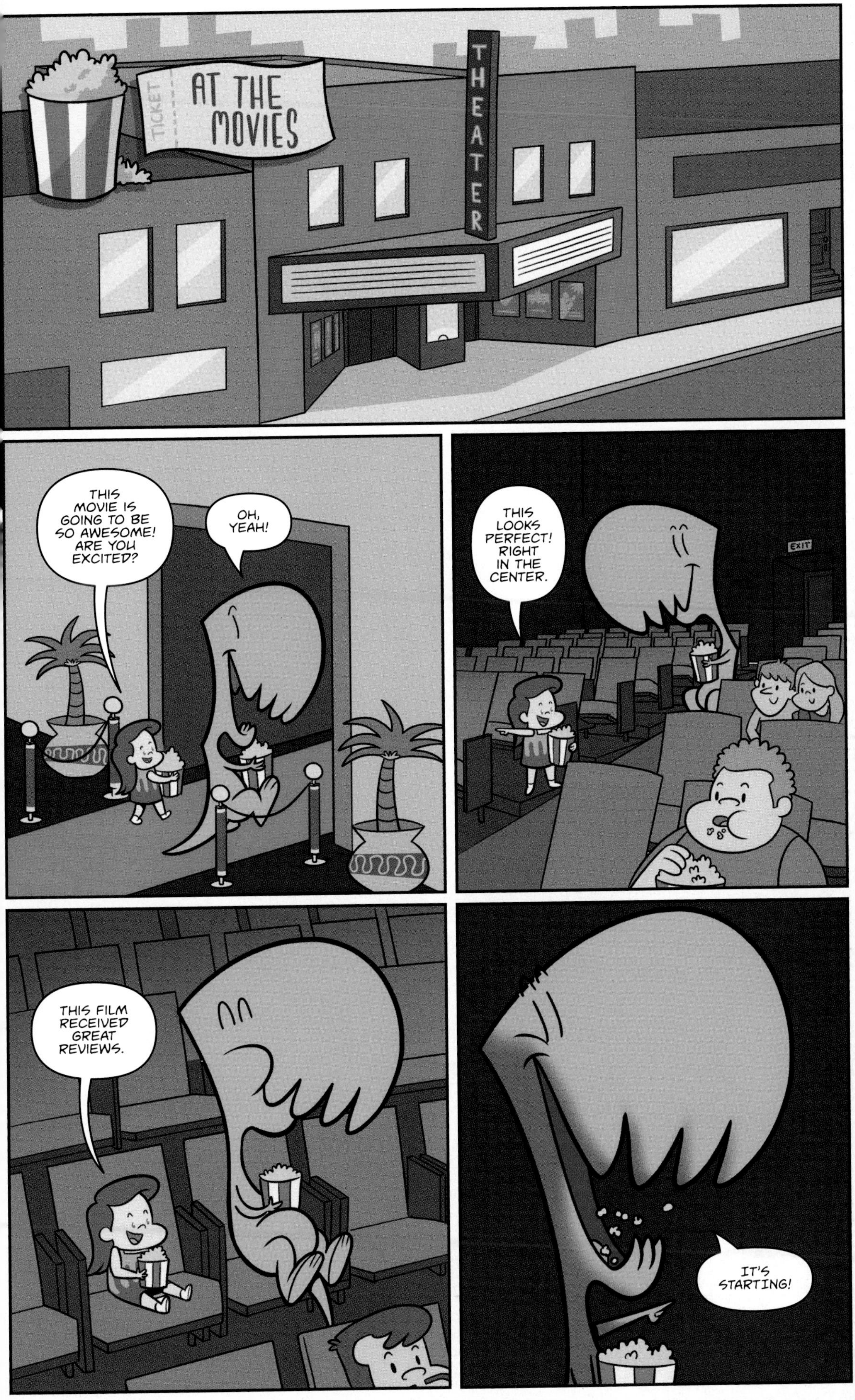
TICKET
AT THE MOVIES
THEATER
THIS MOVIE IS GOING TO BE SO AWESOME! ARE YOU EXCITED?
OH, YEAH!
THIS LOOKS PERFECT! RIGHT IN THE CENTER.
EXIT
THIS FILM RECEIVED GREAT REVIEWS.
IT'S STARTING!

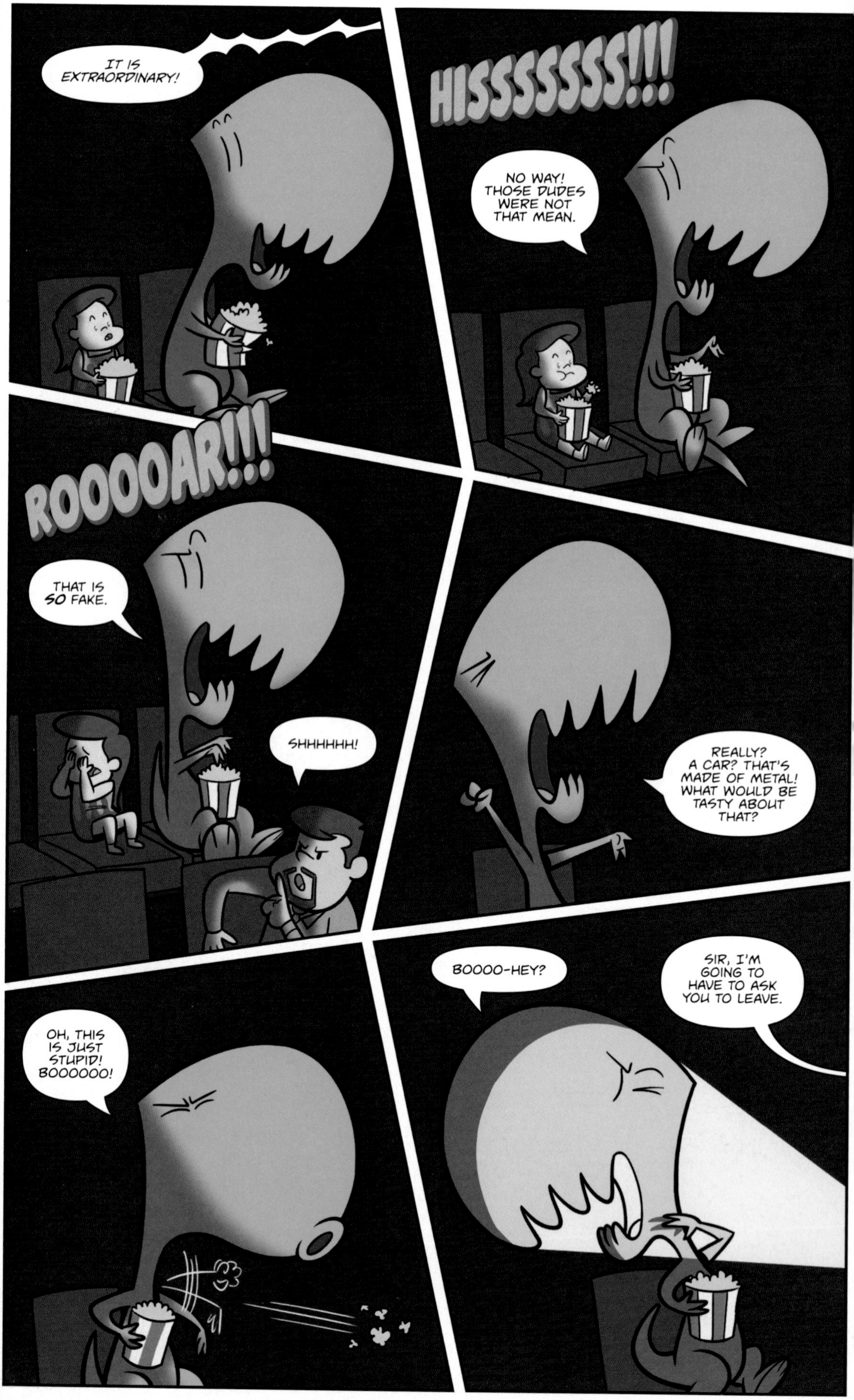
IT IS EXTRAORDINARY!
HISSSSSSS!!!
NO WAY! THOSE DUDES WERE NOT THAT MEAN.
ROOOOAR!!!
THAT IS SO FAKE.
SHHHHHH!
REALLY? A CAR? THAT'S MADE OF METAL! WHAT WOULD BE TASTY ABOUT THAT?
OH, THIS IS JUST STUPID! BOOOOOO!
BOOOO-HEY?
SIR, I'M GOING TO HAVE TO ASK YOU TO LEAVE.

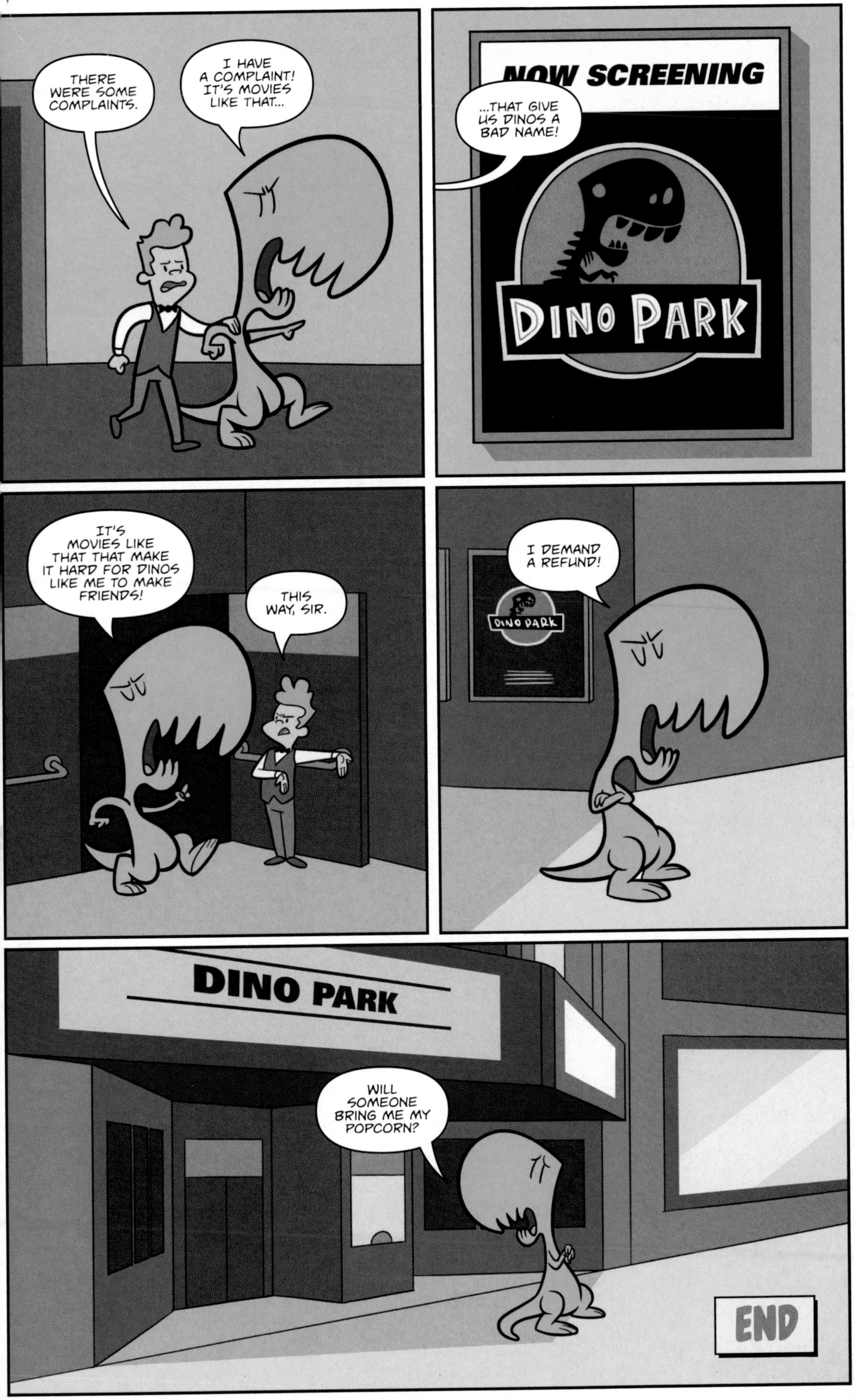
THERE WERE SOME COMPLAINTS.
I HAVE A COMPLAINT! IT'S MOVIES LIKE THAT...
NOW SCREENING
...THAT GIVE US DINOS A BAD NAME!
DINO PARK
IT'S MOVIES LIKE THAT THAT MAKE IT HARD FOR DINOS LIKE ME TO MAKE FRIENDS!
THIS WAY, SIR.
I DEMAND A REFUND!
DINO PARK
DINO PARK
WILL SOMEONE BRING ME MY POPCORN?
END

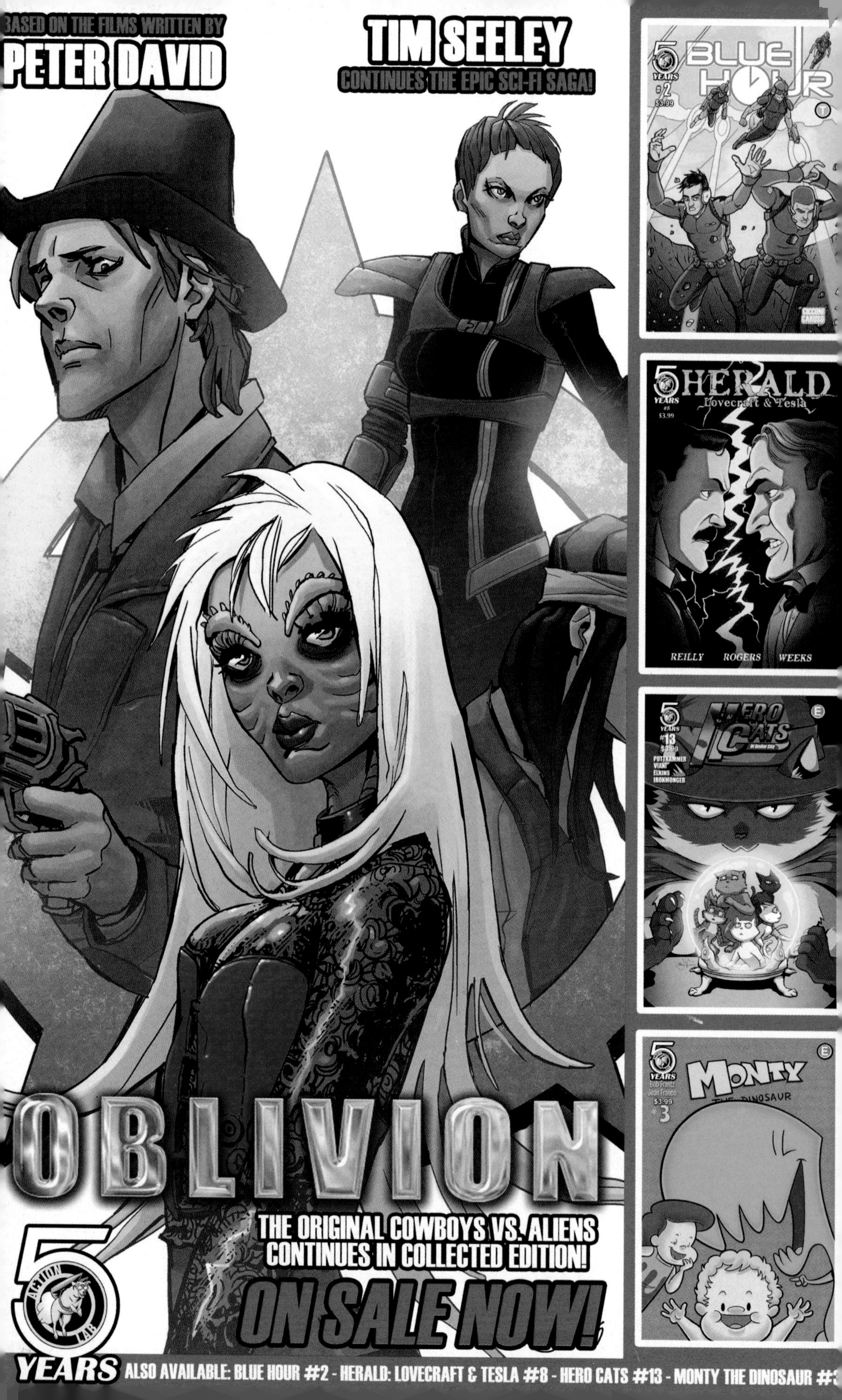

BASED ON THE FILMS WRITTEN BY
PETER DAVID
TIM SEELEY
CONTINUES THE EPIC SCI-FI SAGA!
OBLIVION
THE ORIGINAL COWBOYS VS. ALIENS
CONTINUES IN COLLECTED EDITION!
ON SALE NOW!
5 YEARS
ACTION LAB
BLUE HOUR
#2
$3.99
CICCONI
CARUSO
HERALD
Lovecraft & Tesla
#8
$3.99
REILLY
ROGERS
WEEKS
HERO CATS
#13
$3.99
PUTTKAMMER
VIANI
ELKINS
IRONMONGER
MONTY
THE DINOSAUR
Bob Frantz
Jean Franco
$3.99
#3
ALSO AVAILABLE: BLUE HOUR #2 - HERALD: LOVECRAFT & TESLA #8 - HERO CATS #13 - MONTY THE DINOSAUR #3

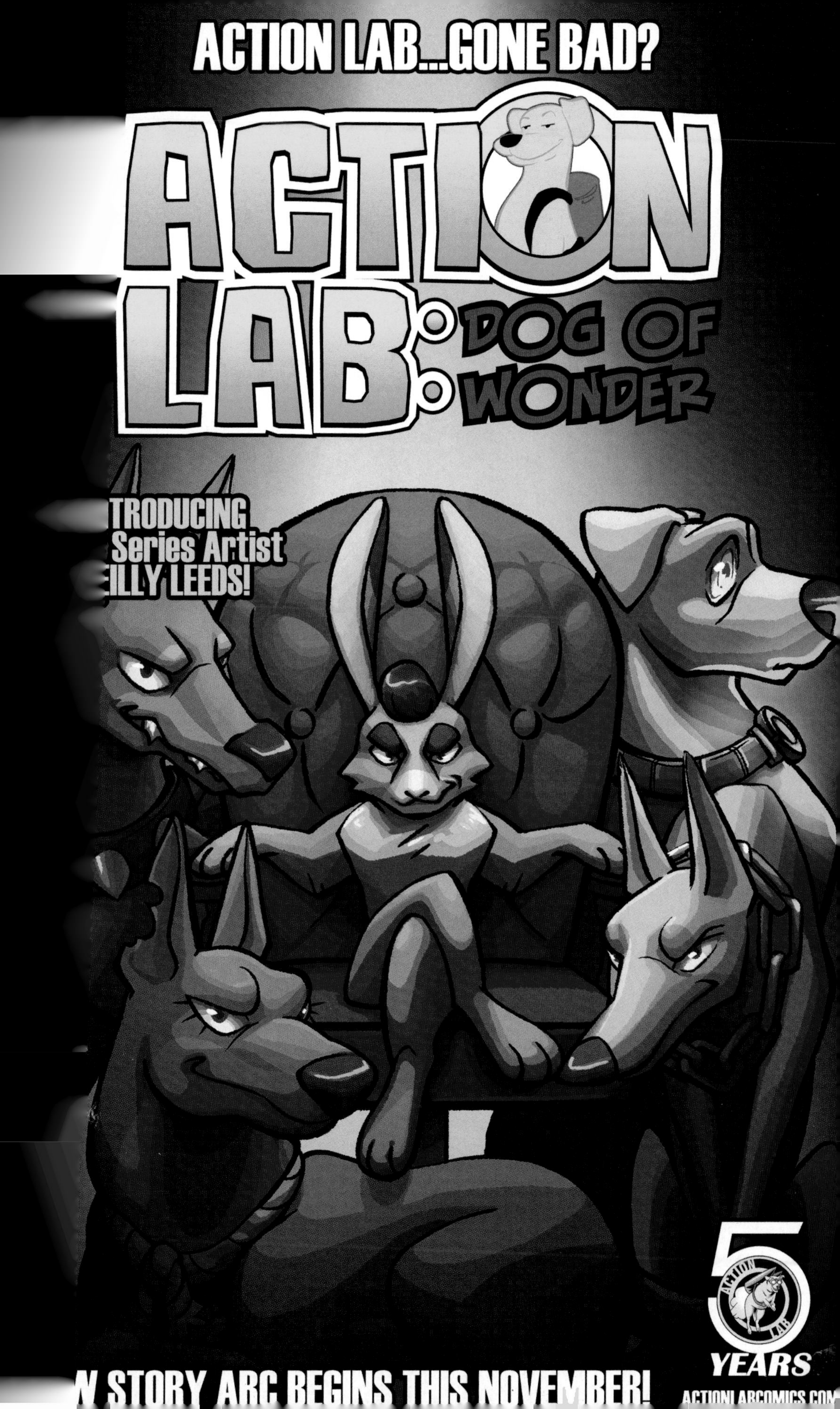

ACTION LAB...GONE BAD?
ACTION LAB: DOG OF WONDER
TRODUCING
Series Artist
EILLY LEEDS!
5 YEARS
ACTION LAB
V STORY ARC BEGINS THIS NOVEMBER!

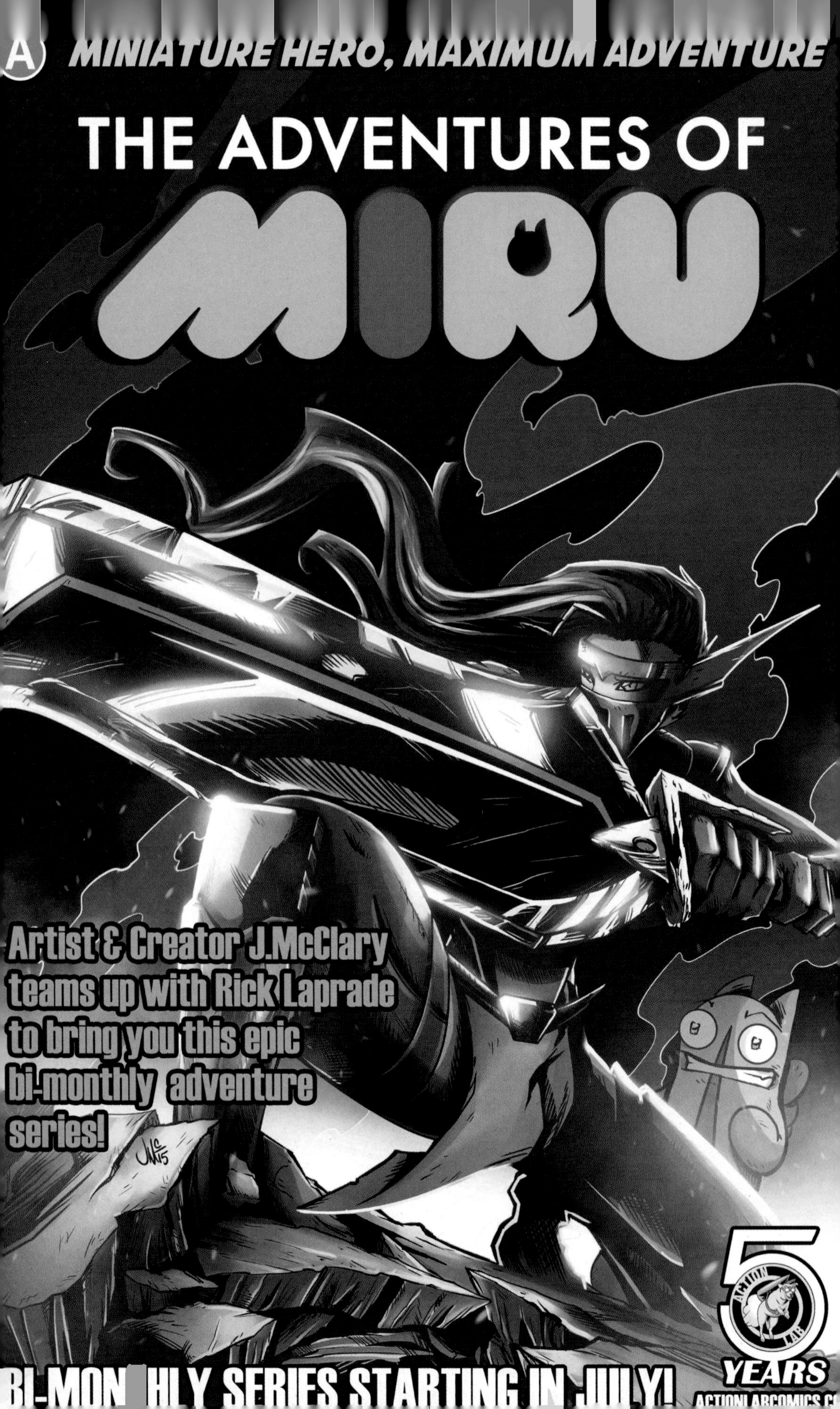
MINIATURE HERO, MAXIMUM ADVENTURE
THE ADVENTURES OF
MIRU
Artist & Creator J.McClary teams up with Rick Laprade to bring you this epic bi-monthly adventure series!
5 YEARS
ACTION LAB
BI-MON HLY SERIES STARTING IN JULY!
ACTIONLABCOMICS.C

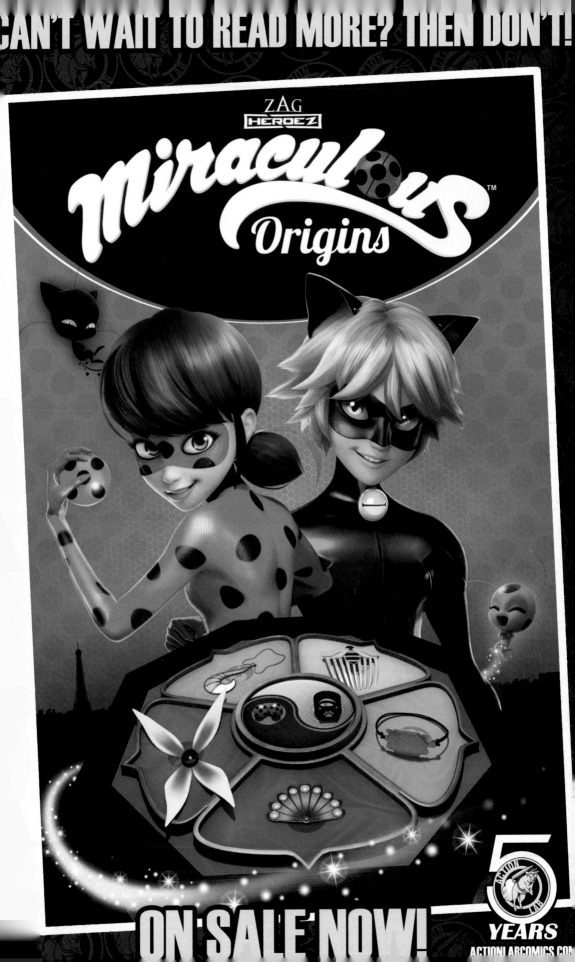

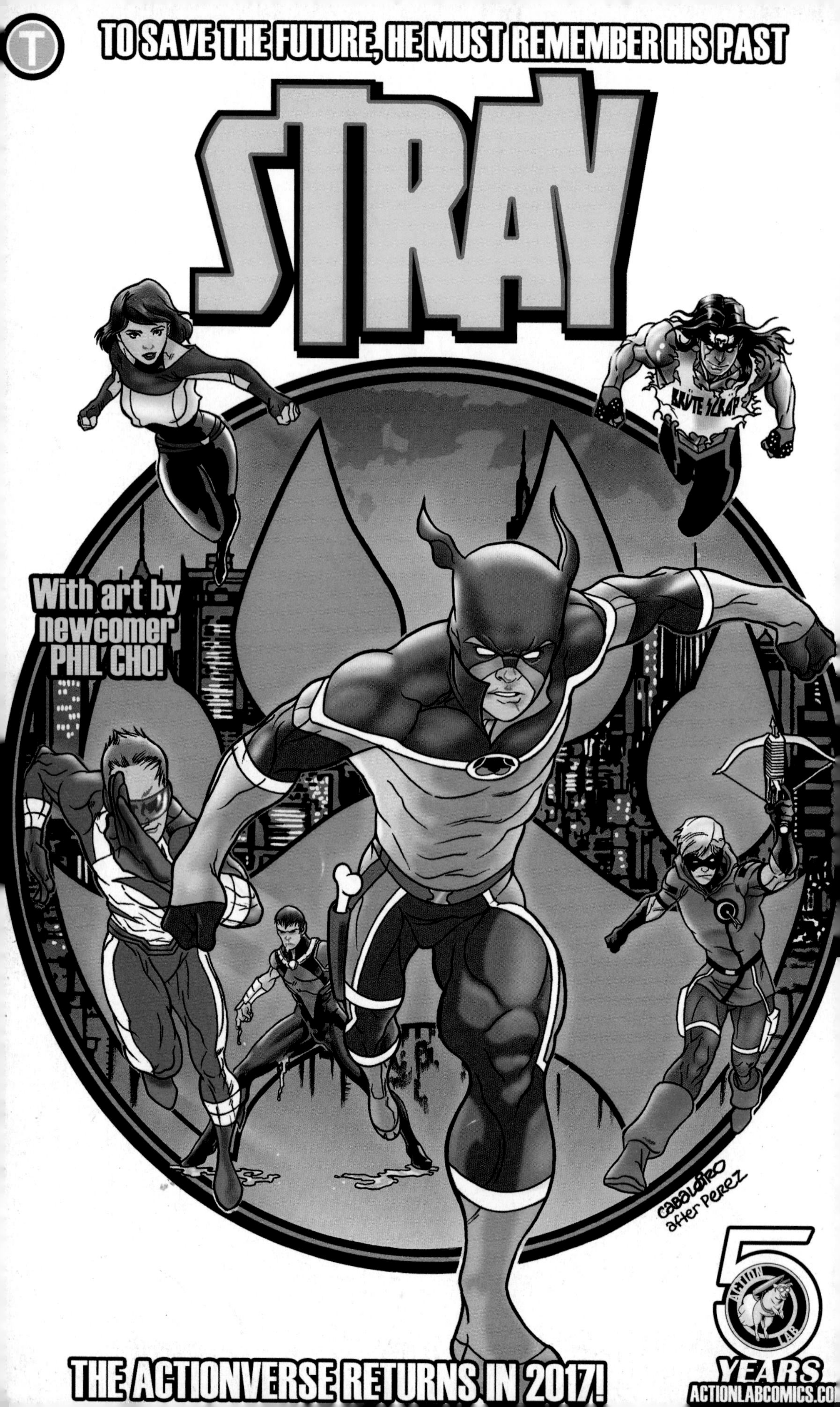
TO SAVE THE FUTURE, HE MUST REMEMBER HIS PAST
STRAY
BRUTE SCRAP
With art by newcomer PHIL CHO!
CABALLERO after PEREZ
5 YEARS
ACTION LAB
THE ACTIONVERSE RETURNS IN 2017!
ACTIONLABCOMICS.CO

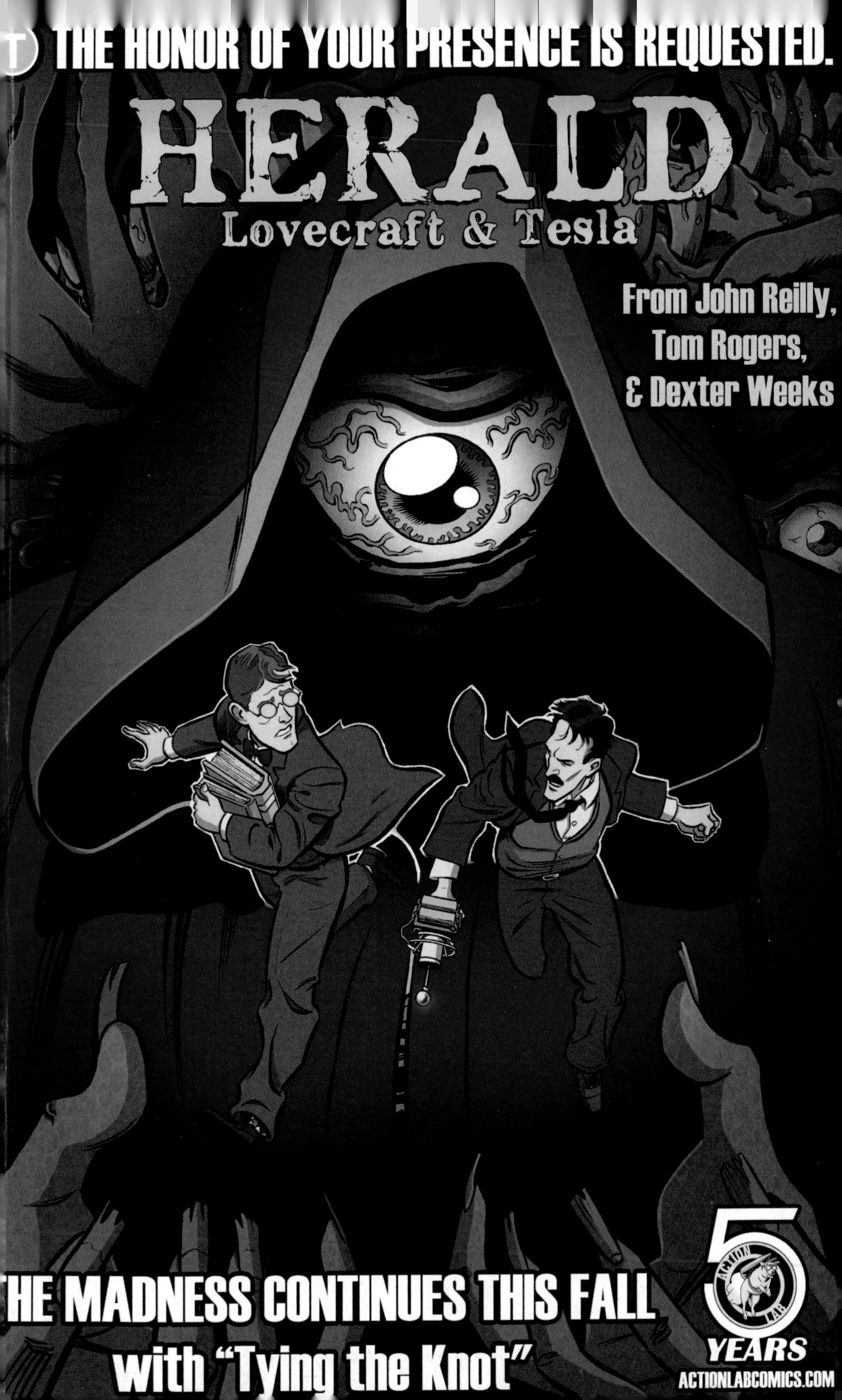
THE HONOR OF YOUR PRESENCE IS REQUESTED.
HERALD
Lovecraft & Tesla
From John Reilly,
Tom Rogers,
& Dexter Weeks
HE MADNESS CONTINUES THIS FALL
with "Tying the Knot"
5 YEARS
ACTIONLABCOMICS.COM

READ MORE NOW

Mony The Dinosaur - Action Lab
www.actionlabcomics.com
00311
7 02382 69143 1